RECKLESS *heart*

BRIGHTON WALSH

COPYRIGHT

Edited by Lisa Hollett of Silently Correcting Your Grammar
Cover Design by Brighton Walsh
Cover Image: Kerry by Wander Aguiar

Digital ISBN: 978-1-68518-030-0
Paperback ISBN: 978-1-68518-031-7
Special Edition ISBN: 978-1-68518-032-4

RECKLESS *heart*

Turns out the gorgeous stranger I had a one-night stand with is not only my sister's best friend but also my new employee.

Worse? I shared a whole lot more with Avery than one mind-blowing night.

I told her my deepest, darkest secret.

Despite my constant worry that she'll let the truth slip to my family, I can't stay away from her. And when we're tossed together for an out of town trip and forced to share a room with only one bed, the chemistry between us finally explodes...again.

I have no problem making her see stars—or breaking the bed. The trouble is, the longer our secret relationship goes on, the more I want to keep her.

But she's eight years my junior, the sunshine to my grump, and I know her free spirit wants more than the small town of Starlight Cove can offer.

I know no one could ever give her more pleasure than I will, but I refuse to hold her back.

Even if that means letting her go when her three month contract is up.

CONTENT NOTES

Please be advised that this book contains content that may be upsetting for some readers. Should you prefer detailed information in order to have the best reading experience, please visit the author's website or scan the QR code below to view a full list of content notes.

AUTHOR'S NOTE

Dear Reader,

While I consider Aiden to be a pleasure Dom and wrote him as such, no formal designations were used in this book. *Reckless Heart* is what we'll call "at home kink," because the MMC doesn't identify as a Dom. Though consent was freely given and aftercare was depicted, no protocols were followed, including the discussion and/or use of safe words.

For those hoping for an instruction manual on pleasure Doms, this ain't it. This book should never be used as any sort of manual to venture into the BDSM lifestyle. Please do your research and practice safely.

For those just here to read about a book boyfriend doing unspeakable things to the FMC, enjoy the ride.

For my grandma who once told me my books could be dirtier. Challenge accepted. But for everyone's sake, I'm gonna need you to not turn this page. (And this better not be like the time you promised you wouldn't read the book and then did anyway.)

CHAPTER ONE

AIDEN

CONSIDERING how my week had been going, it shouldn't have been a surprise that I was standing in the resort's parking lot, wearing a suit covered in glitter, while trying to corral three rolling cases filled with dildos.

It was my fault, really. I was the one who double-booked the resort's only party room. As if that wasn't bad enough, this also happened to be my third fuckup this week. That was par for the course for my youngest brother, Levi, but not me. Never me.

I didn't make mistakes. And I sure as hell didn't fuck up to the extremes I'd done this week. I did what needed to be done when it needed to be done because I handled shit.

Except lately, I hadn't been handling shit *well*. Or at all.

"Sorry about the mix-up, Mabel," I said, pushing one case ahead of me while pulling the other two behind. I didn't claim to be a sex toy expert, but Jesus Christ, that was a lot of dicks. I just hoped like hell the inventory was secured and I wasn't leaving a trail of vibrators in my wake.

"Oh, don't you worry about it." Mabel swept a hand through the air, brushing away my concern. The older woman wore a pair of hot-pink sweatpants and a matching sweatshirt with *I need a cocktail...hold the tail* written in glittery lettering across the front. She was Starlight Cove's surrogate grandma—if your grandma didn't have a filter and was horny 24/7—as well as the town's self-appointed news broadcaster and co-owner of the town's only newspaper. Meaning she had her nose in everyone's business and got away with it because she was "reporting" the goings-on in Starlight Cove via her infamous Facebook Lives. "I actually appreciate the switch to the parlor. All that natural light will better showcase the gemstones in the butt plugs I'm featuring this month!"

No longer at all shocked by the things that came out of this woman's mouth, I gave a short nod. "Happy to help."

"You let me know if I can ever show you anything, honey. Using toys as a part of one's repertoire is totally normal and makes for a very healthy sex life. It can even help loosen up some of the more...*reserved* menfolk." She shot a glance at my suit-and-tie combo, proving I was exactly the "reserved menfolk" she was talking about. "In my opinion, if more men looked at toys as teammates rather than the competition, a lot more women would be able to reach climax right along with their partners. Orgasms aren't just for men, you know."

I couldn't agree more. But I knew better than to tell Mabel anything, least of all that my stance was if a woman didn't get off at least five times to my one, I wasn't doing my job. So instead, I gave a noncommittal hum and kept walking.

"I really love this look, by the way." She gestured to me where I sparkled in the setting sun. "Makes me miss the strip club I used to visit back in the day."

"Thanks," I said dryly. "The high schoolers celebrating homecoming glitter bombed me when I asked them to keep it down."

"Is that why all these hideous vans are here?" She tutted and shook her head. "Never thought I'd see the day that kidnapper vans were the preferred transportation method for homecoming. Kids these days..."

I actually didn't know why all those fucking vans were here, only that they were taking up much-needed real estate in our already small parking lot, and we had nothing on the schedule to account for them. Maybe Mabel was right, and that was what teens did now. What the hell did I know? I hadn't been in high school for more than a decade and a half.

After getting Mabel squared away in the parlor and waving off her offer for a quick demonstration of her most powerful vibrator, I headed to find my sister. Better to get this reaming over with. And Addison was definitely going to dig her claws in. She was already pissed off because of what had happened earlier this week, and my double-booking the party room was going to tip her straight into banshee territory.

Except when I turned the corner into the front room, Addison wasn't alone. The space was filled with more people than the small area could comfortably hold. Especially when several of those people held equipment. Video cameras and microphones and—

Oh, fuck me.

Fuck. Me.

It took barely a second for all the pieces to click into place. The vans in our parking lot housed the crew and equipment for a wedding documentary series featuring engaged couples as they selected every aspect of their wedding as voted on by the viewers. Our resort had been lucky enough to be chosen as the location for this season's couple, and Addison was sure it was going to catapult us to the next level. It had been our second break this year, and things were on the upswing for Starlight Cove Resort.

Although with a fuckup like this, I wasn't so sure it would last.

As I stared at the chaos in front of me, I had a vague recollection of the production team contacting me to schedule a cake tasting on the very day my personal life had imploded. While going viral earlier this year had worked wonders for the resort, the same couldn't be said for me. It had opened doors I'd never thought would be opened for me, but it had also knocked me on my ass. I'd been so distracted with calls and emails and DMs that day that I'd taken the appointment for the cake testing, but I hadn't actually put it on the calendar. Which meant Beck hadn't prepared for it, which meant we had an entire production crew ready to film and an engaged couple ready to taste test, and we didn't have any fucking cakes.

And it was one hundred percent my fault.

"I'm so sorry for the mix-up," Addison said to the production crew, smile firmly in place, though I could read her tells from a mile away. And the twitch at the corner of her eye said she was about to hand someone their ass.

And that someone was me.

"If you'll give me just a second"—she glanced around, her attention snapping to me as soon as she noticed I was in the room, and her lips flattened into a thin line, her eyes narrowing—"Aiden and I will get this sorted out."

Oh yeah. I was totally and completely fucked.

WITH A MURDEROUS GLARE directed up at me, Addison stabbed her finger into my chest and read me the riot act. She was short—just an inch or two over five feet—which meant she was at least a foot shorter than me and our brothers. Despite that, she was a force to be reckoned with...a dictator and a fucking tornado all rolled into one shrimp of a package. And God help any idiot who was in the path of her destruction.

Today, unfortunately, I was that idiot.

"What the hell happened, Aiden?" she barked, and thankfully, we were in a back room, away from guests. "Seriously, what is going on with you lately? As if the *seven hundred* cartons of paper towels instead of the luxury bath towels I asked you to order weren't enough—" She gestured around us to the stacks of boxes currently taking up space in every spare room we had. "Then you put in the wrong price on the booking site, which meant we had five couples reserve their *week-long* stays for a whopping fifty bucks per night because *you* forgot a zero. Mabel is currently in our parlor showing off bejeweled anal plugs to any guest who walks through because *you* double-booked the party room." She ground her teeth together, her eyes narrowing into slits as she pressed her finger harder into my chest. "And now you're telling me you *forgot* to write on the schedule—your precious schedule you won't let anyone else touch, by the way—that a fucking camera crew and the bride and groom we're trying to impress were going to be here for a cake tasting? A cake testing that Beck is not prepared for, nor even aware of?"

I scrubbed a hand over my face, barely restraining a growl of frustration. "Yes, that's what I'm telling you. Look, I get it. I fucked up."

"You didn't just *fuck up*," she hissed. My sister was a tyrant on the best of days, and she didn't have any problem putting people—especially her five older brothers—in their place. When one of those brothers screwed up? The barracuda came out, and she didn't pull her punches. "You may have cost the resort the opportunity of this decade. Of the *whole fucking decade*, Aiden!"

"I got it, Addison," I snapped, no longer able to keep even a modicum of cool as I shoved a hand through my hair in frustration. Except that only made glitter rain down on me, reminding me of exactly how shitty this day had been from the start.

"What the hell are we supposed to do now? We have a whole-ass camera crew in the foyer waiting for something we can't give them. It's not like Beck can magically throw together a wedding cake in the next fifteen minutes!"

"I'll handle it."

She barked out a humorless laugh and shook her head. "Uh, no. Absolutely not. *I'm* handling it, and you're leaving."

"I'm leaving?"

"Yep. While I figure out a solution to this situation and save our asses, I want you gone. I don't want to see your face, or I might claw it off. That means no going upstairs to sulk in your bedroom. Get out, and don't come back until you've gotten your shit together."

With that, she stalked out of the room without a backward glance, and I bit back a litany of curses as I scrubbed a hand over my face. I'd never been the guy who needed to get his shit together, but if these past couple months had shown me anything, it was that I couldn't have it all. I was one hastily pulled Jenga block away from crashing.

I hadn't yet figured out how to balance having personal success while also managing a now-successful resort. Especially because the success was totally new for us. When my siblings and I had taken over running the resort ten years ago after our mom had died at sea, it had been struggling. For a long damn time. Then, several months ago, a viral video sent it soaring.

The power of mass interest wasn't lost on me. It'd taken me—or my pseudonym, anyway—from obscurity to damn near a household name in a couple short months. Suddenly, I had everything I'd ever wanted...everything I'd ever dreamed about...at my fingertips. Amazing opportunities that were all mine.

And my family knew nothing about it.

EVEN THOUGH ADDISON had told me to GTFO, I ran upstairs for a quick shower and to change out of my sparkly suit before heading into town in jeans and a T-shirt. I'd had enough humiliation for the day, and the last thing I needed were catcalls wondering which strip club people could find me at.

As much as I hated receiving a scolding from my baby sister, I couldn't deny any of what she said. I *had* been a mess. And I hadn't been pulling my weight at the resort. Not like I usually did anyway. It'd been my baby for a decade. My older brother Brady might've been the eldest

McKenzie, but he'd already had a career as a police officer —now sheriff—when our world had caved in on itself. The twins, Beck and Ford, had been away at college, my youngest brother Levi's only interest had been in boats, and Addison hadn't even graduated high school yet. So, I'd stepped up. And eventually, with the help of the rest of my siblings, we'd made it work.

But now, I had a whole other aspect of my life pulling me in the opposite direction. I'd been arrogant to think I could juggle it all. That I could accomplish everything thrown at me from all directions. And that I could do it all without my family or this town finding out anything about it.

But if this past week had taught me anything, it was that I was living in a dream world. I physically couldn't do it all. I already wasn't sleeping much—though that was nothing new. If I got more than four hours a night, it was a miracle. And I couldn't ask for help at the resort without my siblings wanting to know why I suddenly couldn't manage what I'd been doing for the past ten years.

So, yeah. I was totally and completely fucked.

I sat at the bar in One Night Stan's, nursing a bottle of beer and contemplating how the hell I was going to make this work. The smart thing—the easiest thing—would be to give up everything else and just focus on the resort.

But I wanted something *more.*

I couldn't remember the last time my life was just for me. For the past ten years, everything I'd done had been done with my family's well-being in mind. But now, I had a glimpse of more. Of something that was just mine. And I wasn't quite ready to give up on that. I just didn't know how to make it work.

I must've been giving off an exceptionally shitty vibe because no one but the bartender had approached me. I was aloof on the best of days, but today, that was cranked to eleven, as proven by the empty spaces on either side of me.

No sooner had the thought passed through my mind than a woman swept in through the front door and strolled straight toward me, dropping her bag on the floor next to the stool on my left.

The bartender lifted his chin at her in greeting. "What can I get you?"

"The best fruity drink you know how to make. And do you have food in this place?"

As the bartender slid a menu her way, she tossed a book faceup on the bar top and settled onto the stool. Out of habit, I glanced over at it, my eyebrows shooting up when I saw a familiar cover. It was *the* dark romance book everyone was talking about right now. And it was *dark*. And dirty. And definitely depraved. Something most people would probably hesitate to read in public.

Most people, but not her.

A small smile tugged at the corner of my mouth. It was clear this woman did not give one single fuck what people thought. And I had to admire her for that. I took a swig of my beer, wondering what that would be like. I couldn't even tell my family I—

She turned toward me then, her whiskey eyes pinning me in place, a devilish smirk on her full pink lips, and a riot of red hair surrounding her like the best kind of distraction. She was stunning, but that wasn't what had me choking on my drink.

I coughed and sputtered as I stared at her chest where her T-shirt proudly proclaimed, *Buy me books and tell me to STFUATTDLAGG.*

Jesus *Christ*, who was this woman?

CHAPTER TWO

AVERY

GETTING STOOD up after driving 1500 miles in three days wasn't exactly how I saw this night ending, yet here we were.

Okay, so I hadn't *exactly* been stood up. I'd received a phone call. But it didn't change the fact that I was alone in Starlight Cove for the evening with no one to keep me company except this week's book boyfriend.

Though that wasn't all that different from what my life had been lately.

It was one of the reasons I'd decided to move back home to Maine following a yearslong stint in Mississippi. While I'd enjoyed my time there, and I'd made some amazing friends, the past few months, I'd started to feel...untethered.

It wasn't that I didn't love my friends there, but they were in a totally different place in their lives—married with kids or kids on the way—and I was out here fumbling through life, just trying to remember to put my clothes in the dryer before they became moldy.

Mississippi had never been in my plans. But I'd made the mistake of following a boy—yes, a boy and definitely not a man—right after college. And while he'd dropped me as soon as his influential—read: snobbish—family got one look at me, I'd gone where the wind had blown me. And it had blown me to Havenbrook, a picturesque small town in the heart of Mississippi.

I didn't live my life with regrets. Boyfriends bailed on me—*men* bailed on me. Friends grew apart. Shit happened, good and bad. And I didn't mind making mistakes—thank God, because I made a ton of them. But I learned from every single one.

And during my time in Havenbrook, I'd learned it wasn't enough to be someone's second or third...or fourth...choice. I'd spent my entire life settling for exactly that, but I was done. I didn't begrudge my friends for slotting me into that space. Of course they would choose their significant others over me. Of course my closest friend there would choose her sisters over me. If I were in their shoes, I'd do the same. Or I would in theory anyway. But what did I know? I was an only child, and *my person* happened to be my mom.

Following the shock of a lifetime, it had been just the two of us against the world. And I needed to get back to that. Needed that connection. Needed an anchor to ground me.

So when I had the chance to pursue what I'd always dreamed of doing—traveling the world as a flight attendant—I'd quit my job, ended my lease, and left Havenbrook behind. I changed everything without a second thought when my mom said her boyfriend of the month could get me into flight attendant training almost immediately by bypassing the waitlist. But changing things on a dime was sort of my superpower.

Like when my dinner date canceled and I had to figure shit out...

Instead of checking in to my cute little boutique hotel and getting ready for a night of fun, I adjusted. No use in getting all done up to eat by myself when I could grab something quick and spend the rest of the night in my room with my book boyfriend and my favorite vibrator.

My phone rang as I pulled up in front of the only bar in town—which happened to be two buildings over from my hotel—and I glanced at the FaceTime request before answering.

"You really miss me, huh?" I said as soon as the video connected.

Willow, aforementioned Havenbrook bestie, huffed out a laugh as her face filled the screen. "Obviously. Was that ever in question? It's not too late for you to come back, you know."

Seeing her smiling face and hearing her sweet,

Southern drawl made me homesick for a place I'd never really seen as home. It was quite the mindfuck.

"Speak for yourself. I just spent the past three days in a car, hopping from motel to motel and subsisting on Twizzlers and Dr Pepper. If you think I'm doing that all over again, the sleep deprivation is really getting to you. Tell Finn he needs to step it up and pull his weight."

She laughed, her smile bright and eyes crinkling, and my heart squeezed. Fuck, I already missed her so much, and it'd only been a couple days. "I just wanted to make sure you got there okay. Are you home?"

"Not yet." I flipped the camera around and gave her a quick view of the adorable downtown before switching it back to me.

"So cute! Where are you?"

"I took a detour through Starlight Cove to visit my best friend and roommate from college, but she had to cancel our dinner plans. Something about an implosion at work, and she had to clean up the mess."

"That sucks. Are you staying there, or are you just gonna head to your momma's?"

"Honestly, I'm dead tired and starving, so I'm here for the night. That way, Addison and I can get breakfast in the morning. I'm going to grab something to eat now and then lock myself in my room with a book and my vibrator."

Willow propped her chin on her hand and let out a dreamy sigh. "Sounds heavenly."

"Oh, don't give me that. You have an actual dick you

can use. Speaking of, what are the chances someone in this bar can decipher my shirt?"

"What shirt is it?"

"Buy me books and tell me to shut the fuck up and take that dick like a good girl..."

She snorted, and her husband's head popped up in the background. "Ask Avery where she got that so I can buy you one, Willowtree!"

"Quit eavesdropping!" she said over her shoulder before bringing her attention back to me with an eye roll.

I laughed. "Oops, my bad. I didn't know there were other ears around."

"Those other ears don't need to get any ideas," she said, loud enough for Finn to hear. "My vagina needs a break from pushing out babies."

Finn walked up behind her and leaned down to murmur in her ear, but he didn't exactly whisper because I could hear every word. "But it doesn't need a break from my di—"

"Oh my *Lord*, would you leave me alone, please?" She pressed a hand to his chest and shoved while he laughed. He slipped out of her reach, only to come back and plant a loud, smacking kiss on the side of her head. The two of them together were so damn cute. It made me sick.

"*Anyway*," she said to me. "I think you're probably in the clear. I'd say you have a slim to none chance of running into a book whore who knows the acronym while you grab a quick bite to eat."

"Honestly, I'd welcome the conversation at this point. It's been *forever* since I've had quality human interaction. I'm starting to get attached to the narrators of the audiobooks I've been listening to."

"It's been three days, you drama queen. And I told you to call me when you got lonely!"

"You're working. And I'm fine."

"Well, I'm not." She stuck out her bottom lip in a pout. "I miss you like hell."

A knot filled my throat, and my eyes stung from unshed tears. I pressed my lips together and nodded. "Me, too," I said thickly. Just because I knew it was time to leave and move on didn't make it hurt any less.

Before I could say anything else, her daughter's cries echoed over the line, and I knew our time was up.

"Sounds like duty calls," I said. "I'll let you know when I get to my mom's, okay?"

She nodded. "Okay. Be safe and I love you."

"Love you, too, Will."

I ended the call, closed my eyes, and rested my head back against the seat. I had no idea if my moving back to Maine was the right choice. Hell, I didn't even know if I'd enjoy the career I'd been building up in my head since I was a kid.

I just knew it was time for a change.

Even though the sun was on its last legs, it was still exceptionally darker inside One Night Stan's. Without allowing my eyes time to adjust to the dimly lit space, I strode blindly toward the bar and dropped my bag next to an empty stool. After partaking in a little small talk with the bartender and giving him my order, I glanced to my right to find the only other person at the bar sitting directly next to me.

I barely had time to register his dark, tousled hair that curled over his ears and the piercing blue eyes that nearly took my breath away before his gaze dropped to my shirt. His eyes widened a fraction...and then he promptly choked on his drink.

Fuck my *life*. Slim to none chance, my ass.

"*Oh my God.*" I slammed my forearm over the acronym, as if that would do anything now that he'd already read it except draw more attention to it. Then under my breath, I hissed, "You know what this means?"

Mr. Hottie was still coughing, his eyes dancing with something I couldn't quite name, and I wasn't sure if I should be mortified or proud. There were worse things than this hot-as-fuck man knowing I wouldn't mind being tossed on a bed and stuffed full of—

"Hadn't been counting on that, huh?" he managed through a rough throat.

And *jeezus*, even his voice was hot as hell, all rumbly and deep and in the exact tenor that made my nipples tighten.

I huffed out a laugh and shook my head. "You're definitely *not* the person I pictured who'd know it. I thought for sure it'd be a fellow smut slut."

His lips twitched, and the barest hint of a dimple peeked out beneath a close-cropped beard. Honestly, it was just getting obscene now. "What makes you think I'm not?"

I lifted my brows, propping my chin on my hand as I gave him a once-over. I couldn't tell how tall he was, but my bet was well over six feet. Tattoos ran up both arms, interspersed randomly from mid-forearm and disappearing beneath the T-shirt sleeves stretched tight over well-defined biceps. The ink was hot as hell, but it was his eyes that held me captive, blue and bottomless and so fucking intense.

"Are you telling me you're a proud member of the smut slut club?" I asked.

He glanced to the back of the bar where the bartender chatted with a group of people before returning his gaze to mine. "I'm not sure I'd categorize myself as that, but I get around."

"*Do you*?" I didn't bother to hide the interest in my voice. Talking about books was quite possibly my favorite thing. Talking about smutty books with this book boyfriend come to life? Fuck me running, my shitty night had taken a sudden turn for the better.

I could discuss books with literally anyone, but I liked to gauge the other person first so I knew what I was getting into—and so I didn't scar them for life. Romance readers came in all different varieties, and what some called spicy was actually just the equivalent of drinking tepid water. I wanted straight up tequila, or I wasn't interested.

"Have you read this one?" I pressed my fingernail on the cover of the book I'd brought inside.

He dipped his chin in a nod. "I have."

My mouth dropped open, and I leaned closer. "No shit?"

"No shit."

My *god*, the filthiness he'd read in this book... Just the thought of it was doing things to me that weren't appropriate for public. While the vast majority of what went on in this novel landed firmly on my side of *fine for a book boyfriend but abso-fucking-lutely not in real life*, it still let me know he was probably open-minded and sexually adventurous. And that only led to more ideas, every single one of them featuring him and me and not a single stitch of clothing between us.

The crowd at the back roared with laughter, and that, paired with the music pumping through the speakers, made it hard to hear.

I leaned closer until our heads were only inches apart, inhaling the crisp, warm scent of him. "What did you think of it?"

He lifted a single broad shoulder, the move brushing his skin against mine and sending a shiver of awareness down my spine. "It was good for research."

The proclamation seemed to surprise him, as if he hadn't meant to say it, and my interest was officially piqued. But before I could say anything, the bartender dropped off my meal, made sure my real-life book boyfriend was good, then headed back to the corner to chat with the raucous group.

"You can't just leave me hanging like that," I said, tucking into my meal. "What kind of research? You planning to kidnap someone or...?"

He laughed, a low, rumbly sound that sank into my bones and settled deep. Christ on a cracker, what was this man doing to me? "It was for...work."

"For work, huh?" I asked, brows up. "You're either a detective or... Yeah, I got nothin'."

His gaze flitted around again as if to catalog the space before landing back on me, hesitation written across his face.

"Oh, come on." I leaned into him, bumping his shoulder with mine. And then I had to force myself to pull away because I wanted to melt into his warmth. I didn't think I'd lost my northernness since I'd grown up here, but four years in Mississippi had made me soft, and I wasn't yet used to Maine Octobers.

It was definitely that and not the fact that he was hot as fuck and it'd been a long-ass time since I'd had my world rocked.

"I won't tell a soul." I mimed zipping my lips and tossed the invisible key over my shoulder. "I'm not even from here —I'm just staying the night, so you don't have to worry about me spilling your secrets around town."

And yes, I was absolutely going to ignore the pang in my gut over the thought that I'd never see this man again. I didn't even *know* him. Why the hell should I care about that?

He stared at his bottle of beer, his long, thick fingers wrapped around the base, thumb stroking up and down the label and gathering condensation in its wake. *Fuck.* That shouldn't have been so hot, and it certainly shouldn't have made my clit throb, but I couldn't stop picturing those hands on my body. Stroking gently… Reverently.

Finally, he tipped his head closer and said, "I'm an author."

My mouth dropped open as I gaped at him. "Seriously? That's so cool! What do you write?"

He lifted his gaze toward the back of the bar once again before meeting my eyes. "Fantasy, but my latest skewed heavily erotic. Hence the research."

"Do a lot of research at strip clubs, do you?"

His brow furrowed as he stared at me. "What?"

I reached out and brushed a finger over his eyebrow and his cheekbone, swiping away the random gold sparkles. Then I spotted another fleck on his jaw and leaned close, softly blowing against his skin to displace it. His Adam's apple bobbed as I pulled back, the tension between us crackling.

"It's a long story," he said, his voice rough. "And I'd rather talk books."

I just blinked at him before shaking my head. "My

God, you're like the perfect man. I wish every guy would read romance novels to get an idea of what women want. There'd be a hell of a lot more satisfied women, that's for sure."

"You have trouble with that?"

It was a more intimate conversation than I usually had after knowing someone for all of twenty minutes, but for some reason, it didn't feel strange or weird with this man. It felt...natural.

I lifted a single shoulder in a shrug. "I think every woman does."

His eyes heated, gaze fixed on mine even while he didn't say a word. But he didn't need to. His stare spoke volumes, and everything screamed, *You wouldn't have any trouble with me.*

I shifted in my seat, my body humming with awareness for him. I wanted to be closer. Hell, I wanted to be in my room and naked with this man, but that wasn't in the cards right now, so I turned toward him. He mirrored my posture, adjusting so his legs were on either side of mine, and the position was so damn intimate. Especially when the insides of his thighs brushed the outsides of mine, the heat even through his jeans and my leggings enough to burn me up.

"So." I cleared my throat, attempting to impart some moisture into my too-dry mouth. "You read smutty books for research... You ever do any real-life research?"

I knew I was pushing the boundaries here, but I was

well past the point of caring. And I didn't want there to be any confusion. I was, without a doubt, interested in him, and I was absolutely down for a single night of fun with this man. A book boyfriend come to life who researched smut for a living? Sign me the fuck up.

The air grew heated, an electric charge sizzling in the space between us, and I felt it from my head to my toes and every neglected inch in between.

"Not usually, and even then, it's probably not how you're thinking." He dropped his gaze, allowing it to roam over my body in a slow perusal I felt all the way to my toes. Then he swiped his thumb across his lower lip and met my eyes again. "But I'm definitely tempted to be a little reckless tonight."

CHAPTER THREE

AIDEN

I DIDN'T EVEN HAVE time to worry about the fact that I'd shared something with this stranger that I'd been keeping to myself for *years*. Didn't have time to analyze why I hadn't instead come up with a plausible explanation to her question, or why it had felt so freeing when I'd told her the truth. Didn't have time to think about any of it before we were crashing through her hotel room door, our lips connected, hands everywhere they could reach.

I cupped her ass and held her against me as I swept my tongue into her mouth, groaning at her taste. That, combined with the noises she made, all needy and breathless, were enough to have me damn near busting out of my jeans. I was so fucking hard for her, but my dick was the last thing on my mind. All I could think about was her. Her taste and her sounds and my desperate need to make her come.

I wasn't this guy. I didn't *do* this. I was careful and methodical. I had situationships that went on until they didn't, and I never cared enough to be bothered by their inevitable end. And yet with this woman—this stranger whose name I didn't even know—I had no idea how I was going to fit everything I wanted to do with her into a single night.

I didn't care that I'd known her for all of an hour. I wanted to fucking *devour* her.

Pinning her against the closed door with my hips, I guided her legs around me. That was all the encouragement she needed to lock her ankles at the base of my spine and grind her pussy down against my cock.

She stared at me, eyes half lidded, as I groaned into her mouth. And then the sexiest fucking smile swept across her lips, and she gave another slow, purposeful roll of her hips.

"You can grind that sweet little cunt down on me all you want, but I'm not coming until you've had your fill."

"I *really* hope you're not talking out of your ass and you can actually deliver on that promise..."

A smile tipped up the corner of my mouth as I brushed my lips along the column of her neck. The barest hint of black ink behind her ear caught my eye, so I swept her hair over her shoulder to get a better look. It was a small bunny tattoo, no bigger than the size of a quarter. I brushed my thumb over it, and she shuddered against me, a soft moan leaving her parted lips.

I pulled back enough that I could watch her reaction, softly tracing the lines with my thumb. "That why you got this here? Is it your on button? If I touch it or kiss it or lick it, are you going to give me more of those needy little moans?"

"Maybe." She turned her head to give me better access and raised a brow in challenge, and *goddamn*, her boldness only got me harder. "You should find out."

Gripping her ass, I lowered my head and brushed my lip over her earlobe before tracing her tattoo with my tongue. At her answering moan, I sucked the spot and hummed against her skin. "I fucking love those sounds."

"Yeah?" she asked, breathless. Her tits brushed against my chest as she arched her back and tightened her legs around me. "I bet you could figure out a way to coax more out of me."

"I bet you're right," I said into her neck. "The real question is if you want me to tell you to shut the fuck up and take my cock, or call you my good girl tonight?"

"*God*," she breathed. "Is it greedy if I say both?"

"Is that what you are, pretty girl?" I pulled back so I could look into her eyes. "You gonna be greedy for me?"

She bit her lip and nodded. And fuck me, this woman was going to be my undoing. I hadn't felt this kind of connection...this kind of chemistry...in years. Maybe ever.

"Then we make a good pair," I said, voice scraped raw.

"Why's that?"

Pressing her to the door with my hips, I braced one

hand over her shoulder and gripped her waist with the other. I slipped my thumb under the hem of her T-shirt, stroking over her pebbled skin and nearly groaning at how responsive she was to me. Especially considering I hadn't even gotten started.

"Because I'm going to love making you come," I admitted.

"That makes two of us."

"Is that your way of telling me you want my hands on you?"

She gave a jerky nod, and I didn't waste any time lowering her feet to the floor before slipping my hand down the front of her leggings and straight into her panties. Bracing one arm on the door above her head, I leaned closer until our noses were nearly touching, her panting breaths ghosting over my mouth. And then I glided my middle finger straight through her pussy lips and hummed in satisfaction when she moaned low and pleasure swept over her face.

"Christ, you're wet," I said against her mouth, our lips brushing with each word. "You want my fingers inside you?"

She lifted her hands to my chest, tightening her fingers in my T-shirt, and nodded. "God yes, please."

"So sweet for me..." I swiped my fingers through her again before gliding my middle two deep into her cunt.

Moaning low, she dropped her head back against the door with a thump. She looked good enough to eat. Her eyes were hooded as she stared at me, lips parted and cheeks flushed, a look of hungry desperation written across her face that I fucking loved.

"How many times do you think I can make you come with just my hand?"

She shook her head before sucking in a sharp gasp as I curled my fingers inside her. "One. If you're lucky."

I didn't have any doubt that I'd be lucky, and I was pretty sure she didn't, either. With the way her pussy fluttered around me, squeezing my fingers every time I stroked her G-spot, there was no denying she was close to tipping over the edge.

I leaned down until my lips hovered over her bunny tattoo, then I stroked it with my tongue. "Can't forget about that needy little clit, can we, bunny?"

I pressed the heel of my hand against it, giving her the friction she needed while I pumped my fingers in and out of her. She gasped, her body going rigid as she held me to her. And then she exploded. Her eyes fluttered closed, and a long moan left her lips, her hips rolling as I stroked her through her orgasm.

But I wasn't done. Not by a fucking long shot.

She stared up at me, eyes wide when I didn't let up, my fingers thrusting into her and exploiting the spot inside her that had her pussy tightening impossibly around me.

"You going to be a good girl and give me another one?"

"I don't— I can't—" She shook her head even as she canted her hips, urging my fingers deeper. Faster.

"You can and you will." I scraped my teeth down the column of her neck, sinking them into the juncture where it met her shoulder. "I'll make sure of it."

Her breaths grew choppy, her body tightening as she clutched me to her, and then she was falling all over again.

"There you go, pretty girl," I murmured against her mouth as her pussy squeezed my fingers. "Come all over my hand."

She moaned, head falling to my chest as she gave herself over to the sensations I was coaxing from her body. I was hard as a fucking rock, every ounce of her pleasure shooting straight to my dick as if I'd been the one racking up those O's. Fuck me, I wanted to taste them. *Needed* to taste just how good I'd made her feel.

Once she sagged back against the door, panting and wrung out, I dropped to my knees, taking her leggings and panties with me before tossing them to the side. Then I hooked her leg over my shoulder and groaned at the sight of her, all pink and swollen and so fucking ready for me.

"Holy shit, is this actually happening?" she asked, her words breathless and disbelieving. "This *can't* be happening. I'm dreaming, aren't I?" She laughed, a half-hinged, hysterical sound, and shook her head as she stared down at me. "Two orgasms from his fingers and now he wants to eat my pussy? Yeah, this is definitely a dream."

"Not a dream, bunny." I swiped my thumb through her slit, my cock throbbing at her unrestrained moan when I passed over her fully exposed clit. "You've already been so fucking good for me. Are you going to let me taste this next one?"

She breathed out a laugh. "The next one? You've already given me double what I usually manage, so let's not get ahead of ourselves."

"That's not an answer."

"What was the question again?"

I let out a low chuckle, so close to her, I had no doubt she could feel it against her skin. "Can I make you come with my tongue?"

"You can sure as hell try." She whipped her shirt over her head—the shirt that had been the catalyst for what was sure to go down as one of the best nights of my life—and tossed it and her bra somewhere over my shoulder. "And for the record, you've got an all-night pass to do whatever you want with your tongue."

My mouth watered at the sight and scent of her, and I couldn't wait another second to have her taste on my tongue. I swept it through her slit, from entrance to clit, groaning when her sweetness flooded my mouth.

"Oh *shit*." She braced herself with one hand against the door, the other on the back of my head, holding me to her pussy. The move was wholly unnecessary because I didn't plan to leave until I'd wrung another two orgasms from her sweet little cunt. I licked her from top to bottom and every place in between, sucking and nipping and humming against her skin every time she gave me a breathy moan.

"God, you're good at this," she said, awe and desire threaded through each word.

"Don't tell me that until you've come down my throat." I turned my head and sank my teeth into the inside of her thigh. Not hard enough to hurt but enough to sting, and a shudder racked her body. "Now ride my face and make yourself come for me."

"Fuck." She dropped her head back to the door, the thump of it mixing with her moans as she rocked her hips against my mouth, doing exactly what I'd instructed her to. With one hand clutching me to her and the other cupping her breast, her thumb and forefinger pinching her nipple, she took her pleasure from me. The sight...the sounds... the fucking taste of her did nothing but make me harder. Make me ache to sink deep inside her and feel her come around my cock.

She ground her hips shamelessly against my face, and I slipped two, then three fingers inside her. I worked her clit with my tongue until I found exactly what made her legs shake, what had her moans increasing and her fingers tightening in my hair. Then I found the rhythm and the speed at which she liked to be fucked—fast and deep, and Jesus *Christ*, I couldn't wait to slide my dick inside her. Couldn't wait to feel this hot, wet heaven between her thighs. To see her dripping down my shaft just like she was my fingers.

"Oh my God," she said, shock ringing in her words. "I'm—*shit*. You're gonna make me come again."

I hummed into her pussy, and she did exactly as promised. She broke against me, her cunt squeezing my fingers while her clit pulsed against my tongue, and I licked up every single drop she gave me.

With her body still shaking, I stood, lifting her against me as I strode straight to the bed and tossed her onto it. Her tits bounced with the movement, her tight nipples begging for my tongue, and I didn't bother to hide my hunger for her. I fucking loved that she was naked, her body flushed and shaking from what I'd done to her, and I hadn't even unbuttoned my jeans.

I wanted to do a thousand different things to her tonight. Wanted to sit her in my lap and make her grind herself down on my cock, guiding her hips until she made a mess all over me. Wanted to suck her tits into my mouth and see if I could get her off by only that. Wanted her to sit on my face and suffocate me with her cunt. I wanted to find every single way I could to make her scream for me. And then I wanted to do it again.

And again.

And again.

She stared up at me with what looked awfully close to awe. "I gotta tell you—your research paid off. You're seriously a book boyfriend come to life, and I'm *not* mad about it."

"Does that mean you're ready for another one?"

Breathing out a laugh like she thought I was joking, she sat up on her knees and shook her head. "It's my turn."

Then she crawled toward me, reaching out and tugging me closer by the waistband of my jeans. With her eyes locked on mine, she undid my fly and pushed my jeans and boxer briefs down until my cock popped free.

She made a noise halfway between a shocked gasp and a moan and shook her head. "Good *God,* you didn't tell me you were hung like a book boyfriend, too."

My chuckle turned into a groan when she lowered her head and sucked me between those gorgeous lips. No lead-in. No preamble. Just the hot wetness of her mouth as she took me deep until the head of my cock touched the back of her throat. The sight of her nearly did me in, bare ass up in the air, her eyes focused on me, and those dark pink lips wrapped around my shaft, trying to suck my goddamn soul from my body.

"Christ, your mouth feels so fucking good."

Too fucking good. If I didn't find a distraction quickly, I was going to come, and I'd promised her I wouldn't until she had her fill.

I slid my hand down her spine, gliding it over the curve of her ass as she sucked me deep. Then I gave it a sharp smack. She jolted then moaned around my cock, eyes blinking up at me with unmistakable hunger. "Still greedy for me, aren't you, bunny?"

She whimpered and nodded, sucking me deep. She was a woman on a mission, but I wasn't going to be derailed, especially when she'd just told me she needed me again.

I pulled back with a groan as my dick slipped from her mouth. "Flip over."

She stared up at me with glassy eyes for only a second before doing what I said and turning to lie on her back, her head hanging over the side of the bed.

"Just like that," I said, stepping up and brushing the head of my cock over her lips.

She opened for me immediately, sucking me into her mouth, her throat working against the head of my dick. Christ, her mouth was fucking nirvana, and she had me too damn close to blowing.

I cupped her tits in my hands, tweaking her nipples, then continued down over her stomach to her pussy. Her legs were bent at the knees and clenched tightly closed, but I pushed them apart, humming in satisfaction when she let them fall to the mattress. And then she was spread open for me and so fucking gorgeous. I swept my fingers over her, coating them in her arousal, before sinking two deep inside.

She moaned around my shaft as I stroked her how she'd shown me she liked, finger-fucking her in the rhythm that would get her off. It didn't take long until she was rocking her hips up to meet my hand. She whimpered as she swallowed around my dick, her hands cupping my ass and tugging me to her, so desperate and needy for me.

"You gonna come again with my cock down your throat, pretty girl?" Just the thought made my words come out hoarse and low, my cock jerking in her mouth, and I was going to make sure she did exactly that.

With my fingers buried deep inside her, I leaned over until I could taste her again. I swept my tongue through her slit before sucking her clit between my lips, and that was all it took.

She whimpered as her orgasm peaked, her body going stiff even as she rolled her hips in time to my fingers. Her moans vibrating down my cock and the sloppy, hungry way she was trying to suck me off were nearly my undoing. I pulled out of her mouth and gripped my shaft firmly at the base. My cock jerked, about two seconds from spilling, but I wasn't ready to come just yet. She hadn't told me she'd had her fill, and I sure as hell hadn't had mine.

"Holy *fuck*," she said, breathless, as the last shudder ran through her. Reaching down, she pushed my hand away from her pussy and squeezed her legs tight. "Oh my God, you're magic."

After a few brief moments when she caught her breath, she rolled onto her side and climbed to her knees, her eyes intent on me. "But I think it's about time you got inside me."

Goddamn, I wanted that, too. More than I'd wanted anything in a long time. But as much as I'd love to stuff her full of my cock, I didn't have any fucking condoms on me. I sure as hell hadn't gone out tonight with the intention of ending up here. And I wasn't one of those guys who carried one around in my wallet, just in case.

I didn't do *just-in-case* sex. I did it on the first and third Tuesday of the month. Or at least I had until the resort went viral, my life was thrown into chaos, and I barely had time for a nightly jerk session, let alone driving to meet my current situationship just to have sex that was mediocre at best and subpar at worst.

Somehow, I knew that wouldn't be the case with this woman. She'd already turned me inside out, made me crave her in ways that were altogether foreign to me.

"I don't have any condoms," I admitted.

She stared at me for long moments before she slipped her hands under my shirt, gliding them up my stomach and chest and taking the material right along with them. I reached back and tugged the neck over my head before tossing it to the side. And god*damn*... How could I be hungry for her when I could still taste her on my tongue?

She reached for me, wrapping her fingers around my obnoxiously hard cock, and grinned up at me, a slow, wicked smile that shot to where she was stroking me. "Good thing I do."

CHAPTER FOUR

AVERY

I'D LIKE to take this moment to thank past me for my insistence on having a condom with me at all times, because you just never knew when you were going to get dicked down. And I was about to get the dicking down of my *life*.

I'd never moved so fast, scrambling off the bed and making a beeline for my purse. Honestly, it was a wonder my legs worked at all with as many times as he'd made me come. Sweet Lord in heaven, the things this man could do...

Before him, I'd never much cared for fingering. After all, I had ten of my own. What the hell did I need his for? But this man took my unvoiced challenge and had me flipping my opinion faster than he coaxed that first O from me. First of four...so far.

This night was probably a mistake.

Sure, when I was ninety years old in a nursing home, I'd be able to brag about the night when this man gave me multiple out-of-body orgasmic experiences, and I'd make all the other old biddies jealous. But at what cost? At the ripe old age of twenty-six, I was about to have my first top-shelf dick but only for a single night. Then I'd have to live the rest of my life knowing exactly what I was missing and exactly what the fuckboys on the dating apps couldn't dream of living up to.

But beggars can't be choosers, and there was no way I was passing up on riding this man like a pony. Not when he was handing out orgasms like candy, and sure as hell not when he was packing *that* below the belt. He could get me off and get me off well, *and* he had the kind of dick I spent all my spare time—and, okay, even some while I should've been working—reading about? It was an enthusiastic yes from me.

After grabbing the condom from my purse, I spun around to face him, holding it up between two fingers like a trophy. The barest hint of a smile tugged up one side of his mouth, making that dimple pop, as he focused those intense blue eyes on me. And *God*, I was going to melt into a puddle right here on the floor.

He should've looked ridiculous standing there, bare chested, jeans open and hanging low on his hips, hand wrapped around his thick cock as it stood proud and jutting from his body. But if anything, the way he held himself, so confident and sure, even half naked, even while stroking himself as he stared at me, just made him all that much hotter.

His dark hair was a mess—thanks to my hands—and his lips still shone from what he'd done to me just moments ago. His shoulders were broad, arms thick and roped with muscle. At least a dozen tattoos were scattered across them, starting from mid-forearm and leading up to his shoulders. His chest was a blank canvas, though, save for a light dusting of dark hair, and I wanted to climb him like a fucking tree.

I still wasn't entirely sure this wasn't some elaborate dream. I would've been less shocked if I witnessed this man walking straight out of my e-reader than I would be to find out he was real.

But I'd be damned if I wasted a second of my very limited time with him, dream incarnation of the perfect book boyfriend or not.

"The way you're looking at me says you want to get fucked. That true, bunny?" he asked, the tenor of his voice making my nipples peak.

"That is absolutely one hundred percent true." I nodded emphatically.

He chuckled under his breath. "Then get over here and climb on the bed. Hands and knees. Show me that perfect ass, and let me see what I've done to that pussy."

Well, fuck me sideways. I didn't think I'd like having a man boss me around. After all, if someone tried to tell me what to do on a day-to-day basis, I'd tell them to fuck all the way off and do so with a smile. But there was something wholly different about being bossed around in the bedroom. And this man could boss me all fucking night.

Without hesitation, I did what he said, dropping the condom next to me as I climbed onto the bed and glanced at him over my shoulder, giving my ass a little shake.

He groaned, palming it before running his hands over the curves of my hips, up to the dip of my waist, and then I felt the slightest pressure against my shoulders as he urged my upper body down until my cheek was flat on the bed. As soon as I was in position, he dropped to his knees behind me, spread me wide with his hands, and licked me from clit to entrance.

"Oh my God, *again*?" I asked, not bothering to hide the shock and excitement in my tone. I curled my fingers into the sheets, my hips rocking with the rhythm of his tongue.

How could I still be so hungry for him? How could I still crave another release? How could I still be desperate for *more* after he'd already given me so much? Regardless of the how, there was no denying the fact that I was. No denying how I arched to give him better access, tipping my hips up so he could reach my clit better. No denying how greedy he made me.

"Again," he answered against my skin as he coaxed another orgasm out of me. With his thumbs running along my pussy lips and his tongue working hard against my clit, I fell over the precipice with little warning, my body thrumming through my release as I buried my moans into the sheets.

I'd never come this much in a single night—hell, I'd never come this much in a single *week*. My body was strung out, shudders sweeping over me in waves, and I collapsed against the mattress as I tried to catch my breath.

"Christ, I love making you come." He ran his hands over me, softly, gently, a soothing touch that had me relaxing even as every nerve ending in my body rang with awareness. "You okay?"

Unable to peel my eyes open, I could only manage a halfhearted grunt and a barely perceptible nod.

"I need your words, pretty girl. Are you okay, or do you want me to stop?"

That made my eyes pop open, and I glanced at him over my shoulder. "No stopping. I'm good. *So* good. But you definitely should have come with a warning label."

With a chuckle, he braced his hands on either side of my head and bent down, brushing a kiss over the tattoo behind my ear. Against it, he murmured, "You did so good for me, bunny."

His words sent a shiver through me, and I twisted, trying to turn beneath him. Ready to wrap my legs around him and pull him deep inside me. But he stilled me before I could.

"Stay just like this." He stared down at me where I was lying half on my stomach, one leg straight and the other bent at the knee. With hooded eyes, he straddled my outstretched leg and tore open the condom before rolling it down his shaft. "I'm going to slide in so deep like this, and I'll still be able to see your face when I fuck another orgasm out of you."

I breathed out a laugh and shook my head, even as I glanced at him over my shoulder. "You've given me five. I'm pretty sure the orgasm factory is closed."

"You think so?" He hooked his hand under my bent knee and pushed it higher on the bed, presenting my pussy to him. His gaze stayed locked on it as he ran the head of his cock through my slit, brushing it against my clit.

I moaned, my eyes fluttering closed as my pussy clenched around nothing, and I lifted my ass back toward him. Aching and desperate for something. For *him*.

He chuckled under his breath. "That little move you just made, trying to get me to slide inside you?" Bracing one hand on my hip, he notched himself at my entrance with his other and pushed in the barest inch. "That tells me this greedy little cunt is hungry for another one. And I intend to give her exactly what she wants."

Before I could respond, he sank inside me in a slow, steady glide. Eyes wide and mouth agape, I stared at him over my shoulder as he filled me. And filled me. And filled me more.

"*God*," I choked out, reaching back to wrap my fingers around his wrist where he held me down and sank deep. He was the biggest man I'd ever been with, without a doubt, and the utter fullness of him inside me stole my breath. I didn't know if it was the fact that he was hung like a goddamn horse or that I was so swollen and oversensitive from all the orgasms he'd already given me, but he felt massive. Massive and so, so good. "Holy fuck. You feel..."

"So fucking *good*," he finished for me, a groan threaded through his words as he mirrored my thoughts.

I nodded my agreement as he pulled back before sinking deep again, dragging a moan straight from my chest.

"Jesus Christ," he muttered under his breath, his gaze pinging between my wide-eyed stare and where I was spread tight around his pumping cock. "Your pussy's taking me so well."

On his next thrust, he hitched my leg even higher, making him sink another inch inside, and I couldn't hold in my moan.

"There you go. Let me hear it," he said, leaning over to brush his lips against my ear. "Your cunt's squeezing me like she wants to come again. Is that true? You want to come all over my cock, pretty girl?"

"Fuck," I whispered. I couldn't believe it, but he was right. I didn't just want to come...I *needed* to. With a desperation that was altogether foreign to me. I felt like I was thirteen all over again, getting acquainted with my body for the first time because my pussy had *never* acted like this in my entire life. She was a one-and-done kind of girl—and those single O's almost always came at my own hands or battery-operated boyfriends. And I'd been satisfied with that because it was all I had known. But after this? After *him*? Now, I'd forever know exactly what I was missing.

It was fruitless to deny what I wanted, especially when he could already read my body so well, so I moaned long and low at his next thrust and nodded against the bed. "*Yes.*"

He hummed, the speed of his thrusts picking up, and I wasn't sure I was going to survive this night. I was pretty sure my pussy would not. "I knew you could give me one more. Reach down and play with your clit. Make that pussy come for me, bunny."

I did what he said, reaching a hand beneath me to the apex of my thighs. My clit was hard and so swollen, a shudder racked my body at the barest glance of my fingers against it. I slid my hand even lower, not stopping until I reached where my pussy lips stretched tight around his thick shaft as he pumped in and out of me.

"Bunny," he said, his tone a warning. "I told you to touch your clit. I didn't say anything about my dick."

I bit my lip to stifle a smile and glanced back at him. "But what if I want to?"

"Too bad." He pushed inside me as far as he could, settling deep and making my eyes roll back. "Your cunt's a fucking dream, and I'm already too damn close. But I'm not coming until you do, so I don't need your hands in the mix, too. Now rub that needy little clit and make yourself come all over my cock like a good girl."

Part of me wanted to see what he would do if I didn't obey his demand. Wanted to see what kind of fun punishment he might have in store for me, because for some reason, with this man, I knew even the punishments would be pleasurable. But the other part of me—the greedy whore who was desperate to come—was far louder and won this battle.

I slipped my hand back up, spreading my fingers in a V on either side of my clit so I could give it the friction I needed without direct contact. As soon as I pinched them closed on either side, my pussy fluttered around him, my body reaching for another release.

"That's it," he said, finally pulling back before pushing into me again. And again. And again. "Let it happen..."

His hips slapped against me in a steady rhythm, the sound a punctuation to each moan and groan that fell from our lips. With his fingers digging into my flesh, he gripped my hip and tugged me against him every time he sank deep, his cock hitting spots inside me even my best vibrator hadn't ever reached.

And then I felt it. That tingle...the build. My pussy tightening and pulsing, desperate to fall over that cliff.

"That's my girl. Give it to me." He dug his fingers deeper into my flesh as he thrust into me. "Just like that. Fuck, look at you. You're taking my cock so well. You ready to come all over me?"

With a whimper, I arched back into him, unable to form words to tell him what I needed. It wouldn't have mattered anyway, because I didn't know. All I knew was I was close...so fucking close but unable to fall over the edge. And then his hand was there, brushing against mine, his finger the lightest touch over my clit, and I exploded. My pussy pulsed around his shaft, and even through my moans and the blood thrumming in my ears, I heard him groan as he settled deep, spilling himself inside me.

He braced his arms on either side of me and curved his body over mine. His panting breaths ghosted against my skin as he rested his forehead on my back. "You did so well for me, bunny," he murmured as he brushed a featherlight kiss against my skin.

That gentle kiss combined with his softly uttered praise swept over my body, sending shivers in its wake.

"*Me*? I can barely move, and that was all you."

"You want another one?"

"Why do I think you're not joking?"

"Because I'm not."

I breathed out a laugh and shook my head. "Are you sure you're real and not just a figment of my imagination?"

"Pretty sure."

"I can't believe I'm saying this, but I don't think I can take another one."

"If you change your mind, you let me know." He pressed another kiss against my back in an oddly intimate gesture before pulling out of me on a groan and heading into the bathroom.

It could've been seconds or minutes later when he returned with a warm washcloth and swiped it between my legs, being gentle and taking care not to brush against my oversensitized clit. And *God,* where had this man been all my life? It was just my luck that I'd found him but couldn't keep him.

After he'd cleaned me up and tossed the cloth back in the bathroom, he settled in the bed next to me. I turned to face him, entwining my legs with his and tipping my head up for a kiss. It was slow and languid, just a soft glide of his tongue against mine. And then he pulled back, pressing a kiss to the side of my mouth, then the underside of my jaw before laying his head on the pillow as he trailed his fingers up and down my spine.

Within seconds, his touch grew short and stilted, his eyelids drooping until they closed completely, his fingers still against me. It took all of thirty seconds before he was lost to the world.

He'd been prepared to keep going...to keep making me come as many times as I wanted. I had no doubt he would've spent all night between my thighs if I hadn't tapped out. Even though he'd obviously been exhausted and he clearly needed the rest, he would have kept going if I'd wanted him to.

I reached up, tracing a finger over his defined brows, down the slope of his nose and the outline of his lips, then

I finally ran my nails through his short beard, loving the feel of it against my fingertips.

His face told a story—from the faint silver scar barely visible at the edge of his eyebrow to the bump at the top of his nose like it'd been broken before to the almost permanent creases between his brows, as if he was constantly stressed—I only wished I'd get a chance to hear it.

I rested my hand over his chest, feeling the strong thrum of his heart beneath it, the rhythm lulling me into sleep right along with him.

CHAPTER FIVE

AIDEN

A LOUD CLICK WOKE ME, and I dragged my eyes open, blinking slowly into the light coming in through the curtains. Curtains I didn't recognize. I glanced around, trying to acclimate myself. This wasn't my bedroom, and it sure as hell wasn't my bed. I couldn't remember the last time I'd woken up and I didn't know where I was... College, probably, but that was almost fifteen years ago and not something I aimed for now as a thirty-four-year-old grown-ass man.

My only excuse was that after a hard night's sleep, I always awoke feeling drugged almost, all languid and slow. My eyes were gritty and tired, made worse by the fact that I fell asleep with my contacts in. I couldn't remember the last time that'd been an issue for me.

As a rule, I didn't sleep, and I certainly didn't sleep

well. And I most definitely did not sleep well in a random place with a stranger sharing the bed.

And yet, I had. Here. With her.

I didn't remember anything after I'd cleaned her up and settled into bed next to her. It was like my head had hit the pillow and I'd been out. Which was unheard of for me. I was a massive insomniac—the wee hours of the night were when I'd started writing my first book—and sleep did not come easy for me. Or at all.

I turned my head to glance around, and flashes of last night came to me unbidden. Her pressed up against the door, staring down at me as I knelt in front of her, devouring her pussy. Her on her hands and knees, wet and swollen and ready for me. Her needy little moans as I'd fucked into her as deep as she could take me...

Christ, I couldn't remember the last time it had been like that for me. Hell, I couldn't remember it *ever* being like that. I didn't know if it was because I'd let my guard down with her—something I hadn't done with a woman since high school. Or if it was because we'd just clicked from the instant we met, an ease in our conversations paired with the undeniable chemistry that crackled between us. Regardless, there was no denying the fact that she'd ruined me in only a few short hours.

But fuck, had it felt good to be ruined.

I had no idea what time it was. Had no idea if I was late for the resort's morning meeting or if I'd missed it entirely. If it was the latter, I had no doubt I'd have a dozen texts from my siblings wondering where the hell I was, because my not showing up wasn't something that happened. Ever.

I rolled over, reaching toward her side of the bed, only to find what I'd anticipated. Cold, empty sheets and just the faint hint of her scent left on her pillow.

While I'd been all too ready to give my mystery woman another half dozen orgasms this morning, it seemed she had other ideas. I had no doubt she was sore, and I hated the fact that I couldn't check on her. Make sure she was okay and then make her come one more time to ease that ache a little... I hated that I couldn't take care of her, period.

But she wasn't mine to take care of.

I lay there, listening for sounds in the room, but it was silent save for the sporadic muted voices coming from the hall. She was definitely gone, swept out of my life as quickly as she'd strolled into it.

With a groan, I threw off the covers, swung my legs over the side of the bed, and braced my elbows on my knees. A folded note on the side table with BB scrawled across the front caught my eye, and I grabbed it, flipping it open to read what was inside.

BB,

And here I thought men like you only existed in books... Thanks for being my real life book boyfriend and for a night I'll never forget.

xoxo, Bunny

PS: I grabbed you a late checkout, so stay as long as you need. You seemed like you could use the rest.

I read the looping script five times before I folded it again and clutched it in my hand.

"Fuck." Releasing a deep sigh, I scrubbed a hand over my face just as my phone rang.

I didn't need to glance at the screen to know it was one of my siblings. Truth be told, it was a miracle they had waited this long.

I reached for my phone from the crumpled pile of my jeans and answered when I saw Brady's name on the screen. "Yeah."

"Who is she?" my older brother asked without preamble.

"Who is who?"

"The woman you spent the night with."

"How do you know I spent the night with someone?"

He didn't dignify that with a response, just waited me out.

I shook my head, no longer surprised at the things he knew as Starlight Cove's sheriff. "I don't know who she is."

He grunted. "Well, I hope she was worth Addison's wrath, because the little tyrant was furious with you this morning—first for all your fuckups this week, then because she had to clean up your mess yesterday. And then you skipped the meeting on top of all that. For the first time ever. So we all got to deal with it instead of you. Thanks for that, by the way."

"You think she's still pissed?"

"Without a doubt," he said. "But one of her friends is in town, and they were going to grab breakfast, so you might just luck out and her ire will have fizzled by the time you see her."

"One can hope..."

"So...was she?"

"Was who what?"

"Worth it? The girl you lost your mind over last night."

"Who said anything about losing my mind?"

His silence spoke volumes, and I breathed out a heavy sigh as I glanced around the empty hotel room. A completely foreign ache bloomed in my chest over the fact that I hadn't gotten to say goodbye. "Yeah. She was worth it."

After I gave him a brief rundown of our introduction last night and keeping most of the rest of it to myself, he said he had to run, but that he'd see me later today at the fall tournament for the Little League team the resort sponsored.

And then I just sat there, unable to force myself to move. I had so much shit to do—baseball notwithstanding. Between righting the colossal mistakes I'd made at the resort this week and meeting my publisher's deadline for turning in my next book, I was spread as thin as one could be without turning into Swiss cheese. And yet, here I sat. Thinking about last night and remembering just how good she'd felt under my fingers and under my tongue... How unbelievable she'd felt wrapped around my cock.

One night with her hadn't been enough, but it didn't matter. She was gone. And didn't it just figure that the first woman I'd met in more than a decade who I was interested in would be someone I'd never see again.

CHAPTER SIX

AVERY

THE SECOND I stepped through the diner doors, Addison greeted me with a warm hug.

She squealed into my ear, her arms banded tight around me. "I'm so happy you're here! Even if I only get to see you for a couple hours."

"Me, too. I can't believe it's been four years since I've gotten one of your boa constrictor hugs." I returned it, squeezing her as tight as I dared, though I knew she could withstand nearly anything. She might've been pint-size, but she was the toughest woman I knew.

We'd met during freshman orientation at the University of Maine, and we quickly became inseparable. Her mom had just died, and she was dealing with some boy bullshit, and I was still reeling from the shock of a lifetime, so we'd naturally gravitated toward each other.

Then we'd pledged the same sorority and became roommates and lifelong sisters. Growing together—*healing* together—forged a bond I'd yet to be able to replicate. Even with Willow, who'd been one of my very best friends the past few years. She didn't even know the parts of me I kept hidden, the secrets I kept buried deep, though Addison did.

With a grin, Addison pulled away and dragged me to a booth tucked in the back corner. "Tell me everything I've missed."

I tossed my bag onto the bench before sliding in across from her with a laugh. "You already know everything. I talk to you at least once a week."

"Yeah, but this is different! I can see your face clearly. FaceTime just doesn't cut it."

"I know, but now that I'll be only a few hours away, we can get together more. Maybe meet in the middle once a month."

"*Or...*" she said with a gleam in her eye. "Maybe I can talk your mom into moving to Starlight Cove, and you can just stay here with me forever."

I rolled my eyes. "Nice try. You know I'm not a stick around forever kind of girl."

She released a heavy sigh. "I do know, and I love you anyway. And now with this new job, flying all over the world? You really are going to be my precious little hummingbird, always flitting away."

"You stole that from my mom."

"Guilty."

With a laugh, I grabbed the menu and scanned it quickly. "What's good here?"

"Everything. But if you don't see something you like, you can order whatever you want. Beck can make you anything."

"Addison," a man snapped from behind the counter. Wearing a backward baseball cap and a scowl, he was tall with an imposing presence that probably intimidated most people. "In case you didn't notice, there are other people in here besides you, so your made-to-order dishes will have to wait for your personal chef."

That had to be one of her infamous pain-in-the-ass brothers. Despite Addison's and my closeness, I had yet to meet any of her siblings. She'd said she'd grown up with them constantly all up in her business, so her college life was just for her. But she knew my mom well enough that the two of them still talked every month or so.

"Oh, relax, Beck." She rolled her eyes, then leaned forward, bracing her arms on the table. On a whisper, she said, "But seriously...anything you want."

A sharp smack sounded from Beck's direction, and I turned to find him pointing a spatula at Addison. "I mean it, or *you're* going to be opening the diner for the next week."

"And what would you be doing?"

"Enjoying some extra time between Everly's—"

"*Okay!*" she yelled, holding up a hand as she cut him off. Then she turned to me with a shudder. "I'm happy for them. I really am. But I've learned more about my brothers' sex lives in the past six months than I ever wanted to know in my entire *life*. And they're falling like dominoes. First Brady, then that grumpy asshole"—she pointed a thumb over her shoulder in Beck's direction—"and now Ford. Who's next? Aiden?" She snorted into her coffee and shook her head.

After putting in our orders—everything from the menu, thanks to an intense stare down from Beck—I sipped my coffee and raised a brow in her direction. "So what happened last night? I can't believe you stood me up."

"God, I'm so sorry!"

"I should let you sweat it longer, but I can't. I'm not even a little bit mad because I got my world absolutely rocked by the hottest man I've ever seen. I've never come so hard in my *life*."

Her mouth dropped open as she stared at me. "*Seriously*? I've lived here my whole fucking life, and my world has *never* been rocked. You're here for, what, twelve hours, and it happens? Unfair. I demand you tell me everything so I can live vicariously through you. Who was he?"

I blew out a sigh and shook my head. "I don't know,

actually. I don't know his name, so I've been calling him BB in my mind."

"BB?"

"Book boyfriend. I swear, it was like he stepped straight out of the pages of one of my filthiest books." I leaned toward her, dropping my voice to barely above a whisper. "He made me come *six times* in like an hour."

She slammed her hand down on the table, drawing the attention of the other patrons. "Shut. Up."

I held up a hand. "Swear it."

"God, you suck. Meanwhile, instead of getting railed into next week, I had to clean up my brother's fuckup."

"Which one?"

"Aiden." She spat his name like a curse word at church.

"What did he fuck up?"

"What *didn't* he fuck up?" Frustration seeped into every word. "I don't know what the hell is going on with him, but it's been one mistake after another. For *months*. Things keep falling through the cracks, and that's completely unlike him. This is the guy who's so buttoned-up, I wouldn't be surprised if he slept in his dress shirts."

I laughed. "He sounds like a lot of fun."

"I just don't know what his issue is. The resort has been a lot busier, so our workload has increased, but that's been going on for months."

"Have you guys hired anyone yet?"

"Nope, even though I've brought it up a dozen times. He

keeps vetoing it because he can't stand the idea of anyone else's hands in his shit." She took a sip of her coffee and shook her head. "I swear, I'm about ready to hire someone behind his back because I can't keep doing my job *and* his. Not now, when the resort is booked solid and we've got that documentary filming here for the next two months. It's already taking up more of my time than I can give."

I hummed. "And how do you think Mr. Buttoned-Up would take it if you did that?"

"Oh, he'd lose his shit, for sure," she said on a laugh.

"And yet you sound absolutely delighted at the thought." I raised a brow at her over my mug. "I see fucking with your brothers is still your favorite pastime..."

She grinned. "It's the best."

"Well, you know my motto... Better to beg forgiveness than ask for permission."

Beck dropped off our meals with a glare at his sister and a slightly less grumpy expression shot my way. "Let me know if you need anything else," he said, tapping his knuckles next to my plate.

"What about me?" Addison called after him.

"Get it yourself," he said without glancing back.

"Are all your brothers this charismatic?"

"If by charismatic, you mean grumpy assholes, then yes, pretty much. Ford's the only nice one, but he's at a tournament for the Little League team he coaches with Aiden, so you won't get to meet either of them. And I won't subject you to Brady or Levi."

Before I could respond, my phone rang.

"One sec." I riffled through my bag until I found it, a picture of my mom and me on the beach flashing on the screen. I glanced at the time with a raised brow. As a rule, she didn't wake up before 10 a.m. And considering it was barely 8, this was unheard of.

"It's my mom." I held up the phone between us, pointing the screen toward Addison.

Her brows lifted the same as mine. "Before 10? You better answer. Maybe she needs bail money."

That should've been something that would garner a laugh, because it obviously wouldn't be true. But my mom had, in fact, called me for bail money. It was during sophomore year, and she'd gotten picked up for trespassing—ie, sunbathing—on a yacht in the harbor. Of course, she hadn't needed us after all because by the time we'd gotten there with the cash, the yacht's owner had not only bailed her out but had taken her back to the scene of the crime, where she stayed for a month as his guest.

"Mom?" I asked after accepting the call. "What's going on? Are you okay?"

She giggled on the other end of the line. "My sweet girl, always looking out for me."

"That's not an answer..."

"I'm fine," she said. "And I'm a grown woman, by the way, so even if I weren't, you don't have to worry about me."

"Well, how can I not when it's 8 o'clock in the morning,

and you told me explicitly if I call you before 10, I better either be bleeding out in a ditch or about to elope in Vegas. Otherwise, you'd disown me."

"And I mean that, too. But this flight is eleven hours, and I knew you'd already be on the road by the time we landed, so I wanted to catch you before that."

"Catch me for what?" I asked before the rest of her sentence caught up to me. "And what do you mean, flight?"

As soon as I was done with breakfast, I was jumping in my car and hitting the road for the three-hour drive to my hometown...where I was supposed to be staying with my mother.

"I have good news and bad news," she said. "Which do you want first?"

"Bad."

She breathed out a long sigh. "Well, it's a funny story, really. It turns out I heard Stewart wrong, and he can't get you into flight attendant training quite yet."

"What does 'quite yet' mean?" I asked with barely restrained patience.

Prior to my coming home, my mom had promised me that her boyfriend of the month was able to pull some strings and get me started on the path of my dream job, but I needed to come *immediately*. It was the entire reason I'd quit my job in Havenbrook and moved halfway across the country in the blink of an eye.

"The next opening is in January."

"*January*?"

Addison's brows flew up at my tone, but I couldn't tamp down my reaction. January was three months away. Not to mention that I'd just quit my job to move home for this supposedly immediate opportunity, and now the opportunity wasn't happening for months.

"Yes," she said. "But just think of how great it will be! You can stay at the house—rent free, of course—so you can take a few months off, relax, enjoy yourself... And Stewart is always happy to give you money if you need it."

"I'm not gonna take some random guy's money, Mom."

"He's not some random guy. I just told you his name is Stewart, and he's been very good to me."

"Good to you for how long?"

She huffed out a laugh. "You know that doesn't matter to me."

I scrubbed a hand across my forehead and blew out a long sigh. "And the good news?"

"Oh! Stewart is taking me to Greece with him, so you'll have the house to yourself for the rest of the month."

I sat there in silence for so long, my mouth hanging open, that Addison lifted a single brow in my direction. But I could only shake my head at her. After a lifetime of growing up with my mom, I shouldn't have been surprised by this. This was her MO, after all. It was one of the many reasons people loved her. One of the reasons *I* loved her. She was spontaneous and charismatic and effervescent—the very epitome of a free spirit. And someone I'd looked up to my entire life.

The only trouble was, she was that person with everyone, not just me. I'd been feeling disconnected for a while now, and I was looking forward to this time with my mom to anchor me again. But it looked like that was going to have to wait.

"The key's under the mat, so you just enjoy yourself while I'm gone."

I huffed out a disbelieving laugh. "It's not that easy, Mom. I've gotta find a job now. Not all of us have sugar daddies to cover the bills."

"That was *one* time."

"Yeah? And what do you call this?"

"Having fun," she said, the shrug clear in her tone. "Now, you have some while I'm gone. I'll let you know when we land. Love you!"

Before I could respond, the line went dead. I stared down at my phone, my mind whirring through all the different possibilities of what was in front of me now that my plan had been pushed back. I no longer had a reason to get to Rosewood today...or this week. Hell, even this whole month. And if I knew my mom—and I did—I wouldn't be surprised if she was gone for months, plural. Especially if she had a chance to avoid a New England winter.

"Well," I said, tucking my phone back into my purse. "It seems I'm no longer in a rush to get home because my mom is flitting off to Greece with her boyfriend of the week. So, what are you doing tonight?"

Addison leaned over the table toward me, her eyes alight with excitement. It was the same look she used to get on her face before suggesting some insane scheme in college. One I always, *always* went along with.

"I have a better question," she said. "What are you doing for the next three months?"

CHAPTER SEVEN

AIDEN

FOR THE PAST COUPLE YEARS, my younger brother Ford and I had been coaching the Little League team the resort sponsored—well, *I* coached, and for the past couple months, he'd been sneaking off with his new wife, Quinn, and leaving me to handle shit on my own. At least today, Brady sat in the dugout with me, lending his unofficial coaching help to the cause.

Sponsoring the team was something our mom had believed in, so it was something we'd worked hard to continue. Even during our lean years—and there had been a fuck-ton of lean years—we'd never cut that from the budget. We'd cut our pay, sure. But taking away these kids' ability to play baseball? Never.

Today was the last hurrah of the fall season—the tournament where we either played all fucking day, or we were out after the first game. I didn't know which I'd prefer. I had so much work to do—both for the resort and my publisher—but being here and focused on the game would keep my mind occupied and off other things.

Namely, the woman I couldn't get out of my head.

"Sorry about that," Ford said as he strolled up to us, his hair mussed, no doubt from his wife's roaming hands. "I just had to—" He cut off then, and I glanced over, finding his mouth agape as he gave me a quick once-over. "Holy shit."

"What?" I asked, turning my attention back to the field.

"You got laid."

It took half a second for his words to register, but when they did, I snapped my head toward him, shock lighting my features before I could school them. *Fuck.* I was usually better than this at keeping shit from my family. First, Brady got me to spill more than I ever normally would have about the woman I'd spent last night with, and now I was apparently wearing a *just got lucky* expression on my face for my brothers to pick apart mercilessly.

"I don't know what you're talking about," I said with as much confidence as I could muster. Which, admittedly, wasn't much because I could still taste her on my tongue.

Ford just laughed. "Sure you don't. There's no use trying to deny it. I can sniff that shit out like a bloodhound. Can't I?" He lifted his chin in Brady's direction.

"You do kind of have something going on there," my traitor brother said, gesturing toward my face as he agreed with Ford. "Is this because of the woman you told me about?"

My gaze shot to his. "Dude. What the fuck."

Brady already fucking knew it was about that woman—we'd just had a ten-minute conversation about her—and him tossing that out like a bone for Ford to sink his teeth into was a seriously shitty move. At only eleven months apart, we'd always been closer to each other than our other siblings, and it had been an unwritten rule between us that what we said to each other stayed between us. But apparently, he was more pissed about this morning's meeting than he'd let on, and this was payback for making him deal with our tyrant of a baby sister without me.

"This is too good." Ford rubbed his hands together, a giant grin splitting his face. "What woman? Tell me *everything*."

I crossed my arms over my chest and glared at them both, then I gazed out at the ball field where our focus should've been and attempted to ignore the assholes.

"Was it the *I can call you Daddy, too* single mom?" Ford asked, referring to one of the Little Leaguer's moms who hadn't been shy about letting me know her interest in me. "Is that why you don't want to talk about it right now?"

I didn't even bother to spare him a glance. "No, it wasn't that woman. I know better than to get involved with someone who'd make my life difficult. And I don't want to talk about it right now because A) we're surrounded by a bunch of little kids and their parents—"

"One of whom is desperate to call you Daddy..." Ford cut in.

"And B) it's none of your fucking business."

Ford laughed. *Laughed.* The irritating little shit. "Oh no. You're the one who showed up at this game with your *I just got laid* face on, thus making it my business." He shrugged and made a show of pulling out his phone to look at the time. "I could also make it Addison's business if you wanted... She'll be here any minute. I can wait."

"You're such a dick."

His smile only grew as he stared at me, one brow raised in challenge. I missed the days when he was shorter than me and I could glare down at him, scare him into doing whatever I wanted with simply a look, but the fucker had been my height since he was seventeen.

Finally, when it was clear he wasn't going to budge, I blew out a long sigh and scrubbed a hand down my face. "It was no big deal, all right? It's been a shitty week, and I needed to blow off some steam. I went to One Night Stan's, had a one-night stand, and that's it. She didn't leave her number, and I don't even know her name—"

Brady cut in, "Just that she's a redheaded smokeshow with a penchant for—"

"Would you shut the fuck up?" I snapped at him. "I didn't even say that. You're just making shit up."

Brady lifted a single shoulder. "You said enough."

"Anyway." I turned around, giving him my back and

doing my best to ignore him. "She's not from around here, so it's done."

"What if she was?" Ford asked.

"What if she was, what?"

He stared at me with raised brows. "From around here?"

Snippets of what that might look like flashed through my mind—her in my room, in my bed, her hair spread out on my pillow while I—

I cleared my throat. "Doesn't matter, because she's not. And we're done talking about it."

Ford lifted his chin toward the bleachers. "If you actually want to be done talking about it, you better do something about your face, because Addison's on her way over here."

I glanced in the direction he'd indicated and found our sister, her powerhouse gait and the way the crowd separated to let her through immediately giving away her position. My gaze strayed to the right of her and out to the field before immediately snapping back when a flash of red caught my eye, and my stomach clenched.

A woman walked next to Addison, laughing at something my sister said. A woman with a waterfall of red hair, a soft smile on those full, pouty lips that had been wrapped tight around my cock, and a tiny bunny tattoo behind her ear that I'd enjoyed the fuck out of exploiting last night.

Jesus Christ. *Jesus. Fucking. Christ.* I'd woken up this

morning, thinking I'd never see her again because she was only passing through, and now she was here…with my sister?

They came to a stop in front of us, and Ford greeted them, but I couldn't find the words. My mouth was dry, all the air sucked from my lungs, and all I could do was stare as Addison gestured to the woman next to her with both hands. The woman whose body I knew intimately but not her name.

"Surprise!" Addison said, gesturing toward my one-night stand with a flourish. "This is Avery, my college bestie! I've managed to sweet-talk her into working at the resort for three months, so you can stop being such a grump all the time, Aiden." Under her breath, she said, "And so I can stop babysitting you and dealing with your fuckups." Then, louder, she added, "You're welcome!"

Addison turned to the woman I'd been inside a mere twelve hours before. "Avery, meet Aiden. One of my brothers and your new boss. Isn't this gonna be *great*?"

Her new boss. Her. New. *Boss.*

Fuck me.

Not only had I, apparently, slept with my new employee, but I'd spilled my guts to her. My sister's best friend. Shared things with her I hadn't shared with anyone before. Things I absolutely did not want my siblings to know. Things I couldn't have anyone else finding out about, for the good of the resort.

And now she stared up at me, confusion and curiosity

and...hurt swimming in those dark eyes, and I knew I was totally and completely fucked.

Avery

I WASN'T sure how long Addison and I had been at the game when Aiden cornered me outside the restrooms in the field house. He looked so different today than he had last night—those tattoos I'd drooled over were now tucked away, hidden beneath a white button-down shirt rolled up at the cuffs, and he had a weight to him that he hadn't had last night.

Last night, when he'd made me come more times than I ever had before.

Last night, when he'd slept next to me, his arm banded around my waist.

Last night, when he'd talked books with me and told me he was an *author*. Not that he owned and ran a beachfront resort.

"Avery," he said, and I didn't want to think about how much I loved the sound of my name on his lips. "Can we talk?"

"I'm not interested in talking to liars," I said, stepping around him and not sparing him a glance.

"Wait, I can explain." His words made me pause, but it

was his softly uttered, "Please," that had me stopping in my tracks.

Slowly, I turned around to face him and crossed my arms over my chest. "Explain what? The fact that you apparently felt the need to lie to get into my pants?"

"I didn't lie."

I breathed out a laugh. "No? So you *don't* own and run your family's resort?"

"I do..."

"That's not what you told me last night."

He ran a hand through his hair and glanced around. Then he wrapped his fingers around my wrist and tugged me behind the field house, out of sight from any onlookers. Quietly, he said, "I do that, but I'm *also* an author. Which is the part I need you to keep to yourself."

"You what?" I asked, unable to keep the sharpness from my tone.

"Look, no one else knows about that. Not Addison. Not any of my brothers. No one in town. Just my agent, my publisher..." He sucked in a deep breath and blew it out slowly, those intense eyes locked on mine. "And now you."

I ignored the thrill that shot through me over that and shook my head. "You can't be serious."

The tick of his jaw was his only response.

I huffed out an incredulous laugh. "So, let me get this straight—it wasn't bad enough that you lied to me, but now you want me to lie to my best friend *for you* and keep this secret from her? You don't even know me. Do you know how shitty it is to ask me to do that?"

"Yes." He stared down at me, those bright-blue eyes remorseful but determined. "But it doesn't change the fact that I don't want anyone else to know. And you're the only other one with the knowledge to tell them."

"Why?"

"Why what?"

I crossed my arms over my chest and raised a brow. "Why don't you want them to know?"

He pressed his lips together and shook his head. "It doesn't matter."

I stared up at him, blinking slowly. "Okay, *wow*. Because of last night when you absolutely destroyed my vagina—thanks for that, by the way—I already know what you're packing, but *Jesus*. You've got quite a pair to demand this of me without providing any answers after you lied to my face."

"I didn't lie," he said firmly. He cleared his throat and leaned closer, lowering his voice. "But *you* did. You told me you weren't sticking around, which was the only reason I told you in the first place. And now I find out you're not only staying in Starlight Cove, but you're going to be working at the resort for the rest of the year?"

"Not that I owe you an explanation, but I hadn't agreed to stay until a couple hours ago when your sister begged me to. And if I hadn't signed the contract already, I'd just leave so I wouldn't have to deal with any of this." I pressed my thumb and forefinger against my eyes and breathed out a sigh before dropping my hand to my side. "You didn't have to lie. You could have just told me the truth."

"I *did* tell you the truth," he said, his voice low and thick with something I couldn't quite name. "You're the only one I've told the truth to." He stared at me, his gaze scanning my face, though I wasn't quite sure what he was looking for. "Please don't make me regret it."

Without another word, he stepped around me, his shoulder brushing against mine and sending a ripple of awareness through my body, reminding me exactly what he'd been able to coax from me last night. And then he was gone, and I was left there, reeling.

I hated lies and I hated secrets. Hated the weight of them, hated when they came out, hated the aftermath. And he'd just asked me to keep one from my best friend. Something I'd never done once during our entire friendship.

I had no idea what I was going to do. Just that I'd have to do everything in my power to avoid him until I could figure it out.

CHAPTER EIGHT

AIDEN

I COULDN'T REMEMBER the last time I'd been this mad. And that was saying something, considering the fact that I'd been dealing with my sister every day for the vast majority of her twenty-seven years. But I'd had enough with that overstepping little shit.

The system we had at the resort may not have been perfect, but it was ours. One that had been working for years. When we'd been thrown into the deep end ten years ago, following our mother's death and our father completely shutting down after it, we'd had to figure shit out. Quickly. While the day-to-day operations were mostly run by Addison and me, with Beck taking on the responsibility of the diner, it was still a collaborative family effort. Ford did repairs around the resort and any new builds, Levi ran boat tours, and Brady had picked up the monetary slack for years.

Yet Addison had taken it upon herself to hire a new employee without so much as whispering the mere suggestion to *any* of us. It was complete bullshit, and I was pissed enough to corner her about it without allowing myself time to cool down.

She might have been upset with me for what had been going on this week—okay, these past couple months—but it had nothing on how I was feeling right now. Frustration over the fact that I couldn't get my shit done. Worry about whether I'd be able to meet my publisher's deadline. Regret over the fact that I'd shared my secret with someone I absolutely shouldn't have. And anger that my meddling sister had brought that mistake directly to my doorstep.

Once I was back at the resort after a day full of games, I strode into the main inn, spotting Brady's girlfriend, Luna, behind the desk, with Levi lounging on the couch, reading a book.

Luna was fairly new around here. She'd caught the eye of my older brother when she'd chained herself to a tree on our property's border to protest a new development in town. While she'd been a pain in the ass for me and this resort in the beginning, she'd eventually become the reason we were finally standing on two feet. Since she and Brady had officially become a couple, she now worked for the resort, providing in-room massages to guests and hosting daily yoga classes on the beach.

And, apparently, covering the main inn when my sister fucked off to play with her friend.

"Either of you see Addison around?" I asked.

Levi grunted out something I took to mean no, and Luna shook her head. "Not since earlier when she introduced us to Avery." She grinned. "I'm so excited to have another girl join the crew! Even if it's only for a few months."

I stumbled to a stop and glanced at Luna over my shoulder. "Wait. Addison told you we were hiring Avery?"

"Yeah." She lifted a single shoulder in a shrug. "This morning when she asked Levi and me over to cover for her."

I clenched my jaw and gave a stilted nod before storming through the house to find my pain-in-the-ass sister. She didn't think it prudent to touch base with me—the guy in charge of all the financials—before bringing on a new hire, but she *did* discuss it with Brady's girlfriend and the resort's yoga instructor?

Complete and utter bullshit.

That wasn't how we did things around here, and I had no qualms about reminding her of that fact. Loudly and vehemently until she got it through her thick skull.

The main inn wasn't ostentatiously large, but it was big enough that it had held a family of eight comfortably for years. Now, Addison and I were the only two who resided in it, leaving the vast majority of the rooms empty—or empty when they weren't filled with cases of paper towels, thanks to my most recent screw-up.

Since one had to be cleared out for Avery to use, it could've been any of the four bedrooms available. I could only hope Addison put her on the other side of the house where her room was, rather than in the only other bedroom on my side. One that wasn't just close but also happened to be connected by a bathroom.

I had no idea how I'd handle being that close to Avery, day in and day out, for the next three months. Because not only was she a walking, talking time bomb, but she was someone I was uncontrollably attracted to.

But Addison wouldn't do that. She'd want her friend close to her. She wouldn't—

I stopped dead in my tracks when I strode through my bathroom and into the connecting bedroom that had once been Brady's. It had been cleared of all paper towel cartons, leaving only the few furnishings in it—a bed, dresser, and nightstand. But clearly, my hope that Addison wouldn't put her friend directly next to me had merely been wishful thinking. Because there, on top of the navy comforter, were Avery's bags.

"Fuck me," I muttered under my breath, scrubbing a hand down my face.

I had no idea how the fuck I was going to handle this. Having the woman I'd had a one-night stand with, who was now my employee and knew the secret I couldn't have getting out, only two doors away was going to be a challenge I hadn't anticipated. Add that to the already precarious tower of bricks my life was, and I didn't know how I was going to make it through without everything tumbling down around me.

I gritted my teeth and stormed out into the hallway, intent on finding Addison. Something out the window caught my eye, and I glanced down to see my sister leading Avery around, obviously giving her a tour of the resort. I stopped in front of the window and braced my hands on the sill, my shoulders sagging as I blew out a frustrated breath.

Apparently our little chat was going to have to wait.

Since Luna and Levi were watching the inn and Addison wasn't available for me to lay into, I might as well make use of this time and put all these feelings to work in my writing.

I was currently struggling my way through a sex scene that I'd been blocked on for a while, but if there was one good thing about all this anger and frustration bubbling up inside, it was that I could release some of that onto the page.

I DIDN'T KNOW how much later it was when my sister came stomping down the hallway, her obnoxious laugh breaking my train of thought. Though it didn't matter much because I'd spent the past hour staring at a blank document, my mind not coming up with anything constructive. Instead, it'd constantly strayed to last night and how Avery had looked every time I'd made her come. Even without trying, she rattled my concentration, something I couldn't afford with everything I had on the line.

I listened as Avery and my sister said their goodnights, and then a door closed and retreating footsteps sounded, signaling my cue as Addison left.

After closing my laptop, I tore out of my room, taking a second glance toward Avery's now-shut door to ensure she was tucked away. It took only three strides before I caught up with Addison, and I gripped my sister's wrist to haul her to a stop. "We need to talk."

She turned to face me with a raised brow. "Oh, *now* you want to talk? Where was that interest this morning when you ditched the meeting?"

"I was busy. And so were you, apparently." I clenched my jaw, crossing my arms over my chest as I glowered down at her. "I want to know what made you think it was a good idea to hire a new employee without discussing it with anyone."

"Well, if you hadn't been fucking off wherever you were this morning, I could have discussed it with you."

"Nice try, but I was out coaching the Little League team we sponsor when you decided to go Maverick on us."

"What's even the big deal, Aiden? We need the help. Desperately."

"What's the big deal?" I asked incredulously. "You have no idea about the resort's financials. How do you even know if we can afford to pay someone?"

"Are you kidding? I have to listen to you drone on about it every week! Of course I know we can afford to pay someone. And the only reason I took it upon myself to handle it is because I knew you never would. You *haven't.* You can never ask for help, even when you're drowning. So I did what needed to be done."

"What's that supposed to mean?"

"It means you haven't been handling yourself or your duties at the resort. Shit has been slipping through the cracks for months. Something had to give, because I can't keep pulling your weight *and* my own." She shrugged. "Avery's plans fell through, and she doesn't have anywhere to be until January. This was the perfect solution."

"The perfect solution for whom?"

"All of us, obviously." She rolled her eyes. "I can focus on our social media and marketing and getting this documentary handled, you can focus on the boring spreadsheets that you love to bury your face in all day long and whatever the hell else has been taking your attention, and Avery can deal with the day-to-day guest interactions. Getting my bestie here to help even out the overwhelming testosterone I choke on every day is just a bonus."

I clenched my jaw, unable to dispute any of her claims but hating every bit of it. "You still should've talked to us before you made that decision on your own."

"Maybe. But it's already done." She shrugged, like she hadn't thrown a wrench the size of Europe into my life. "Look, we needed help, Aiden. And it's not like we don't have the room for her."

I narrowed my eyes. "Yeah, four open bedrooms, and yet you pick the only one next to me. There a reason for that?"

She sniffed, tucking her hair behind her ear as she looked up at me with an innocent face she'd perfected over the years. One that had always had our mom blaming me or one of my brothers for something our brat of a sister had done. One I didn't believe for a second. "I don't know what you're insinuating, but Brady's room had the fewest amount of paper towel cartons in it, so it was easiest to disperse the overflow to the other rooms. I could've put her in the one next to mine, but it's bursting with your last mistake..."

I clenched my jaw, my hands curling into fists as I stared down at her. Was there anything in the world that got someone more enraged than a headstrong baby sister who thought she knew best? If there was, I hadn't yet come across it.

"You can give me your BS excuses all you want, but I know you," I said. "And I know when you're meddling."

"I'm not—"

"Lay off, Addison," I snapped. "I mean it. Stop fucking around in other people's lives."

With that, I stormed back to my room, slamming my

door like I was fourteen all over again instead of a thirty-four-year-old man who normally had a better handle on his emotions.

On a groan, I dropped down on the edge of my bed. I hung my head, elbows braced on my knees, and admitted the truth to myself. My sister wasn't who I was mad at. That award lay firmly on my shoulders.

I'd gotten myself into this mess. I was the one who'd written a book that had gone viral. I was the one who'd accepted a lucrative publishing deal to finish out the series. I was the one who'd been trying to juggle it all, while making an active choice to keep it from my family and the rest of the town.

There had been so many times in the past five years when I'd had the opportunity to come clean. At first, I'd kept it a secret because of those whispers in the back of my mind, courtesy of our father. We'd grown up in a house where genre fiction was a dirty word. As a man who'd spent his life attempting to write the next great American novel, he held the viewpoint that if you weren't reading the classics, you might as well not be reading at all because everything else was trash. It was a bullshit stance that I'd since shed, but when I'd first started writing, I'd had no idea if my siblings had. I'd been rightfully apprehensive over their finding out that I not only wrote fantasy, but erotic fantasy at that.

It wasn't until years and half a dozen books later when I'd come to the realization that my siblings cared about that elitist outlook as much as I did. Which was to say, not at all. But at that point, the hole I'd dug had gotten so deep that it had become easier just to keep going along with the status quo than it had been to come clean. Then, suddenly, five years had gone by, and my tally of lies had just kept stacking up.

And now, with the resort in the limelight, I was worried about what would happen to its success if it became widely known that one of the owners of the resort and A.M. Kinsey were one and the same.

While it was great to hope that everyone in the world would be open and accepting about it, the truth of the matter was that just wasn't the case. People judged harshly for far less, and I didn't want my choices to negatively affect my family or the success we were just starting to see.

With a sigh, I stood and unbuttoned my dress shirt, ready to call it a night. It was clear I wasn't going to accomplish anything more today, and the best thing was probably for me to sleep it off—or attempt to, anyway. And to do so while trying to forget the fact that the sweetest pussy I'd ever tasted was less than fifteen feet away.

I could hear her shuffling around in the bathroom as I stripped down to my boxer briefs, not bothering to tamp down my body's reaction to her. My cock was hard and thick, thanks only to her remembered taste and those damn noises she'd made through each one of her orgasms.

Bracing my hands against the frame of the closed bathroom door, I hung my head and shut my eyes, taking a few deep breaths in an attempt to get my shit under control. Normally, I'd take care of this problem in the shower, but that felt exceptionally risky, considering Avery and I now shared this bathroom.

But would she feel the same way? Or would she have no problem getting herself off in there with the detachable showerhead, pointing the pulsing spray against her sweet little clit? Teasing herself until she was crying out in pleasure, biting her lip in an attempt to stifle her moans...

I was just reaching down to adjust myself when the bathroom door flew open, and Avery walked out of the bathroom and straight into my chest.

With a yelp, she jerked back, confusion on her face that quickly morphed into anger. "What're you doing in my room?"

I raised a brow at her and lifted my chin toward the identical-looking door on the other side of the bathroom. The one she'd obviously mistaken mine for. "Wrong door, bunny."

She glanced around, her eyes shifting behind me until she took in my bedroom, clearly different from the one she was staying in. Then her gaze traveled over me from my face and down my chest until her attention stuttered briefly on the beast that was dying to be let out of my boxers, before snapping her eyes up to mine.

"Right. I got mixed up. I'll just—" She jerked her thumb over her shoulder, giving me another once-over before she spun around and headed back to her room.

With a groan, I cupped a hand over my eyes and shut the bathroom door, cutting off my view of her in the tiny shorts she wore beneath a threadbare T-shirt. But it didn't matter. The sight of her walking away was seared into my retinas, and I had no doubt it would be keeping me company as I attempted—and failed at—sleep.

CHAPTER NINE

AVERY

AVOIDING Aiden was more difficult than I'd anticipated. I didn't realize how often we'd cross paths, especially since my room was directly next to his. And especially since I'd confused his door for my own more than once.

Though I'd tried my best to avoid him, I could feel his eyes on me whenever we were in the same space. And I'd like to say I didn't watch him when he wasn't looking, but that would be a lie.

I caught dozens of glimpses of him sitting behind his desk, those sexy-as-fuck black-framed glasses perched on his nose, his brow pinched and mouth set a firm line as he went over financials or files or spreadsheets.

I knew by heart the transition of his attire from completely buttoned-up at the beginning of the day to how it was when he finally headed up to his room for the night—tie loosened, the top couple buttons of his shirt undone, and his sleeves rolled up.

More than once, I'd been forced to witness him hauling guests' luggage or loading boxes for Beck at the diner or helping the production crew carry their equipment where it needed to go, watching the bunch and flex of all those muscles.

And that didn't even mention all the times I'd run into him in the middle of the night, him shirtless and me not wearing nearly enough to keep what he did to me under wraps. His eyes were usually tired but sharp, proving he hadn't yet been to sleep. I couldn't help but wonder how often that happened. And why he'd been able to fall asleep so quickly and sleep so soundly when he'd been with me.

I also didn't anticipate how many times I'd be getting myself off to memories of what he'd done to me, stifling my moans into my pillow or hoping the shower spray covered them all while he was just a door away.

Thankfully, Addison had been my touchstone for my new job, so I'd been able to steer clear of the man who'd taken up permanent residence in my fantasies, managing to avoid any more one-on-one conversations with him for more than a week. I knew that couldn't possibly last, especially considering I'd be here for three months, but I was going to do everything in my power to extend it as long as possible.

Because I still didn't know what to do.

I was torn, one part of me yearning for the man he'd

been that night in my hotel room, and the other part hating the one who'd asked me to keep a secret from his entire family. It was shitty, no doubt, but I couldn't help but wonder if I'd hate his request as much if my life hadn't happened the way it had… If my mom and I hadn't had the rug pulled out from under us, our lives irrevocably altered by someone's kept secret.

"Hey." Addison pulled me out of my thoughts, tearing into the front room of the inn like a tiny tornado. In the years we'd been apart, I'd somehow managed to forget how she was always on the go, never standing still. She moved at the speed of a freight train, and God help anyone who got in her way. "Are you busy?"

"Nope, just checking on tomorrow's reservations. What's up?"

"The crew didn't finish cleaning the Bayside Room when they were done filming in there, and it's booked for tomorrow. Can you take care of it before you clock out?"

I gave her a nod. "Sure."

"Great." She shot me a beaming smile. "I should be done soon. You want to grab dinner? We could head into town and go to One Night Stan's."

At her words, I tripped over absolutely nothing and stumbled straight into the wall, flashes of the last time I was at that bar accosting me. Aiden's smile, how his dimple popped when we'd been talking, and his low, rumbling laugh. A laugh I hadn't heard once in the time I'd been staying here…

"Shit," Addison said with a giggle. "Are you all right?"

"You're supposed to ask me that *before* you start laughing."

She snorted, obviously trying to hold it in. "I'm sorry."

"No, you're not."

"You're right. I'm not." She stopped trying to hold it in and let out a loud guffaw. "You remember that time you tripped up the steps at a football game, and your popcorn and slushie flew everywhere?"

"No," I said flatly. "I'd forgotten all about one of the most embarrassing moments of my life. But thanks for reminding me."

"Oh, it wasn't that bad."

I pinned her with a look, one brow raised. "I spilled my entire cherry slushie onto Ben Forester's lap, so it looked like he had a period."

That only made her giggle harder. The thing about Addison's laugh was that it was infectious as fuck, so even if she was laughing *at* you, pretty soon, you were laughing *with* her. It didn't take long before we were leaning into each other, tears streaming down our faces until we were out of breath and attempting to hold each other up.

God, I'd missed this. Missed *her*. There was something special about friends who had known you for so long. Friends you'd grown up with and had inside jokes with. The kind you had your own shorthand language with. The kind who knew you, inside and out. Knew all your baggage, who'd seen you at your best and helped you through your worst and loved you fiercely all the same.

"Okay," I said on a giggle, straightening as I wiped tears from the corners of my eyes. "I'll go clean up, then I'll change, and we can head out when you're done."

"Sounds good." She nodded. Then, with a completely straight face, she asked, "Do you think you'll get a chance to sit at a stranger's table and eat their food tonight?"

It was a callback to senior year when I'd unknowingly done exactly that. Except it hadn't just been a stranger...it'd been one of my professors, and I hadn't realized that until he'd returned to the table just in time to see me inhale a mouthful of his french fries.

Without bothering to reply, I flipped her off over my shoulder, her laughter following me as I headed toward the Bayside Room. My stomach was growling like no one's business, so hopefully it wouldn't take me too long to straighten up.

I turned the corner into the room and jerked to a stop just inside the door. Aiden stood in the corner, his back to me as he handled what Addison had sent me to do. While I'd done my best to restrain my roaming eyes this week, the chance to look at him while he was unaware was too good to pass up.

His shoulders were broad, filling out that gray dress shirt in a way that should've been illegal, but that had *nothing* on his ass in those suit pants. I'd never been one for the whole businessman look, but there was something delicious about *this* man in it. Maybe it was because I'd already seen him dressed down in a T-shirt and jeans, and I'd seen him in nothing at all. And because of that, I knew exactly what he was hiding beneath his buttoned-up attire.

It felt like a secret just between us, and I hated how much I loved it.

I leaned a little too hard against the door, causing it to knock softly into the wall behind it. He froze, then straightened as he turned his head to look over his shoulder. With a muttered curse, I slipped out and around the doorway, pressing myself against the wall and holding my breath. Hoping like hell he hadn't seen me.

After a few tense moments, I finally exhaled slowly when I heard him go back to what he'd been doing and thanked whoever was looking out for me that I'd have at least one more day of reprieve.

A COUPLE DAYS LATER, Addison strolled into the front entry as I was researching a day-trip the couple in Cottage Twelve had asked me to arrange. Thankfully, I had taken to the job they'd needed me to fill easily and without much training. It wasn't all that different from what I'd done in Havenbrook—taking care of people and making sure they had what they needed. Except here, it was the guests I needed to look out for.

"Hey," she said, stopping on the other side of the desk. "How's it going today?"

"Good. Scheduled a fall foliage tour for Cottage Seven, organized a private fishing charter with Levi for the group of friends staying in Cottages Three, Four, and Five, and I'm working on putting together a day-trip for the couple in Cottage Twelve."

She shot me a grin. "I don't like to brag or anything—"

I snorted since we both knew that was a blatant lie, but she continued on as if she hadn't heard me.

"But hiring you was a stroke of genius on my part."

"Well, I'm glad it's helping."

"More than I can tell you. Seriously. It's such a load off not to have to stop what I'm doing every ten minutes to handle something for a guest. And Aiden hasn't fucked up all week! I'm calling that a win all around."

A familiar wave of uneasiness washed over me, same as it did anytime Addison complained about him. That wasn't anything new with us—it was something she'd done frequently in college—but it felt oddly intrusive now, considering how intimately I knew the brother she was complaining about.

Except she didn't know that tiny little detail...

Since the start of Addison's and my friendship, we hadn't kept secrets from each other. That was probably what had bonded us so quickly and so permanently. But I was keeping a secret from her now. Multiple, actually.

I might've been mad at Aiden for asking me to lie to

Addison and keep his secret, but wasn't I doing the exact same thing by keeping my involvement with him under wraps?

"Can you do me a favor and help unload the truck out front?" she asked. "It's the supplies we ordered for Mabel and George's anniversary party this weekend. Everything should go to the Bayside Room."

"Sure." I strolled toward the front door and glanced out the window, my steps faltering when I saw not only the delivery truck and driver, but also Aiden standing at the back, helping to unload the equipment. The dress shirt he wore did nothing to disguise the way his arms and back muscles rippled with the effort. His forehead was creased, eyes focused and intent, and *God*, I remembered what it felt like to have all that intensity directed at me.

While I was naked and moaning for him.

In the time I'd been working at the resort, I'd become so aware of his schedule that I knew at this point in the day, he was usually poring over his spreadsheets and doing the day's reconciliation. Which meant the only reason he was out there in the first place was because *someone* had asked him to be.

The very same someone who'd stuck me in a room directly next to her brother. The same someone who'd tried to throw us together earlier in the week when she'd asked me to clean up after the crew. And the same someone whom Aiden had told, firmly and loudly enough for me to hear it through my closed door, to stop meddling in other people's lives.

I turned back to Addison with narrowed eyes. "That's weird... Aiden's already out there. Doing exactly what you just asked me to."

She stared back at me sweetly, not an ounce of deceit on her face. "Really? That is weird. But if you go help, you'll get it done in half the time."

Oh, she was good. But we'd played enough poker in college that she should know I'd always call her bluff. "Nah. There's no need for me to go out and help, because Aiden's already taking care of it."

"Well, I say there is a need, and I'm your boss, so..."

"Actually, when I took this job, you explicitly told me you *weren't* my boss. Aiden was. And I'm pretty sure my boss would want me to stay where I'm supposed to be in case any guests need attention." I patted the front desk and shot her a smile.

She stared at me for long moments, the tiniest twitch at the corner of her eye the only sign of her irritation. Then it was wiped clear from her face, and she beamed at me, all frustration gone. "Fine. The garbage needs to be gathered up and taken out anyway. And after you're done with that, you can check all the mousetraps."

And then she swept past me with a blinding smile, the brat, and I could only shake my head at her retreating form. I didn't know what she was up to, but meddling was her middle name. And there was little doubt she was attempting to meddle with Aiden and me. In an effort to… what? Throw us together?

Little did she know, we'd already been thrown together. Naked. And I couldn't even close my eyes without remembering exactly how good it had been between us.

I obviously couldn't tell her why it was a bad idea to keep forcing us together. But I was getting dangerously close to saying fuck it, just a frayed thread away from throwing my ire out the window and climbing him like a tree. Again.

AVERY:

I know what you're doing.

ADDISON:

Recording videos for this week's social media posts?

AVERY:

Don't play dumb with me. I was there when you made dean's list all four years, remember?

ADDISON:

Yes, yes, I'm incredibly smart

What does that have to do with anything?

AVERY:

You know damn well that's not what I mean.

ADDISON:

I have no idea what you're talking about

AVERY:

I'm talking about the fact that refilling the snack station in the parlor isn't a two person job, yet you asked me to do it. Along with your brother.

ADDISON:

Well, you're kind of short

I thought you might need help reaching the granola bars

I was just looking out for you

Is that so wrong?

AVERY:

You just can't help yourself, can you?

ADDISON:

Self-control isn't my best quality, no

CHAPTER TEN

AIDEN

"WHAT DO YOU MEAN, you're sending us to Vermont?" I asked, a bite to my tone I didn't bother to hide.

Addison stared back at me with a single brow raised. "I'm not sure what's so hard to understand about this, Aiden. Honestly."

Avery stood next to my sister, arms crossed as she stared at Addison, something that looked awfully close to suspicion written on her face. Maybe she'd also noticed Addison's thinly veiled attempts at matchmaking. If I weren't hanging on by a thread, worried that Avery would spill my secret at any second, I'd think it was downright hilarious. Especially considering the people Addison was trying to hook up had already done so. Spectacularly.

I pressed my thumb and forefinger to my eyes, gritting my teeth in an effort to bite back the litany of curses I wanted to hurl my sister's way. As if it hadn't been torturous enough living in close proximity to Avery these past couple weeks... Running into her more times than I could count while she was wearing the tiniest garments of clothing that she somehow thought passed for sleepwear. Or being attuned to every move she made, every sound that escaped her lips, and being able to catalog each one. Even her fucking scent got me hard.

The worst part was I was still walking on eggshells around her, because she'd never agreed to keep my secret. Never agreed that she wouldn't tell Addison or the rest of my family or, hell, anyone in town.

And now my sister had the bright idea to send us on a weekend trip. Alone.

"You can't just decide shit for everyone else, Addison," I snapped. "You need to stop meddling in other people's lives."

"When those people work for the resort and I am the one making sure shit gets done around here, sometimes meddling is required."

Closing my eyes, I pinched the bridge of my nose, praying for an ounce of patience I knew would never come. Especially where my sister was involved. Blowing out a deep breath, I said, "What the fuck is even in Vermont, and why do we need to go there?"

She raised a brow. "Didn't you just get on Levi's case last week for dropping an f-bomb in the presence of guests?"

It was midafternoon on a Thursday, and no guests were

milling around, which was pretty normal, given the day. We always had a lull during the middle of the week.

I made a big show of looking around at the otherwise empty space, save for me, Addison, and Avery. "Do you see any guests around here?"

"Mabel's right over there." Addison tipped her head in the direction of the parlor.

"Mabel is here for the free snacks we set out for paying guests," I said. "She doesn't count."

"I'm also here to discuss details about our anniversary party this weekend!" the older woman yelled from the other room. "But Aiden's right. It's mostly the snacks."

I raised my brow at Addison in a silent, *see*?

She blew out a long-suffering sigh and pinned me with a look, as if *I* was the issue here. "I know this isn't on your precious schedule, but I need you to deal. Unless, of course, *you'd* like to handle all the requested special arrangements for Mabel and George's anniversary party, not to mention making sure it goes off without a hitch, and also find time to do the interviews—yes, multiple—for the documentary. I'd be *happy* to go to Vermont in your place like I originally planned. I'd love to act like a tourist with Avery for three days if you'd take those off my plate." She stared up at me with a sweet smile, but she wasn't fooling me. There was nothing sweet about her. She had me, and she knew it, because I'd rather pluck out each one of my eyelashes than do any of those things.

"Fine." This was the absolute worst time for me to be

taking a long weekend for a frivolous and totally unnecessary trip to, apparently, play tourist—whatever the fuck that meant. My publisher-assigned deadline was next week, and I absolutely could not miss it. I'd just have to figure out how to make it work. "I'll go, but Avery doesn't have to suffer, too. She can stay here."

"It won't be suffering. Don't be so dramatic." Addison rolled her eyes. "You're going to enjoy their festival and see what sorts of ideas we can bring back to implement in Starlight Cove. Plus, I need Avery's outlook and magic brain on the case. All you're going to see is how much everything is going to cost. She'll be able to envision how we can rework it here so we're able to bring in more tourists, which means more bookings for the resort, which means more money for us."

"Addison," I said, my tone sharp. "You can't just—"

"It's fine," Avery cut in, shooting a glance my way before focusing on my sister. "I'm happy to take a trip on your dime. Where exactly are we going?"

Addison beamed at Avery, her irritation with me wiped clear off her face. "Maplewood, Vermont."

"Did you say Maplewood?" Mabel hustled in, the material of her purple tracksuit swish-swish-swishing as she walked, eyes brimming with excitement. "Well, damn. If this weren't my own anniversary celebration this weekend, I'd tag along and scope things out! That's one of the more substantiated guesses for where my new favorite author lives! A. M. Kinsey? Have you heard of him? He's real secretive online, no headshot or anything and a generic bio. That, of course, has all the fans foaming at the mouth to dig up the details. But I tell you what, I haven't devoured a book like *The Flames of Heat and Desire* in years! And I can't wait for *The Realm of Storm and Shadow*."

Jesus Christ.

Jesus fucking *Christ*.

At her words, every ounce of color leached from my face, and I had no idea how I was going to make it through this conversation without giving myself away. When my book had gone viral...and then continued to go viral anytime someone posted about it...I'd always known there was the possibility of people in Starlight Cove coming across it. It had been sitting on the *New York Times* list for seven straight weeks, after all. But given our town's small population, I'd always thought that was a stretch and that I didn't need to worry about it coming to fruition.

And then Mabel happened.

There she stood, casually name-dropping the titles of both the book that had rocketed me to stardom and the one that was releasing the first part of next year.

I made the mistake of looking at Avery, only to find her eyes already on me. Her gaze scanned over my features, no doubt taking in my ghastly appearance, and I knew it was too late to school my expression.

From the way she was staring at me, she knew. She knew Mabel was talking about *my* book, which meant she now knew the pseudonym. I hadn't had to admit to a damn thing—my guilt was written all over my face.

My stomach churned over the possibility that this was it. All my hard work—years of keeping this part of myself locked away in an effort to maintain separation between this part of my life and my family's business—would all be for nothing if she spilled my secret. She had the power to ruin all my efforts in just a few short words.

"I don't think I've heard of that one," my sister said, continuing on as if I wasn't having an existential crisis right next to her.

"You have to read it! *Storm and Shadow* doesn't release until next year, but *Heat and Desire* is out now." Mabel pulled out her phone and scrolled to something before holding it at arm's length as she squinted down at the screen. Then aloud, she read, *"In a world on the brink of annihilation, an ordinary woman's forbidden love affair with the Prince of Shadows, cursed heir to the realm of Eternal Twilight, sets off a chain reaction of secrets, prophecies, and peril. The pair explore each other's deepest desires as they navigate the treacherous darkness and unravel the mysteries that bind them, all while racing against time in a trek that will either shatter their worlds or become the salvation they both desperately seek."*

"Ohhh, that does sound good," Addison said, and I had to work hard to keep my poker face on. The thought of my sister reading my highly erotic novels was negative twelve thousand sixty-two on my list of shit I'd like to happen in my lifetime.

"It's the best book I've read all year," Mabel said with conviction. "I shared my hardcover copy with a friend, but as soon as Charlene is done, I'll have her pass it on to you. The storytelling was beautifully done, but the *spice*..." Mabel fanned her face and then shot us a wink. "Whew! That miracle of a book was single-handedly to thank for getting me and George out of a little slump. I can't keep my hands off him! I bought the e-book, too, just to make sure I had access to my favorite parts, if you know what I mean."

"I think everyone knows what you mean," Addison said dryly.

Mabel swiped a hand through the air. "Oh, come on now. I know you're not that big of a prude, Addison! Certainly not like those old fuddy-duddies in my book club. *Former* book club," she corrected with an upturned nose.

"Former? What happened?" Avery asked. And I took it as a hopeful sign that her first words weren't, "*He's been lying to you!*" But there was no way I was letting my guard down just yet.

Mabel pursed her lips and blew a raspberry. "I nominated *The Flames of Heat and Desire* for this month's pick, but I got vetoed. And rudely at that. They said they were a 'reputable' book club and 'reputable' book clubs don't read *those* kinds of books. So I told them I was going to start my own book club." She sniffed. "One that *isn't* reputable so we can read the good stuff. Who wants to trudge their way through *Ulysses* when you can read about two people engaging in a passionate, forbidden love affair instead?"

"That's a very good point," Addison said.

"They told me I should be ashamed of myself for even suggesting it, but I lived a lot of years doing just that, and do you know what I realized?"

"What's that?" Avery rested her elbow on the front desk, propping her chin in her hand as she stared at Mabel.

"I cannot find a single hoot to give. It took me— Well, a long time until I finally got to the point of not caring, but I'll be damned if I go back. They can boycott the newspaper all they want."

Avery's brows flew up, and I couldn't help but mirror the expression. "They're boycotting the newspaper?"

"So they say. But George's and my little paper is the only game in town. Where do they think they're going to get their news from? Facebook?" Mabel tossed her head back in a gleeful cackle. "I've already blocked them and put them on my Dead to Me list. Buncha old prudes," she muttered. "They probably haven't seen the other side of an orgasm since the last Bush administration."

My sister let out a loud guffaw, and Avery snorted a laugh, bringing her hand up to cover her mouth as if trying to hold it in. I didn't know whether to laugh, flee, or stand as still as a statue and hope no one noticed I was still in the room. My palms were sweating, my heartbeat frantic, and my body hadn't decided on fight or flight just yet.

"It's true!" Mabel said. "I have no doubt they were the ones who complained about my booth at the farmers market and forced me to keep all my sex toys and various paraphernalia under the table. The mayor's wife is in that book club, you know, and she's a stick-in-the-mud. Has her hands in *everything* in Starlight Cove, too. Poor Ernest can't even grow his cannabis in his yard anymore."

"She sounds like a real fun-ruiner," Avery said.

"Oh honey, she *is*," Mabel agreed. "And I don't even see what the big deal is. It's just sex. I don't know what they're so scared of."

I didn't either, but it was clear they were terrified enough to attempt to put a small family business under. A small family business that wasn't all that different from ours.

This was exactly what I'd been afraid of. And knowing a small group of influential women in town were boycotting the newspaper simply because of Mabel *reading* a book was just more confirmation of my fears. Starlight Cove was tiny and tight-knit enough that it wouldn't take a group of naysayers to ruin my family's business. All it would take was *one*.

I wasn't ready to gamble that because of a selfish dream I just couldn't let die.

I glanced at Avery and found her staring at me, her

bottom lip caught between her teeth and a furrow between her brows. I had no idea what was going through her pretty little head, but I could only hope that after hearing what Mabel had to say, she was starting to understand my perspective. Starting to realize I couldn't possibly come out as the author of this kind of book without the resort and my family suffering the very real ramifications of such a reveal.

I could only hope that after this, she kept my secret a little longer.

WITH MABEL TALKING Addison's ear off about the party this weekend, I followed Avery up the stairs to our side of the house to get packed for our apparent weekend away. Before she could disappear into her room, I wrapped my fingers around her wrist and tugged her to a stop, that ever-present hum of awareness zipping up my arm at the contact. She twisted to look at me, and I scanned her face, trying to get a read on where her head was right now after everything she'd heard.

"Hey." I leaned close, keeping my voice low so it wouldn't carry downstairs. "I know you need to pack, but I just wanted to say thank you."

She leaned back against her closed door, one brow raised. "For what?"

"You know what." I tipped my head in the direction

we'd come from. "Downstairs. Not saying anything when you very easily could have."

She lifted a single shoulder in a shrug but otherwise didn't say anything. She didn't tell me she understood now. Understood why I'd been lying for so long. Didn't tell me she'd keep my secret as I'd asked of her. A shrug was all I was going to get.

I scanned her face, looking for any sign of apprehension or uneasiness over our impending trip, but I couldn't find any. Still, three nights together was going to be unbearably long if she didn't want to be there, so I wanted to give her the out if she wanted it.

"You don't have to do this, you know," I said. "Despite Addison being a tyrant and throwing us into this situation without our input, she can't force you to go. If you'd rather stay here, I can tell her to fuck off and deal with it."

She stared at me for long moments, her eyes dropping briefly to my lips before scanning the rest of my face. There was no denying the chemistry between us still crackled. A charge was in the air when we were this close... A pull that was tugging me closer to her with every second that passed. One that had been damn hard to ignore.

One that would be even harder to ignore on a trip with just the two of us.

She shook her head and glanced down, breaking the connection. "No, it's fine. We can handle being in the same car for a few hours, right?"

With this woman? I truly wasn't so sure. Being this

close to her for weeks and not being able to touch her had been testing my limits. Every fucking day. And that was when I had my own space to escape to for a reprieve. But driving four hours with her in the close confines of my car, the memories of that night playing on a loop in my mind? Well, that was going to be a challenge I hadn't expected.

"Right." My voice was too low, too rough, but it couldn't be helped. "We'll have separate rooms, so we can each do our own thing. I'll stay out of your way so you're not uncomfortable."

"I'm not uncomfortable around you, Aiden," she said, truth ringing in every word.

I lifted my gaze to meet hers, my body leaning into her space without my permission. It would be so easy to close the distance. To press her against the door, drop my face into her neck, brush my lips against her bunny tattoo, and soak in the little whimper that would escape her at that contact.

But I couldn't do that. We weren't there. We might never be again. And I should've been happy about that. Should've been happy I wouldn't have a distraction like her diverting me from everything on my plate.

Clearing my throat, I stepped back and turned toward my bedroom. "We'll leave in an hour."

"Hey, Aiden," she called just as I turned my doorknob. When I glanced back at her, she said, "Was that why you did it?"

"What?"

"Why you've kept the secret for so long... Because of what Mabel said down there? Because of those women boycotting her business? You're worried the same thing will happen to the resort, aren't you?"

I stared at her for a long moment and swallowed. Finally, I gave her a short nod. There was no use in denying it anymore. No use in pretending my choices didn't have the very real ramifications of fucking up my entire family's lives.

And no use denying that even knowing all that, I'd still signed on the dotted line.

CHAPTER ELEVEN

AVERY

IT WAS late by the time Aiden pulled up in front of The Cozy Maple Inn, the bed-and-breakfast we'd be staying at during our time in Vermont, and I couldn't get out of the car fast enough.

I didn't give more than a cursory glance at the ivy trailing up the brick exterior or the cobblestone path lit by old-fashioned lampposts or all the trees that surrounded the property in their varying shades of crimson, orange, and gold. Instead, I closed my eyes and sucked in a lungful of air that, thankfully, wasn't tinged with the spicy warmth of Aiden that I'd been inhaling for the past four hours straight.

I thought I'd be fine. I'd managed the entirety of my stay thus far with him just on the other side of a shared bathroom, all while being thrown together at every opportunity by my so-called best friend. And also while working with him day after day, hearing that low, rumbling voice when he walked me through a task, or watching him roll up his sleeves midafternoon, carefully and methodically, his attention never leaving his laptop, and my attention never leaving *him*. But being stuck in a closed-in box for hours on end tested my resolve in a way I hadn't been prepared for.

Aiden had let me pick the music for the trip, and even my extensive playlist of every Taylor Swift song ever released didn't help. We hadn't spoken for most of the ride, but the silence between us hadn't been the comfortable kind. Nope, this had been laced with the kind of sexual tension I loved to read about in books. The kind that would normally have me squirming in my seat and inhaling the pages as fast as I could to get to the good parts. Except in this version—in my very much real-life version—there would be no good parts. No release.

Because of me.

I'd drawn a very clear line in the sand that morning following our night together, and Aiden respected that boundary. A boundary I wasn't even sure I needed to have anymore. Not after that encounter with Mabel. Not after he'd admitted exactly why he kept his secret. And I couldn't blame him.

Which was a real mindfuck when my body was on high alert around him anyway.

Like now, when he stood with his hand hovering at the small of my back as he held the front door to the inn open for me. Just that barest touch—innocent for all intents and purposes—and I was ready to fold and beg him to fuck me all over again.

It was honestly a miracle I could control myself enough not to push up on my toes, press my nose into his neck, and lick him from collarbone to chin.

And just what kind of crazy-ass horny motherfucker daydreamed about licking someone's neck, just to get the taste of it on their tongue?

This man had ruined me, though I'd known he would. From the second we'd met, I knew. What I didn't know was just how much it would fuck with me. And how much it would have me questioning my preconceived notions.

Just as I was stepping past him, my resolve crumbling with every brush of my shoulder against his chest, my phone rang. I was so keyed up, I nearly jumped out of my skin at the sound.

"Whoa." He pressed his hand to the curve of my waist to steady me, his eyes concerned as he stared down at me. With a raised brow, he asked, "You okay?"

I cleared my throat and nodded in a spastic, jerky fashion that probably made me look like I'd just taken a hit of something. "Yeah, fine. Just, um, just let me check this."

I pulled my phone from my bag, my mom's contact image lighting up the screen. We'd been playing phone tag for two weeks—it was one of the longest stretches I'd gone without talking to her, and I was desperate to. Especially with everything going on with Aiden. I could use her brand of advice right about now.

I held up my phone, turning the screen toward him. “It’s my mom. I’m just gonna take this really quick.” I jerked a thumb over my shoulder, indicating the bench just off the walkway.

He nodded, his gaze roaming my body in a quick once-over. Though the speed didn’t lessen my reaction to it whatsoever. “Take your time. I’ll go get us checked in.”

I watched him walk away, and I absolutely did *not* stare at the way those jeans hugged his ass or how that long-sleeved Henley stretched over him like a second skin, putting every flex and bunch of his muscles on display for my very horny perusal.

Blowing out a shaky breath, I shook my head and answered the call. “Hey, Mom.”

“Oh!” she said, sounding surprised. Like she hadn’t been the one who’d called me. “It’s you.”

“Did you mean to call your other daughter?”

She laughed, breathy and light. “No, I just mean I thought this was a replay of that time someone stole your phone and it ended up in Florida.”

“Why would you think that?”

“I got a notification that you were in Vermont, which is definitely not Rosewood.”

I could count on one hand the number of times my mom had checked in on me via the location-sharing app. It was and had always been more for my peace of mind than hers.

"But yet you didn't call when it showed I was still in Starlight Cove..."

"Our cell service has been spotty here in Fiji, so the app hasn't been working very well. And I'm—wait, did you say you were still in Starlight Cove?"

"Took you a minute, huh?"

"Oh, shut up, you. Stewart's been keeping my champagne flute filled with Cristal all day. I'm a little tipsy. Now, quit dodging the question, missy."

"Yes, I'm still in Starlight Cove. Well, not this very second, but generally speaking, yes."

"What're you still doing there?"

I leaned back against the bench and stared out at the front lawn of the bed-and-breakfast, the lampposts softly illuminating the leaves as they cascaded down from the trees. "I needed a temporary job. Addison offered me one."

"Really? That's great! And how fun that the two of you are together again! You better stay out of trouble, though. I'm not there to bail you out of jail."

"That was *you*, Mom."

"Oh. Right. Well, still. I'm glad you've got a friend close. Especially because Stewart's asked me to accompany him for a few more weeks, so it turns out I won't be home before Thanksgiving."

"Really? Didn't see that one coming."

Her laughter rang over the line. "Oh, stop."

"It's fine, Mom." And I meant that. I loved her more than anyone else in the world, but I'd learned a long time ago not to put too much stock in her plans until they were staring me in the face. "I hope you have fun."

"I will. And maybe you'll find a man to pass the time with while you're there and have some fun of your own."

I shifted on the bench, twirling a lock of hair around my finger. "Actually..."

"Actually?" she prompted, voice bright, and I could picture her—elbow on the table, chin propped in her hand, eyes wide. "Who is he? Where did you meet him? How's the sex?"

"Oh my God."

"What? No point in sticking around if it's not good, honey. And don't you fake it to save his pride. If he can't find your clit, he deserves to hear nothing but silence coming from you."

"I know, Mom. Play silent library until they figure it out. You've gone over this many, *many* times." I closed my eyes on a laugh, dropping my head back on my shoulders as flashes of Aiden's and my single night together flitted through my mind. "Believe me, that's not an issue with this one."

"But there *is* an issue..."

It wasn't a question, and I wasn't surprised she'd been able to suss that out, even over the phone.

"Kind of, yeah."

"Well, let's talk it out," she said. "What's going on?"

"You sure you have time?"

"Of course I have time! Stewart can wait. Now tell me what's up."

I blew out a heavy breath. "Okay, well, we met my first night in town, when Addison had to bail on dinner. I went to grab something to eat at the bar next to my hotel, and he was there. We clicked right away, you know?" At her knowing hum, I continued, "We had an *amazing* night together and then we went our separate ways, and I thought I'd never see him again."

"But?"

"*But*...it turns out he's Addison's brother, my new boss, and he lied to me that night." I cringed because what he'd done hadn't exactly been lying, even though it had felt that way when I'd found out the truth. "Kind of."

"And we both know how you feel about lies."

I sagged back against the bench. "Yeah."

"You said kind of... What does that mean?"

"He didn't lie exactly. He just...didn't tell me the whole truth. It's really a convoluted mess that I can't tell you without *really* telling you, and that's the problem. He wants me to keep it from everyone. Addison included."

"And have you?"

"Yes." I hadn't allowed myself much time to think about the why of that. Initially, I'd brushed it off as the fact that I just hadn't had the opportunity to spill the secret. It would be weird to randomly bring it up. *Oh hey, your brother is an erotic fantasy author, and he's been lying to you about it for years. I've also been lying by omission because we fucked like bunnies that night you stood me up, and I'd do it again in a heartbeat.*

Except I'd had the perfect opportunity earlier today. I couldn't have coordinated a better setup if I tried. But then I'd seen his face, the fear and panic written all over it, and I couldn't do it. I couldn't throw him under the bus when it was clear he wasn't keeping this secret to himself to be malicious.

He was doing it to *protect* his family, not ruin it.

"You sound like someone kicked your puppy," she said. "You know, it's not the worst thing in the world to keep secrets. If they're important or for someone who is."

I hummed noncommittally but otherwise didn't respond. Secrets were what had torn our family apart—broken as it had been in the first place—and I knew that clouded my judgment on the subject. It was hard to come at this from a neutral position when my stance on it since I was sixteen years old had been negative.

"Not everyone is like your father," my mom said softly. "And not every secret is of that magnitude. Haven't you ever kept a secret from someone? Big or small?"

I had. Obviously, I had. I was doing it right now with Addison. I wasn't only keeping Aiden's secret from her, but also the fact that I'd slept with him. And it was clear I didn't even need to with how forcefully she was throwing the two of us together. It was easier to justify to myself because I knew my intentions weren't malicious. But after talking with him in the hallway outside our rooms, it was clear his weren't, either.

"I'm going to take your silence as affirmation," she said.

"It's different."

"It *is*," she agreed. "And that's okay. What your father did was unforgivable. But you can't live your life scared of it happening again or shoving every person and situation into the same box, because they're not all created equal. Don't make yourself or those in your life pay for a mistake *he* made. And don't think for a second that you looking past it or forgiving someone for doing it means you have to forgive your father. They're not the same."

I swallowed hard over the lump in my throat and nodded even though she couldn't see me.

"If you like this man," she continued. "If you clicked as much as you say you did, then why not give him a chance? Maybe he has a good excuse for keeping the secret."

There was no maybe about it, and though I'd wondered about that since that day at the ball game, he'd confirmed it just before we'd left.

"Did any of that help, honey?"

Honestly? I wasn't sure. I knew I didn't have to be mad at him anymore, but I wasn't sure that getting involved with him was the best idea, even though, with how Addison was throwing us together, there clearly wasn't a fraternization policy I had to worry about. But look how upset I'd been after only a single night with him. What would happen if we spent days, weeks, or even months together? Where would that leave me in the end?

Instead of voicing any of my fears, I just said, "Yeah."

"Good. Stewart's waving me over, so I've gotta run. He's taking me island-hopping in a helicopter. But you think about what I said, okay? I'll call again when I've got good service."

"Okay, Mom. Have fun and be safe."

"You have fun…and be *wild*, my little hummingbird. Love you!"

After ending the call, I strode through the front door of the bed-and-breakfast and toward the welcome desk where Aiden stood. His posture was stiff, his hands braced on the counter as he spoke in a low but firm tone to the front desk attendant.

"There has to be a mistake," he said.

"I'm afraid not, Mr. McKenzie. We have the note right here. Ms. Addison McKenzie made the reservation for the Cozy Garden Hideaway, and that's the only room I have booked for you."

"Can you check again, please." The way Aiden said it was less question and more demand, but the man behind the counter simply smiled and did as Aiden had requested.

"Hey," I said, splitting my gaze between him and the front desk attendant, whose name tag read Mark. "Everything all right?"

Aiden slid his gaze to me, giving me a slow once-over. I'd noticed he did that every time I walked into the room.

It felt less like he was checking me out and more like he was checking to make sure I was okay. And my body reacted every damn time, goose bumps sweeping over my skin and a warmth blooming low in my belly. "We'll see," he said.

Mark made a low hum in his throat. "I'm afraid we just have you down for the Cozy Garden Hideaway, sir."

Aiden hung his head and blew out a heavy breath. "Fine. Do you have another room available that I can also reserve?"

"Unfortunately, we're all booked, thanks to the fall festival taking place this weekend."

"Let me guess," Aiden said flatly. "It'll be the same for every other place in town."

"I would assume so, sir."

I glanced between Aiden and Mark, brows raised. "What does that mean?"

Aiden curled his hands over the front desk ledge, tension coming off him in waves. "It means Addison 'forgot' to add another room to our reservation. And she booked the smallest room while she was at it."

Mark's gaze bounced between Aiden and me. "If you're worried about the accommodations, I can assure you the room is cozy and quaint—"

"Read: small as fuck," Aiden muttered under his breath.

"With a double bed and a gorgeous view of our back garden, which is full of a kaleidoscope of colors right now.

The trees are just breathtaking. You've really picked a beautiful time of year to visit!"

Aiden glanced at me then, a brow raised. "It's your call. We can turn around, and I'll drive us right back home tonight."

"It's almost ten."

"Doesn't matter. I don't want you to be uncomfortable, especially when my sister strong-armed you into this," he said, as if *he* was the one making me uncomfortable.

And he was, but not for the reasons he probably thought. I wanted him—hadn't *stopped* wanting him—but I didn't know if it was a good idea.

Still, I wasn't going to sabotage this weekend. Even if Addison's intentions were nefarious, that didn't change the fact that she really did want me to scope out the festival and return to Starlight Cove with a bunch of ideas we could implement there. And I really was excited about doing it.

I held Aiden's gaze as I spoke to the front desk attendant. "We'll stay."

"An excellent choice!" Mark said, typing away on his computer. "All our previous guests who've stayed in that room have enjoyed their time immensely, so I have no doubt you will, too."

I wasn't so sure about that. Three evenings with Aiden in a tiny room that held only one bed? I was pretty sure this was going to be torture.

CHAPTER TWELVE

AIDEN

THIS WAS FUCKING TORTURE.

We'd been in the room for all of seventeen minutes, and I wasn't sure I'd make it three nights with Avery in these cramped quarters. I had no idea how this room was classified as anything but a closet. While it had large windows on three of the walls, which helped with the whole claustrophobia thing, the double bed took up the vast majority of the space. The only other furnishing was a luggage rack that sat tucked into the corner.

When Mark had shown us to the room and Avery and I had settled in, we'd danced around each other as best we could. Which, in a space this size, did fuck all. It felt like I couldn't even breathe without brushing against her. And if I somehow managed to avoid that, I still sucked in a lungful of air laced with her sweetness. Which, as previously established, only made my dick hard.

So, basically, I was fucked.

Now, I lay on the bed on top of the white down comforter, my arm tucked behind my head as I listened to the sounds of her getting ready on the other side of the bathroom door. The only saving grace in the laughably small Cozy Garden Hideaway was its surprisingly spacious bathroom, which was damn near the size of the bedroom. Avery's eyes had lit up when they'd landed on the old-fashioned claw-foot tub, so it wasn't a total loss.

Pretty fucking close, though. Because not only was our room tiny, but it was also freezing. I'd changed into a pair of sweatpants and kept on my long-sleeved Henley, and still, my nipples were hard enough to cut glass. I only hoped Avery had brought something besides the minuscule doll clothes she usually wore to bed. Otherwise, she'd be an ice cube by morning.

The bathroom door creaked open, and I didn't know if it was a blessing or a curse that the room was nearly pitch black so I could barely see her. Only the nearly full moon illuminated the space, but it didn't lend enough light for me to make out more than her shape. It wouldn't have mattered anyway for the swiftness with which she dive-bombed the bed and burrowed beneath the comforter.

"Fuck me," she said through chattering teeth, clamoring to cover herself up. "Did we have to pay extra for an igloo room?"

I huffed out a laugh, surprised I couldn't see my breath.

"Knowing Addison, I wouldn't put it past her. She's conniving when she sets her mind to something."

"And her mind is set on forcing us together?" Avery turned away from me even as she asked the question, as if she was trying to put as much space between us as possible.

But that did fuck all in a bed this size. She didn't take up much of it, but at 6'4", I wasn't exactly a small guy, and a double bed wasn't exactly grown-ass-man-sized. That meant I could feel every shift she made, and my dick was one hundred percent aware of that fact. I'd just managed to talk it down while she was in the bathroom, and now it was back with a vengeance and hard as a fucking rock, wondering why the hell we weren't doing what we'd done the last time we were in a hotel room together.

I grunted in the affirmative. "Seems that way."

"If only she knew," she said, so quiet I wasn't sure I was supposed to hear. She probably thought I wouldn't be able to over the loud chattering of her teeth.

I figured her shivers would settle after a few minutes of being under the covers. Instead, they only seemed to worsen until I could feel the entire bed vibrating with them. Even though I'd seen every inch of this woman—kissed and licked and sucked all of them...even though I'd been *inside* her—I'd lain on top of the covers to give her the only bit of separation I could.

But that had been before I knew she was a human popsicle. And I wasn't about to lie here and let her suffer.

Especially when it was clear that though she obviously needed me to lend her some body heat to warm up, she'd never ask for it.

She snapped her head toward me when I shifted to stand so I could slip under the covers. "You're leaving?" she asked, her voice tinged with panic.

I paused, wondering if I should've offered to sleep in the car... "Do you want me to?"

She was silent for a beat...two...and then she said, "You were the only warm thing in this bed, so not particularly."

And that was all the confirmation I needed—never mind that it was all I was going to get—so I lifted my corner of the comforter and slipped under it.

"What are you—" Her words shut off on a shudder when I slipped in directly behind her. I curled my body around hers, pressing my front to her back, my knees tucked beneath hers, and wrapped my arm around her waist.

"I'm getting you warm," I said into her hair. "If you died of hypothermia while I lay on top of the covers and watched, Addison would never forgive me."

She huffed out a laugh but otherwise didn't say anything. But she also didn't move away, and I took that as a good sign. Finally, her body started relaxing by degrees. Soon enough, she melted into me, pressing every inch of herself against me. Including her cold-as-fuck feet, the chill of which seeped through the material of my sweatpants.

"Jesus Christ, woman," I muttered, even as I curled myself tighter around her. Even as I tucked those blocks of ice she called feet between my calves in an effort to warm them faster. "I can feel those through my sweatpants. Did you take an ice bath before you came to bed?"

"I should've taken a hot bath, actually. It's the only thing that warms me up when I get cold like this. My body has this superfun quirk where my feet are, like, twenty degrees colder than the rest of me at all times. Same with my nose." As if to prove her point, she lifted my hand that was resting on her stomach to her face and pressed her nose against it.

She wasn't wrong. And though I had no idea how to warm up her nose, I'd try my hardest to take care of the rest of her. I tucked one arm under the pillow beneath her head and wrapped the other arm around her, my forearm between her breasts, hand flat against her chest. Attempting to imbue as much of my heat into her as I could.

Her chattering teeth had finally subsided, and her breathing had evened out until I was sure she'd nearly fallen asleep.

Then the noises started.

It was quiet at first, just the whisper of a moan. Something that could be written off as a dozen different things. But then there was the hushed murmur of voices interspersed with more moans. And then came the soft, rhythmic thumping of a bed being put to good use.

If I thought I was hard before, it had nothing on the solidness of my dick right now. Holding Avery this close and listening to the ASMR version of amateur porn had my cock ready to bust through my sweatpants. I could only hope I'd shifted my hips back far enough so she couldn't feel it.

She must've heard the noises next door, though, because her body stiffened. And then she started squirming against me. Subtle at first, and then more pronounced. Like she was just as affected by this as I was. When she shifted again, this time brushing over the beast in my pants, she sucked in a sharp breath and froze.

So much for my hope that she wouldn't notice.

"Ignore it," I said into her hair.

She huffed out a laugh. "I hate to be the first one to tell you this, big guy, but you're not exactly packing something that's easy to ignore."

Jesus Christ, this woman was trying to kill me.

I shifted my hand to cup the front of her neck, just resting it there as I ran my thumb up and down the length of it in an effort to relax her all over again. If she didn't fall asleep soon, I had no doubt where this night would lead. And I also had no doubt she wasn't ready for that yet. When...*if*...she was? Well, that was a different story entirely.

"Go to sleep, bunny," I murmured into her neck, my thumb soft against her skin.

Before long, despite the pornographic soundtrack

coming from the other side of the wall and my cock trying to break through the barrier of my sweatpants and burrow its way into its favorite place, she did just that. And though I assumed I'd be up for hours, kept awake by my incessant insomnia and the horny bastards next door—or the horny bastard in my pants—it only took minutes for me to fall into a deep sleep, just like the last time I'd held her in my arms.

CHAPTER THIRTEEN

AVERY

I COULDN'T REMEMBER the last time I'd woken up this comfortable. This cozy. This…turned on.

My eyes popped open as soon as the realization of exactly where I was hit me, and last night came rushing back. The last-minute trip to Vermont. The tiny room Addison had booked for Aiden and me. The single bed that was the size of a Matchbox car. And the fact that the room was a good fifteen degrees cooler than anywhere else in the inn. How last night, when my body had been so cold I was shaking, my teeth chattering, Aiden had barely paused before he'd wrapped his arms around me and pulled me back against his chest. Having him there, his body flush along my back, had been tempting.

Then came the pornographic soundtrack from next door, which had made it infinitely worse. Not to mention the feel of him, hard and ready, against my ass… That had all been bad enough. But this?

This was so much worse.

Because he wasn't curled around me to keep me warm. Nope. Instead, I was fully on top of him, my head on his chest, my arms tucked beneath him, hands curling under his back to grip his shoulders, his hands low on my back just above the curve of my ass, and my legs spread around his hips. Which placed me directly on top of the part of him I'd gotten to know best. The part that was, once again, hard and ready for me. The part I was currently dry humping with everything I had.

Yeah, *that* was the problem.

As soon as I registered my position, I scrambled out of bed and threw myself across the room—which wasn't much of a feat, considering its size.

At my sudden movement, Aiden bolted upright in bed, his hair mussed, cheeks rosy from sleep, but his eyes were sharp and alert as he scanned the room for whatever had spooked me. Unfortunately, the room didn't have any mirrors in it, so he wouldn't find the culprit.

When his gaze landed on me, his eyes scanning me from head to toe, I felt it *everywhere*. Not just a little tingle, either. Nope, my body was obnoxious about it—nipples hardening, goose bumps scattering across every inch of flesh, and we weren't even going to talk about the state of my pussy. How the hell did this man always do that to me?

"What happened?" he asked, his tone all business. "What's wrong?"

"Nothing," I said too quickly, shaking my head just as fast. "No problem here. None at all." I jerked my thumb over my shoulder toward the bathroom. "But Addison's given us a pretty packed schedule for today, so I'm going to get ready."

Without allowing him time to voice the concerns his narrowed eyes very clearly portrayed, I slipped into the other room and sagged back against the closed door, grateful for this tiny bit of separation between us.

I needed to get my shit together. Especially since we were only at the start of this trip. And considering how worked up I already was, I had no idea how I was going to have enough willpower to withstand jumping his bones over the course of three whole days.

After I was cool, calm, collected, and presentable for the day, I slipped out of the bathroom, only to stop dead in my tracks at the sight that greeted me. Over the past couple weeks, I'd seen Aiden in various states of dress. From fully buttoned-up and professional to slightly rumpled—tie loosened, sleeves rolled up—at the end of the day. I'd seen him in jeans or sweatpants and a T-shirt a handful of times. But this? This was new. And fucking indecent.

He sat on the bed, propped against the headboard, his legs outstretched in front of him. He wore black pants and a white button-up, except none of the buttons were done—

like he'd been in the middle of getting dressed and had gotten distracted. The shirt lay open, revealing his chest and that smattering of dark hair that made my mouth water. An open laptop rested on his thighs, and those black-framed glasses sat perched on his nose.

And fuck me running, but how did this man always look like he'd just stepped out of the pages of a magazine whose sole purpose was to be used as fap material?

As soon as I stepped into the room, he lifted his gaze toward me, dropping his eyes to do a quick scan from head to toe. Unsurprisingly, a full-body shiver zipped down my spine, and yeah... This was never going to work.

There was no way I was going to be able to spend this amount of time with him, alone, without throwing all my hesitations straight out the window and falling right back into bed with him.

"Morning," he said, his voice just a low rasp that shot straight to all my horny girl parts. "Everything okay?"

I plastered on a smile and nodded, forcing my eyes away from him. Unfortunately, there wasn't much else in the room to look at, so my gaze landed right back on him. "I'm good. Great, even! Ready to head out for the day."

"About that," he said, hesitation in his tone. "I know Addison wants us to do this together, but it's really more of your area of expertise than it is mine. And..." His apprehension was evident as he studied me. After a moment, he continued, "My deadline for this publisher is next week, and I'm scrambling to meet it. Especially when my sister decides on a whim to send me to another state. I had an idea as I was getting dressed and wanted to run with it."

"Oh, okay." I nodded, grasping at this tiny nugget of reprieve. "Do you want to stay here and write while I check out the festival?"

"Really?" he asked, brows up. "You wouldn't mind?"

Would I *mind*? Fuck no, I wouldn't mind. The relief that swept over me at the fact that I wouldn't have to spend the entire day fighting this attraction to him was laughable.

"Nope! Not at all!" My voice was too high, too chipper, and could I sound like any more of an idiot? "I'll run through the schedule today by myself. And you'll stay here, doing...that." I gestured to him in all his fuckhot glory. "And then we'll touch base later tonight. Or not! Maybe you'll be exhausted from a hard day of writing and crash before I even get back. Which would be totally fine with me, by the way. No need to wait up or anything. In fact, you probably shouldn't. Who knows what kinds of things your sister has me doing or how long they'll take." I breathed out the fakest laugh I'd ever made in my life and grabbed my purse. "See you later!"

With that, I slipped out the door, shutting it harder than necessary, and rested my back against it. I closed my eyes and breathed out a sigh of relief, grateful I had a little reprieve before I'd have to face this undeniable attraction I had to Aiden. An attraction I didn't see fading anytime soon.

Group text message with Aiden, Avery, and Addison

4:57 p.m.

ADDISON:

I forgot to tell you

You have a reservation at 6

AIDEN:

For what?

ADDISON:

The rooftop experience

AIDEN:

What the fuck is the rooftop experience?

ADDISON:

Wine tasting

And a five course meal

AIDEN:

Isn't it a little cold for outdoor dining?

ADDISON:

They have heat lamps

Don't be such a diva

AVERY:

Sounds nice. What aren't you telling us?

ADDISON:

Why would you think I'm not telling you something?

AVERY:

Because I know you.

ADDISON:

Just checked the calendar

I also forgot to mention you've got an appointment at 9

AIDEN:

Tomorrow morning?

ADDISON:

Tonight

AIDEN:

What kind of appointment do you have us booked for at 9 p.m.?

ADDISON:

A couples massage

AIDEN:

A what?

ADDISON:

Exactly what I said

I thought it might be a good option for Luna to offer

So I want you to check it out

Report back with what you think

AIDEN:

You booked a couples massage.

ADDISON:

Yes

AIDEN:

For a trip you were originally supposed to take with Avery.

ADDISON:

Yes, Aiden

Your point?

AIDEN:

My point is this is getting ridiculous. You need to worry more about the shit going on at the resort and less about us.

ADDISON:

I AM worried about the resort

This streak of luck won't last forever

Bookings could dry up tomorrow

And when that happens, I want to make sure we have unique offerings to draw people in

So suck it up and deal

AVERY:

Just tell us where to be and when.

ADDISON:

I knew you were my favorite for a reason!

There's a curved staircase at the back of the B&B

Someone should be there to get you to where you need to be

Oh and I forgot to mention something…

AIDEN:

Jesus, Addison. What now?

ADDISON:

All the foods they serve for the experience are supposedly aphrodisiacs

But that's all probably made up

So you guys should have nothing to worry about

Anyway, have fun!

CHAPTER FOURTEEN

AVERY

I MIGHT'VE LEFT this morning with nothing but Aiden on my mind, but it hadn't taken me long to settle into the festivities. Between the Harvest Market, the Food Truck Alley, and the Octoberfest celebration, my attention was consumed, and Aiden was barely more than a blip in my thoughts throughout the day.

That was until I'd received the text from Addison, letting Aiden and me know of our evening plans. There was no denying she was a mastermind with her nefarious schemes. And fucking relentless. I'd forgotten just how much she loved having her hand in other people's business. I would've found it funny if I weren't trying so hard to resist her brother.

Why? Well, that I didn't quite know anymore...

My resolve was slipping away more and more, day after day, and now it was nothing more than wisps of smoke at my feet. I could admit now, thanks to that ever-helpful hindsight, that my initial reaction had more to do with my history than it did with Aiden or what he'd done. He'd just borne the brunt of it.

But my hesitation about getting involved with him was still present. If for nothing else than to keep my wits about me. Because I knew if any man was going to have me losing myself again, it would be him.

And I had no intention of traveling down that path. Been there, done that, adjusted my life for it. Never again.

Just before 6, I swung by our room to change into something more presentable than what I'd been wearing around the festival all day. An oversize sweatshirt and leggings were great for strolling the beer garden, but they probably weren't going to cut it at any sort of event that was titled an *experience*.

Thankfully, I'd packed my *just-in-case* outfit—a two-piece black set with a long-sleeved, off-the-shoulder, smocked crop top and a high-waisted skirt. After a quick touch-up to my hair and a few swipes of mascara—nothing too elaborate because this absolutely was *not* a date—I headed around back to where Addison had indicated.

The maître d' greeted me immediately and led me up the spiral staircase, the brisk evening air making me shiver. Fortunately, the chill dissipated as soon as I stepped onto the rooftop. A dozen heat lamps were placed around the intimate space, and in the middle of it all sat a candlelit table set for two. The maître d' dipped his head and held his arm outstretched toward the man who was definitely *not* my date and then took his leave, heading back down the stairs and leaving Aiden and me alone.

The man I'd spent all day trying not to think about stood from his chair, his eyes drinking me in as I walked toward him, and I couldn't help but do the same to him. He wore dark gray pants and a black button-down with the sleeves rolled to mid-forearm. If I squinted, I could just make out the barest hint of a tattoo peeking out from beneath it, and it gave me a sharp thrill that I knew what he looked like under that professional façade. Knew what he looked like when he was completely undone.

"Avery." He stepped around the table to my side, placed a hand on my waist, and dipped his head to press a kiss just below my ear. It wasn't quite the spot I'd come to think of as his—and that said it all, didn't it? That I'd known him for only a couple weeks and had already marked a part of my body as his—but it was close enough that a shiver swept through me. I had to stiffen my spine in an effort to hold myself back from melting into him. From pressing my body against his, rubbing myself all over him, and letting this thing between us consume me like it was so desperate to.

He pulled back enough so he could meet my eyes, though his hand never left my waist. He stroked his thumb over the sliver of exposed skin on my abdomen, the light touch like lightning. Then, in a low murmur, he said, "You're stunning."

I'd been called a lot of things in my life. Pretty, cute, hot. Sometimes even beautiful. But stunning? Never. And the best part—or worst, depending on how you looked at it —was that I *felt* it. Coming from Aiden, in that soft, serious tone, those intense eyes never leaving mine, I felt it. Straight to my bones.

"Thank you," I said. "You look good, too."

Understatement of the century. He must've swapped his glasses for his contacts, because nothing was blocking those gorgeous baby blues from me or the way they raked over me. He didn't even try to hide it, that slow perusal over every inch of me, and I didn't want him to. There was something decadent about the way he looked at me. Like I was the only woman in the room.

The only woman in the whole fucking world.

He pulled out my chair for me—another first…the guys I usually dated weren't at all concerned with taking care of me, in big or small ways. I murmured my thanks as Aiden slipped into the chair to my right. They'd set up the table so Aiden and I were directly next to each other rather than across, and I didn't know how I was going to make it through a five-course meal and wine tasting with him close enough that our arms brushed with every movement.

I just knew if I gave him the green light, this would be on. No holding back. There was no denying that we flared bright when we were together, but I wasn't sure I was ready to get burned.

In an effort to distract myself from his nearness and how much I was enjoying it, I glanced around at the deck, taking mental notes to bring back some ideas for the resort. The space was...lush. And romantic. Ivy-covered trellises bordered the deck on all sides, creating a secluded, intimate area, and string lights hung in a canopy above, giving off a soft glow. This tiny little pocket of paradise felt like a getaway all on its own, and it would be even better in Starlight Cove, with the ocean as its backdrop.

"Wow," I breathed. "It's beautiful up here."

"It is." At Aiden's low, reverent tone, I glanced over, but he wasn't taking in our surroundings like I'd been. Instead, his eyes were focused intently on me, that look sending a bolt of lightning through my insides, and my stomach dipped and swooped for no good reason.

Okay, not for no good reason. Because I was remembering, in great detail, what it had felt like to have his attention on me in an entirely different manner. That intensity focused solely on my pleasure...on making me feel good. On taking care of me. And, honestly, it was a wonder I didn't melt into a puddle at his feet.

Thankfully, our waiter chose that moment to greet us, allowing me time to cool myself down.

"Aiden and Avery, we're so happy to have you dining with us tonight." He dipped his head and gave us a warm smile. "Welcome to The Rooftop Experience. My name is David, and I'll be taking care of you this evening. Our chef has curated for you a five-course meal accompanied by carefully selected wine pairings. Each of the dishes has been prepared with the finest ingredients, locally sourced where possible, with an emphasis on aphrodisiacs. To give you privacy during your dining experience, I'll make myself scarce this evening, other than to bring your dishes out to you." He pointed to a small item that looked similar to a doorbell, set in front of the vase of flowers on the other side of our table. "But should you need anything at all, just press that button and I'll be right up."

With that, he left us with our first course—Oysters Rockefeller, natch—and slipped down the spiral staircase, leaving Aiden and me alone with nothing to do but get drunk on this never-ending supply of wine and eat food designed to make us horny.

But I was sure that was fine. I could handle this and keep my head on straight. I could make it through one evening without jumping his bones.

Right?

Aiden gestured for me to dig into the oysters first and leaned back in his chair, bringing the glass of wine to his lips. "How'd today go?"

I smiled, grateful for a safe topic to discuss. "It was really fun. Considering this town isn't much bigger than Starlight Cove, I wasn't expecting this event to be so big. Or so impressive. And that's even with most of the festivities not starting until tomorrow. I can't wait to poke around and see what other things they're doing. My notes are getting obnoxious. I know Addison sent us here with ulterior motives, but I really think you guys can make this work in Starlight Cove. And I was thinking that if—" I cut off, finally realizing Aiden was just...staring as I babbled on. "What?" I reached up, brushing a hand over my mouth. "Do I have something on my face?"

His lips twitched, that dimple popping out, and shook his head. "I just like listening to you talk. Especially about things you love. Books. This. It's obvious you enjoy it."

"I do, actually."

He raised a brow. "You sound surprised."

"I am." I lifted a shoulder. "I didn't think I'd have as much fun as I did, but the second I stepped out there, my brain was spinning with ideas to bring back to the resort. And I loved talking with all the different people, learning their stories."

"So what you're saying is, I need to give my sister some credit. She had the right idea shipping you up here, even if her original plan was just to force us together."

I breathed out a laugh. "I guess so."

"Is this what you saw yourself doing?"

"In life?" I clarified. At his nod, I continued, "Not even a little. I've always wanted to travel, all over the world. And I figured the best way to do that and not go broke is as a flight attendant."

"Really?" he asked, brows up.

"Yep."

"So why aren't you doing that?"

"Actually…that's why I'm here. My mom got me an opportunity to skip to the front of the line, so to speak. Training starts in January."

He stilled, his brows lifting as he studied me intently. "And then you're off," he said, his voice just a murmur.

"And then I'm off," I agreed. The words felt heavy. Wrong. But I didn't know why.

This was what I'd been dreaming about my whole life…the chance to experience different places and cultures, learn about different people. To explore the world. I had a tattoo of a plane inked on the top of my foot to remind me of exactly that, for fuck's sake. So why did it feel like I just wanted to explore *him*?

"What about you?" I asked, desperate to get the topic off me. "How'd writing go today?"

He froze with his wineglass halfway to his mouth, and I worried I'd overstepped. Maybe he didn't like talking about his work with other people. After all, he hadn't told a single soul about it other than his agent and publisher. And the only reason he'd confided in me in the first place was because he thought he'd never see me again.

That conversation with Mabel proved why he kept his mouth shut. I wasn't sure why I thought it would be any different with me. It was clear Aiden kept things close to his chest. He was a man of many secrets, and he had no reason to share them with me.

"I'm sorry. I don't want to badger you like Mabel did—even if she didn't realize she was doing it. You don't have to tell me that." I waved a hand through the air. "Forget I asked."

"No," he said, sharp at first, then he cleared his throat and spoke again, softer this time. "No, I was just... surprised. I'm not used to people asking. And Mabel is an entirely different beast. If she knows something, the whole town knows it. And you saw how well that went for her. I don't want to think about what it would do to the—" He cut himself off with a shake of his head and cleared his throat. "Anyway. You really want to hear about it?"

"Of course." I'd take any nugget of information about him that I could get, but I wasn't about to say that. "Why wouldn't I?"

He raised a brow but otherwise didn't say anything.

"Right." Because it was the reason our relationship—whatever it may be—hadn't gotten off on the best foot. The reason I hadn't been riding the Aiden train every night while I was staying in the room next to his. "I owe you an apology for that."

"You don't."

"I do," I insisted. "My reaction was more a reflection of me, not you. I...don't have the best history with secrets. Let's just say my dad kept some pretty important shit from me and my mom, and I've been soured to them ever since."

He studied me for long moments, no doubt wanting to ask me about it. But he must've read the closed-off expression on my face because he just dipped his chin in a nod. "Fair enough."

"But I do want to hear about this. If you want to tell me. I mean, you don't have anyone else to talk to about this stuff, right?"

"Just you," he confirmed after a long moment, and the weight of those two little words settled deep in my chest, a flurry of butterflies taking flight in my stomach.

Ignoring how much I loved that I was the only person he'd entrusted his secret to, I raised a brow and lifted my wineglass. "Then I'm all ears."

Then, like a switch had been flipped in him, his entire being lit up with every word that passed his lips as he discussed realms and enchantments and evil forces dead set on keeping the hero and heroine apart. It was as if whatever front he put on for other people dissipated completely as he shared this part of himself with me. A part he'd never shared with anyone else.

This was the real Aiden. Not the guy who was stressed all the time or who wore a scowl like a second skin or who barked orders at his sister and never had enough time to get everything done. This man, who gave me all his smiles. Who talked about tropes and archetypes and casually asked if I thought twelve sex scenes were enough in an erotic novel or if he should add one more... That was who he truly was when he wasn't fearing judgment or ridicule or the demise of his family's business.

That was who he was with me.

"So, it went well, then?" I said on a laugh when he finally paused long enough to take a bite of our entree.

He chuckled lowly, dipping his eyes to the plate of grilled steak with red wine reduction in front of him before lifting his gaze to meet mine. "Surprisingly, yes. It was the best writing day I've had."

"On this book? Nice."

"No. Ever."

I stared at him with wide eyes. "Seriously?"

He breathed out a disbelieving laugh and shook his head, like he couldn't believe it himself. "Seriously. I wrote as much today as I usually do in a week, sometimes two."

"That's amazing, Aiden! What do you think did it?"

"I'm not sure. I guess we'll see if it happens again tomorrow."

"Does that mean you feel better about meeting your deadline?"

"If I can have a couple more days like this? Yeah. I have no doubt I'll get it done on time."

"So you just need to spend the rest of your time here pounding away."

Aiden choked on the sip of wine he'd just taken, and my eyes widened when I realized how that sounded. "At the keyboard!" I clarified. "Pounding away at the *keyboard*. Not at—" I gestured wildly with my hand, although I had no idea what that was going to accomplish. All it did for me was conjure up images of our night together, his hips slapping against me as he sank inside me over and over and over again, all while whispering the filthiest things in my ear...

I couldn't even blame my overheated cheeks on the temperature. From the way Aiden's gaze pinned me in place, his eyes heavy with something that looked an awful lot like lust, he knew exactly what I was thinking about. And there was no denying his thoughts mirrored my own.

I didn't know if it was the aphrodisiac ingredients we'd been shoving into our mouths for the past two hours and that I was a little tipsy on all this wine, or the fact that Aiden and I had chemistry in spades, or that I knew exactly what he could do to my body, but I couldn't ignore it anymore.

I wanted him. Badly. And it was getting harder and harder to deny.

I could only hope this upcoming couples massage was actually relaxing and I'd somehow be able to ignore the fact that Aiden was lying next to me. Naked.

Truly, what was the worst that could happen?

CHAPTER FIFTEEN

AVERY

WELP. I really put out a challenge to the universe when I asked that stupid question, didn't I? I was an idiot, because it turned out the worst was not, in fact, lying next to a naked Aiden while I was equally naked, both of us getting separate massages.

Nope. The worst was being the one performing that sensual massage on his naked body and then having him reciprocate, all while I was turned on enough to power a small village.

Meanwhile, Aiden seemed to keep his cool. While he didn't try to hide the fact that he wanted me, he was being so damn respectful about it, I wanted to scream. At first, I'd welcomed it. Appreciated that boundary he'd put in place without my asking him to.

But now? I wanted it gone. I wanted him as keyed up for me as I was for him. I wanted him to bend me over the bed, shove up my skirt, and plant his face between my thighs. Lick me until I was screaming his name and coming all over his face. I wanted him to see if we could crack my record of six orgasms.

I wanted him, period. Naked and inside me, preferably.

Instead, I got a silent walk back to our room, Aiden's hand hovering just over the small of my back and those eyes following every single move I made. Never overstepping. Never pushing. Being respectful as fuck.

It was infuriating, honestly.

I'd spent the past twenty-four hours—though, if you wanted to get technical, it was more like weeks—being turned on by him, and I was going to combust if I didn't get some damn relief.

I glanced back at him as the door to our room shut behind us, and I allowed my gaze to travel down the length of his body. I didn't know how this man got hotter the longer I was in his presence, but somehow he did. Either that or the aphrodisiacs we'd indulged in for hours really did work.

Of course, it also could've been the fact that I'd had my hands on a naked Aiden not long ago. And forget about when he'd reciprocated. His strong hands had rubbed out every ounce of bottled-up tension I'd been holding in my body, while simultaneously replacing it with a totally different kind. One that only he could alleviate.

And my *god*, this man was good with his hands. Something I'd already known intimately. Though tonight, he'd never once strayed in a way that could be construed as inappropriate. Didn't slip his hand up my side toward my breasts or along my inner thighs to where I throbbed for him, though I'd silently begged for both.

Now he was looking at me with one brow raised in an unasked question. And that question was, *what the fuck is going on, and why the fuck are you scowling at me*? Because, yeah. Apparently when I became exceptionally horny, I turned into a grouch.

"I'm sorry Addison scheduled that and thought it would be appropriate," he said. "I'll handle it."

He thought *that* was why I was wound so tight? Because my bestie forced me and the man starring in my wet dreams together for what was essentially the perfect beginning to a porno? Jesus, for someone who'd become so attuned to me in such a short period of time, he was really missing the mark with this one.

"It's fine," I said, sharper than I'd intended, but I was on fire.

Could I die of horniness? Because with the way my body was a live wire, every nerve ending zinging with awareness of him, it felt a little like I'd be meeting my end any second.

Aiden's brows lifted the slightest bit at my tone, his lips twitching. Like he found the whole thing amusing. Then he tipped his head toward the bathroom. "Would a bath help with whatever you've got going on here?" He gestured toward me in what I assumed was meant to encompass my shittastic attitude.

Would a *bath* help? No, a fucking bath wouldn't help. Not even a full blast from a fire hydrant directly on my clit would. What would he say if I told him the only thing that would help me out of this was his dick?

"No," I said firmly, leaving it at that. I glanced to the bed...to the tiny space we'd be forced into again, and there was no way I could slip under those covers without first having a minute or twenty to myself. "But I'm going to take one anyway. Do you need to get in there before I do?"

"I'm good. You relax and enjoy it." He lifted his chin toward the other room. "I had them deliver some bubble bath while you were gone today. It should be on the vanity."

So he'd noticed I'd nearly had an orgasm with my eyes last night when I'd seen the gorgeous tub for the first time, but he hadn't noticed how much I needed to come right now? If I wasn't sure he'd enjoyed himself when we'd slept together, I'd be second-guessing whether he found me attractive and this was just his way of letting me down gently.

But this had to be some sort of ridiculous, misguided attempt to be respectful of my boundaries, even after I'd dropped a dozen hints tonight that I was done trying to stay away from him. That I wanted him, badly. But it was clear I wasn't going to have him. Not tonight, at least.

I shut the door behind me harder than necessary and

started the bath, grabbing the bottle of bubbles he'd left for me on the counter.

If I didn't know better, I'd think he was doing this on purpose. First, greeting me with that view this morning, his shirt unbuttoned and those glasses on, looking hot as hell and so fucking *capable* it was ridiculous. Then giving me space to do my own thing today before meeting back together tonight. How he hung on every word that left my lips, his gaze never leaving mine as I told him my ideas for the resort and my dreams for my life. The low rumble of his laugh and the sparkle in his eye when he spoke about writing. The soft, subtle touches he gave me seemingly without thought. Simply because he *had* to...

I stepped into the steaming hot water, sighing as I settled into the deep tub, my body melting even as parts of me were still wound up and in need of relief.

A single candle sat on a ledge, softly lighting the space, and though only a door separated Aiden and me, I had to strain to make out the sounds of him moving around in the bedroom.

Was it the same for him?

Could he hear me in here, splashing around?

More importantly...would he be able to hear if I took care of my little problem?

"Aiden..." I whispered.

And I didn't know if I wanted him to answer me or not. Didn't know if I'd rather he burst into the room, eyes heated as he found me with my fingers buried inside my pussy, or if I wanted him completely unaware of what I was doing. There was something so decadent about making myself come to thoughts of him when he was just on the other side of the door, without a clue.

After calling out his name twice more, a little louder each time, and not receiving an answer, I settled back against the tub and slipped my hands into the water. Not stopping until they were between my thighs. If my only options were to sleep next to him all night with my clit thrumming and begging for attention or this, I could be quiet. I'd get myself off in silence, and he never had to know.

Aiden

TONIGHT HADN'T GONE how I thought it would. Though, truthfully, this entire day hadn't.

From this morning when I'd woken up to Avery's sweet pussy grinding down against me before she'd flown out of bed. Then how I'd been struck with inspiration for a scene I'd been stuck on, letting the words pour out of me all day in a way they never had before. And then dinner...

The entire evening had been unexpected in the best kind of way. Not just the meal—one I had no doubt Beck could recreate even better—but just being with Avery. Talking with her. *Really* talking. About things that mattered. Things we both loved. Things I normally kept hidden from everyone.

I'd never once had that. Never once been able to be my true self—my *whole* self—with another person. Not even Brady, who I was closest to in my family. And it was some twist that I'd found that now with her...

My sister's best friend.

My employee.

And the woman who was leaving to pursue her dreams in a couple short months. A woman who'd drawn a very clear line in the sand between us. One I could not—*would* not—cross without her express permission. Not when we had this power dynamic between us. Not only was I eight years older than her, but I was also her boss.

I'd thought that line had been fading. After everything, it had seemed the wall she'd built between us had been crumbling brick by brick. Especially when I'd shown her the parts of me no one else had ever seen.

And then we'd gotten back here following the massage—one in which I'd been hard as a fucking rock the entire time, wishing so badly I could touch her how I wanted to—and the soft warmth she'd been giving off was gone, replaced by nothing but attitude.

There were no two ways about it—she was acting like a little brat, and I wanted to know why. Wanted to know what caused the sudden shift. Wanted to know how we could get back to the connection we'd had over dinner.

A soft groan sounded from the bathroom, and I paused

in unbuttoning my shirt to glance toward the door. I cocked my head to listen for anything more, but it was silent on the other side. Just when I'd written it off as a fluke, she groaned again, but this time, frustration laced the sound.

I'd heard it only a couple times before. On the night when I'd had her spread out for me. When her clit had been begging for my fingers and my tongue. When I'd made her come again and again.

She was getting herself off. Or trying to anyway. And not having much success, by the sounds of it.

I walked over and braced my hands against the doorframe. Hanging my head, I closed my eyes and just listened. A soft moan. A splash. A whimper that went straight to my cock. And then that frustrated groan again.

I curled my fingers around the frame, my entire body strung tight over the thought of her on the other side of this door. Head resting back against the tub, eyes closed, fingers playing with her pussy as she tried in vain to get herself where she needed to go.

"Aiden..."

At first, I thought it was part of the fantasy playing through my mind. Then my name fell from her lips again, louder this time and tinged with desperation, and there was no more denying it. Avery was in there, naked, failing to get herself off. And she was calling out for me in her frustration.

Because she knew I was the one who could give her

exactly what she needed. *I* was the one who could help her.

We might not have sorted out all of our problems, and I had no doubt she didn't fully trust me with everything yet —something that went both ways. But she trusted me with this. Trusted I could take care of her.

"Bunny." The single word was barely more than a breath, so it was no surprise she didn't hear me, another soft whimper her only response. Louder, I said, "Avery."

As if I'd startled her, a loud splash sounded, and she responded with a breathy, "Yeah?"

I closed my eyes and stifled a groan, remembering her uttering that same word, in that same cadence. On that night weeks ago, her eyes had pleaded with me then when I'd asked her if she wanted me to make her come.

And we were right back there. Her desperate for release. Her cunt begging for my touch.

"Do you want my help?" I asked.

"With what?"

"You know what," I said, the words like sandpaper in my throat, my cock so hard it hurt.

She didn't respond, and I could picture her there, eyes half lidded as she stared at the door, full tits playing peekaboo through the bubbles, her hand disappearing between her thighs...

It all came perfectly clear then. This wasn't something that had suddenly arisen since she'd climbed into the tub. She'd been fighting this level of arousal all night.

She could've said something to me at any time, and I'd have taken care of her—hell, I would've slipped my hand under the table and fingered her to an orgasm while David served our dark chocolate raspberry tart. Instead, she worked herself up, made a mess in her panties, and then got mad at me for it.

With that thought in my mind, my patience officially snapped. "Stay or leave, Avery."

"What?"

"Do you want me to stay and give you what you need or leave you alone to handle it?"

I should've taught her a lesson and left her to deal with it. See how long it'd take her to get herself off. But the thought of her in the other room, naked and needy, her little pussy desperate to come, made me unhinged.

There was a beat of silence. Two. Three. Then she whispered, "Stay."

CHAPTER SIXTEEN

AIDEN

SHE'D BARELY GIVEN me the green light before I turned the knob and opened the bathroom door to a sight that nearly had me stumbling straight to my knees.

Flickering candlelight illuminated Avery as she rested her head back against the tub, her hair piled on top in a careless bun. And I'd been right about those perfect tits—bubbles skimmed the surface of the water, covering most of her skin, but every once in a while, a rosy nipple, tight with need, peeked through. Her hands were nowhere to be seen, though the soft, rhythmic waves of the water gave away exactly what she was doing beneath its surface.

"Bunny," I said, voice low with barely restrained need. "Are you in here playing with your pussy?"

Her movements stilled then, and she looked at me with pleading eyes. For me to touch her. Push her. Give her exactly what she needed. But she'd thought her hand was good enough, so we'd see how far that would take her.

"Don't let me stop you." I leaned against the doorframe, crossing my arms over my chest as I stared down at her. "Show me how you make yourself come."

She scraped her teeth over her bottom lip, her eyes connected with mine as she swept her hands through the water. The movement broke apart the bubbles on the surface, enough so I could see exactly what she was doing. Or *wasn't* doing, as it were.

I gave a low sound of disapproval and pushed off the doorframe to stride toward her. "Don't be shy now. You sure as hell weren't when you were fingering yourself, even knowing I was just on the other side of this door."

After the briefest pause, she slipped her hands down the insides of her thighs, not stopping until they hovered just above her pussy. She started slow...soft. Building herself up, though I had no idea why. It was clear she was strung tight with need, desperate for release. Before long, soft and slow turned into tight strokes across her clit as she sank her fingers inside in a quick rhythm designed to get herself off.

I squatted next to the tub, bracing my arm on the edge. Close enough to see the flush of her cheeks had spread down her neck to her freckle-dotted chest. Past the trio of star signs she had tattooed below her collarbone and continuing even farther before it disappeared beneath the water. And there was no hiding her widely blown pupils as she stared up at me, lips parted, tits rising and falling with each panting breath.

"What if I'd heard you?"

The ripples grew faster, the pink of her cheeks deepening even more. Finally, she admitted, "I was hoping you would."

"Why?"

"I don't know."

"You know what I think?"

"What?" she whispered.

"I think this was payback," I said, dipping my fingers into the nearly scalding water and swiping a path through the bubbles again. It gave me an unencumbered view of her hands as they disappeared between her thighs, both working her toward release. "You spent the past couple weeks mad at me, and instead of talking about it, you avoided it altogether. You wanted the space from me but then hated when I gave it to you."

Her lips parted as she dipped her gaze away from mine for a brief moment, and that was all the confirmation I needed.

I hummed low in my throat. "And now? Tonight? You wanted to see how far you could push me before I snapped. Wanted to drive me out of my fucking mind, didn't you? Make sure I could hear you in here, playing with that greedy little cunt, and knowing I couldn't touch you."

"I wanted you to," she admitted, her eyes locked with mine. "I *want* you to."

I didn't know what she'd worked through in her mind or what conclusion she'd suddenly come to that made this all okay, but my control was already on a frayed leash, ready to snap. There was no fucking way I could resist her plea.

I lowered my hand into the water, uncaring as it soaked my shirtsleeve, just needing to feel her. She sighed, goose bumps erupting on her skin at the first brush of my fingers against her inner thigh.

"That was naughty of you, bunny." I swiped my fingers through her slit, barely a brush of skin against skin. And though it killed me, I ignored how she chased them, lifting her hips, desperate for more contact. "Especially after you were a brat out there, pretending to be mad at me when it was just your needy pussy wanting some attention."

She whimpered at the next brush of my thumb against her clit and then moaned, long and low, as I slipped one of my fingers inside next to her own.

"Take off your shirt," she begged, her gaze darting to where it was plastered to my skin.

"You aren't the one making demands here, pretty girl."

"But I want to see you."

"And I've wanted to make you come all day—hell, I've wanted to for weeks—but instead, you've been acting like a little brat, so it looks like neither of us is getting what we wanted."

She rocked her hips in time to our thrusting fingers, lips parted as she worked her clit faster. Quietly, she said, "Are you mad at me?"

I studied her for a moment, trying to figure out where she needed this to go. I didn't know her cues enough yet to be able to guess, and I hated that. Hated not instinctively knowing exactly what she needed so I could give it to her. "Do you want me to be?"

"I don't know."

If she wasn't sure, then that told me she didn't want soft and sweet from me tonight. Which was fine. I wasn't feeling very soft or sweet at the moment. I was feeling fucking ravenous.

"I'm not mad," I said, realizing it was the truth. Even after weeks of cold shoulders. Even after her shutting me out and not entertaining any kind of conversation. Even after her attitude out there... It seemed it'd take a hell of a lot for me to get mad at this girl. "But I am frustrated. I don't like knowing you wanted me and didn't say anything. Hate knowing this pussy was needy for me. And it is, isn't it?"

"Yes."

"And how long has it been needy for me?"

Guilt flashed over her face, and she bit her lower lip, slowing her fingers against her clit.

"Tell me."

"The whole time," she whispered.

I nearly groaned at that, thoughts of her in the next

room over, her pussy aching and desperate for my touch, and her too stubborn to admit it. To ask for it.

"You want me to make you come?"

"*Yes*. Please, Aiden. I need it."

"I know you do," I murmured, watching her expression change as I toyed with her pussy, cataloging every reaction that flitted across her beautiful face. "But instead of telling me that...instead of telling me how desperate you were to come, you ran away."

From the look she gave me, she knew I was talking about so much more than just earlier today. I was talking about the entire time she'd been in Starlight Cove. From the moment my sister had introduced us. She'd assumed the worst and hadn't listened to anything else—she'd done the equivalent of plugging her ears like a child and *la-la-la-ing* her way to ignoring me.

"I'm sorry. I—" Her words cut off on a low moan when I sped up my pumping finger and curled it to brush against that spot inside her, her breaths growing choppy as she rocked her hips to meet every thrust.

She dropped her head back on a whimper, eyes fluttering closed as she strummed frantically against her clit. Her pussy tightened around our pumping fingers, and it would be so easy. So fucking easy to guide her through this orgasm and straight into the next.

I'd thought of little else these past couple weeks but how beautiful she looked when she came, and I wanted to see it more than anything. But instead of doing just that and giving us what we both craved, I slipped my finger from inside her and removed my hand from the bath entirely.

She snapped her head up, eyes popping open as she stared at me openmouthed. "Aiden..."

Part of me wanted nothing more than to go right back to what I'd been doing and get her off like she needed. With how worked up she was, it'd barely take anything at all. I bet I could work her through three...maybe four while she lay there under the water. One after another after another.

But neither of us was going to get what we wanted tonight.

I'd be damned if she walked away from this thinking it was ever a good idea not to tell me exactly what she needed. That was how this had to work—she'd tell me, and I'd give it to her. Without question. Without hesitation. Without fail.

But that meant she had to be honest with me and couldn't run away.

I stood, grabbing one of the oversize bath towels from the cabinet, and held it open for her. "C'mere."

She blinked up at me, confusion written on her face. "What?"

"I said, c'mere. It's time to get out."

"But... But I didn't..."

"I know."

She was frozen for long moments, just staring up at me

with wide eyes. But when I didn't offer any further explanation, she finally braced herself on the edge of the tub and stood, giving me an unencumbered view of her. Her entire body was flushed, her nipples tight, and goose bumps dotted every inch of her skin like the freckles and tiny tattoos scattered everywhere. She was so fucking gorgeous, I wanted to spend hours...days...*weeks*... worshipping her.

But not tonight.

I reached down to drain the water, then wrapped the towel around her shoulders and dried her off. She shifted with each movement, the barest hint of a moan leaving her lips every time I passed over her breasts, across her ass, between her thighs...

Brushing my lips against the tattoo behind her ear, I whispered, "Still needy, bunny?"

She huffed out a sound halfway between a whimper and a groan. "You know I am."

"Good."

"What do you mean, good?" she asked, a snotty lilt to her voice.

"Exactly what I said." I lifted her into my arms and carried her into the bedroom where I sat her on the bed. Once I'd peeled the towel from her and tossed it into the bathroom, I gripped her behind the knees and pushed up and out, spreading her open for me. I stared down at her as I brushed my hands along her inner thighs, not stopping until I was nearly to her pussy, all pink and swollen and so fucking wet for me.

She shifted under my gaze, her body restless, her fingers twitching at her sides. And then she lifted them from the bed and ran them over her breasts and down her stomach, straight for where she was no doubt aching for relief.

But before she could make contact, I said, "Hands off," my tone brooking no argument.

She stopped immediately and let out a low groan. "Aiden. Please."

"No touching." I unbuttoned my shirt and slipped it off before undoing the fly of my pants and giving my cock a little room to breathe. Bracing my hands on either side of her hips, I leaned over her, bringing our faces inches apart. "You had your chance in the bathroom, and you couldn't make it happen. So that means this pussy is mine to make come tonight. If I want to."

"Oh my God," she said, eyes wide, fingers curled around my forearms. "Please don't leave me wound up like this..."

I lifted a brow at her. "The next time you get like this, are you going to act like a brat who's desperate to have her clit spanked, or are you going to be a good girl and tell me what you need?"

Indecision flashed across her face, as if what I'd said interested her. And if I'd been uncertain about the two of us clicking before, that simple move wiped every ounce of hesitation away. I'd met my match in Avery. She yielded to me...but only after a fight. She was pliant...but only after she made me work for it. And I fucking loved that push and pull between us. Loved how she gave just as good as she got.

"Not sure, bunny? Let's test it out." I ran my hand down her inner thigh, not stopping until I brushed over the length of her slit. She moaned at the barest contact of my thumb against her swollen clit, peeking out from beneath its hood. Then I brought my fingers down hard, a sharp smack sounding in the room.

She jerked, letting out a squeak of surprise as she snapped her legs together. "Aiden!"

"Open for me." I pressed my hand against her inner thigh and waited until she complied, letting her legs fall to the sides once again. "Good girl," I murmured, gliding my fingers over her pussy in a soft caress.

Once she settled, her body melting into the bed at my gentle strokes, I brought my hand down against her again. This time, her sharp gasp was followed by a long, low moan, and I reveled in the sound. Wanted to hear it again and again.

But as much as I loved it, it was far too fucking loud.

I lifted my gaze to the wall the pornographic soundtrack had come from last night. If we were able to hear them, no doubt they could hear Avery, and I wasn't ready to share her sounds with anyone. They were mine and mine alone.

"Shh, bunny. You've gotta be quiet, or everyone's going to know exactly how needy this pussy is." Reaching up, I cupped my hand over her mouth to stifle her sounds, and that only seemed to make her hotter, a muffled moan slipping free. "Do you like this?"

She murmured against my palm, a subtle nod showing her agreement as she attempted to shift closer.

"Look at you, arching your hips up for another spanking. You're a dirty fucking girl, aren't you? Acting like a brat just to get your clit slapped."

She fisted the sheets on either side of her hips and stared up at me with wide eyes, a whimper vibrating against my palm.

I cupped her pussy with my other hand, brushing the heel of my palm against her clit in soft circles to keep her right on the edge, aching for relief. "If you would've just told me how desperate your cunt was for me to own it instead of acting like a brat, I would've given you exactly what you wanted. Would've made you come on my fingers and my tongue and my cock. Over and over again until you begged me to stop." I slid my hand up, swiping my fingers through her wetness before bringing them down against her on another loud smack.

Her entire body jolted, her eyes rolling back and her legs curling up toward her chest as she shuddered and moaned. Her pussy was a deep, dark pink, swollen and dripping wet, thanks to my hand. I wanted to sink my cock inside her so fucking bad, watch as her pussy stretched around me, taking me deep. Wanted to taste all this sweetness I'd coaxed out of her. Wanted her to come so many times she'd soak the sheets beneath her. And then again, just because I could.

"But now?" I brushed my fingers through her slit. Not giving her the pressure or the speed she needed. "You're getting one."

Her wide eyes shot to mine, and she let out a whimper of disappointment behind my hand.

"Just one," I confirmed as I continued the too-light pressure against her. "And it's not going to be from my tongue or from my fingers buried deep inside you. It's not going to be from my cock fucking one out of you. It's going to be from me slapping your clit like the naughty girl you are."

I didn't know if it was my words or my actions—the soft glide of my fingers against her, dipping just inside to tease, followed by a sharp slap to her clit, but she came then, her back arching, legs curled toward her chest as she shuddered and shook through her release. I caught her moans against my hand, my gaze soaking in every inch of her body as waves of pleasure rolled through her and her pussy pulsed against my fingers.

My cock was a steel pipe in my pants. Angry and hard and fucking desperate to feel the sweet heaven of her cunt squeezing the life out of it as she came until she couldn't anymore.

But I wasn't fucking her tonight. We needed to talk before we did that again, and now was not the time.

So instead of giving in to what I knew we both wanted, I headed into the bathroom and wet a washcloth with warm water. When I stepped back into the bedroom, I found her exactly where I'd left her, in the middle of the bed, limbs spread out, pussy still wet and needy.

With soft strokes, I cleaned her off, taking care to be gentle. After I tossed the cloth into the bathroom, I slipped out of my pants and into bed, gathering her in my arms as I tucked us both beneath the covers. She curled immediately into my side, her head resting on my chest as I stroked my fingers down her back.

"You okay?" I asked, my lips against her forehead.

She gave a soft hum and nodded, wrapping her arm across my stomach and draping a leg over my hips to snuggle closer. After long moments of silence, she whispered, "Tomorrow, can I have it?"

"Have what?"

"Everything," she said, tipping her head back to look up at me. "All of it. Just like you said."

I reached up and swiped the hair back from her face, brushing my thumb down her jaw. "If you want it."

And I knew she could read in those words everything I wasn't saying. We could go back to how things were—no touching, no intimacy. Addison could continue to throw us together, and we could continue to fight it.

Or we could see where this thing between us could go. It was her choice.

"I do."

I lowered my mouth to hers then, groaning when she slipped her tongue into my mouth and relishing in the taste of her. After a moment, I pulled back and murmured against her lips, "I'll give you whatever you want, bunny. You just have to tell me what that is."

CHAPTER SEVENTEEN

AVERY

I'D BARELY BEEN UP for thirty seconds before I tested exactly what Aiden had told me last night—all I had to do was tell him what I wanted, and he'd give it to me. He'd made me come last night, but it had only been once. And while that used to be my usual, it now felt like a punishment when I knew what he was capable of. When I knew what my body was capable of under his attention.

I rolled over and propped my hand on his chest, ready to beg for a morning O when he blinked open his sleepy eyes.

"Morning, bunny," he said, his voice a low rasp that shot straight to my nipples. He brushed a hand down my back, not stopping until he had an entire palmful of my ass. "How're you feeling?"

"Horny." I raised a brow. "Did you mean what you said last night?"

"Without question."

"Good." I grabbed his other hand and tugged it down between my thighs. No sense in beating around the bush. I'd been aching and desperate for him last night, and that came back full force at the first brush of his fingers against me. I shuddered at just that barest touch before he flipped me onto my back.

He braced himself over me and lowered his head to kiss me. I fell into it immediately, melting against him as he stroked my tongue with his own. God, this man. He made my body come alive in ways I'd never thought possible. In ways I'd never even dreamed it could.

"I was mean to your little pussy last night, wasn't I?" he murmured, his eyes heated.

I bit my lip because I wouldn't exactly call a mind-blowing orgasm mean, despite getting me there with pain-laced pleasure. But I was one hundred percent here for whatever he had in mind to make up for it, so I gave a short nod.

"Can you be quiet while I kiss it and make it better?"

My nod was more enthusiastic this time, remembering exactly what Aiden could do with his tongue. Then, with a gleam in his eyes, he disappeared beneath the comforter, settling his wide shoulders between my spread legs and giving a soft hum of approval I heard even through the covers.

And then he proceeded to give me the best apology I'd ever received in my *life*. He licked up the seam of my slit, sucking my pussy lips into his mouth before laving my sensitive clit with his tongue. He worked me up quickly, like he'd been playing my body for years. Like he knew exactly what I needed to send me flying and he was ready to give it to me.

Before long, I had his head gripped in my hands, my hips rolling in time with his thrusting fingers. And then I was coming all over his face, a loud moan leaving my lips as I shuddered through my release.

With a nip at my inner thigh, he popped his head up from beneath the comforter, his eyes bright but serious, his mouth still wet from me. "That wasn't very quiet, bunny."

I breathed out a laugh and tossed an arm over my eyes, utterly blissed out and loving the hell out of it. I'd like every morning wake-up to be just like this, please and thanks. "Sorry to tell you this, but I'm never going to be quiet with you."

"I'll have to remember that for tonight."

"Tonight?" I asked, my voice nearly a shriek as I jerked my arm away from my eyes to stare up at him.

With a raised brow, he said, "Yes, tonight. I've gotta pick up some condoms because I didn't bring any with me."

Fuck. I didn't either because I thought it'd be a deterrent. If I didn't have any, that would stop me from giving in to my desires and falling into bed with him. So much for that theory.

"I have an IUD," I said, not bothering to hide the

hopeful plea in my voice. "And I got tested a few months ago. I haven't been with anyone since."

He stared at me for a beat, then dropped his face into my neck and released a low groan. "Bunny. Are you telling me you want me to fuck you bare?"

"If your tests are clear, too, then yes, please." I nodded enthusiastically, pushing against his chest.

Though he definitely didn't have to, he allowed me to flip our positions so he was flat on his back. After shoving off his boxer briefs, I settled astride him, rolling my hips and gliding my pussy directly over where he was so hard for me. The head of his cock bumped against my clit with every pass, and I tossed my head back on a moan.

Aiden cupped a hand over my mouth, his eyes hot as he watched me ride him. "What'd I tell you? Gotta be quieter, pretty girl. No one else in this place needs to hear how fucking sexy you sound when you come on my cock. That's just for me."

I whimpered against his hand, gliding my hips faster, so close to my release. I had no idea what it was about this man or why it was like this with him, but I'd become insatiable in a way I'd never been before.

"Such a greedy little thing, aren't you?" he murmured, gripping my hip in his other hand as he helped guide my movements. "Rocking that sweet little cunt against my cock. Look at you, making a mess all over me." He groaned, glancing between us at the slickness coating his length. "You gonna come for me, baby? Come all over my dick so I can slide nice and deep. Gonna fill you up until you beg me to stop."

My orgasm was just out of reach, the peak so close I could taste it, when there was a knock at the door. With a groan, I deflated against Aiden, my orgasm receding in a flash.

"Ignore them," he said, fingers digging into my flesh as he guided me against him once again.

With a nod, I closed my eyes and rocked over him, grinding down as I started the climb all over again. I was nearly there when another knock sounded. I whimpered, sagging against him as the orgasm slipped through my fingers just like before.

"Fuck," he snapped under his breath. Then louder to reach whoever was on the other side of our door, he said, "What?"

The person cleared their throat. "Pardon me, sir, but it's Mark from the front desk. I have an urgent message from your sister? She called as she wasn't able to get through on your phones. She set an appointment for you this morning and was adamant I made sure to contact you so you wouldn't miss it."

"I'm going to kill her," Aiden muttered, one hand on my hip, the other still cupping my mouth. "Going to straight up murder her in her sleep."

At this point, with my clit throbbing, my pussy aching for the relief it'd been denied not once, but twice, I wasn't so sure I wouldn't help him.

"Give us a minute," Aiden called toward the door. Then, quietly so only I could hear, he said, "Need to take care of this greedy little pussy first. Need to make sure my bunny's satisfied before I send her off for the day, don't I?"

With that, he gripped my hip, guiding me back and forth over his cock in a firm grind designed to get me off.

"You gonna come with him just outside the door?" he murmured, low enough for only me to hear, his fingers digging into the flesh of my hip. "You are, aren't you? My dirty fucking girl. You're going to gush all over my cock while he's standing out there waiting for us."

That was all it took. My eyes rolled back in my head as I shuddered and shook, coming apart on top of him. He caught my moans in his hand, his answering groan and murmured encouragement extending every ounce of my pleasure.

When I was sated and boneless on top of him, he brushed his hands down my back and pressed a kiss to my forehead. "You're not *really* close to Addison, right? You won't miss her when she's gone?"

I huffed out a laugh and rested my hand on his chest, propping my chin on top. "Don't put a hit out on her. Without her scheming, we wouldn't be here right now."

"Being forced apart by the world's most clever cockblock?"

With a grin, I rolled out of bed, loving how Aiden's gaze followed my every movement. "I've got the festival all day, but there's always tonight."

He tossed the covers aside and stood, striding toward me. He was completely naked, his cock jutting out thick and proud, proving I'd been the only one who'd gotten relief this morning.

Crowding me against the wall, he brought one hand up, placing the other on my hip. "Oh, bunny. You think I'm going to wait for tonight and leave this pussy needy all day? Not a fucking chance."

CHAPTER EIGHTEEN

AVERY

AIDEN MADE good on his promise. And though I'd been strung tight all day, I'd also had the time of my life. While I'd explored, taking notes and brainstorming ideas to bring back to the resort, he'd stayed at the bed-and-breakfast to write again. Except, unlike yesterday, he'd slipped away a couple times to meet up with me throughout the day, each encounter hotter than the last.

First had been midmorning in the corn maze—the appointment Addison had booked for us that she'd thought so urgent we needed to receive a wake-up call about it. Aiden and I had slunk off into a corner, and he'd stood in front of me, blocking my body from any nosy onlookers. And then he'd shoved his fingers into my panties and made me come, all while whispering what a good, dirty girl I was being for him and how he couldn't wait to taste me again.

Then we'd met up for lunch, where he'd casually touched me throughout the meal, dropping lingering kisses on my lips, my jaw, my neck but never giving me what my body was hungry for. At least until he'd asked for the bill. As we were waiting, he'd tugged me into his lap. With the tablecloth as our only barrier, he'd touched me over my clothes until I'd come, biting back a moan. All while I'd stared out at the oblivious patrons filling the restaurant.

And finally, he'd called me late in the afternoon, double-checking that we were still on for dinner. When I'd asked how writing had been going, he'd read me what he'd written—a filthy exhibitionist sex scene that had my panties wet immediately. It'd barely taken more than a brush of my fingers against my clit as I was hidden away in a single-stall bathroom before I was flying, Aiden murmuring praise on the other end.

Needless to say, he was a distraction in the best possible way. But even with those interruptions, I'd still managed to get in a full day's worth of activities, had taken five screenfuls of notes and talked with a dozen different people by the time he met up with me in the evening.

Our plan was dinner and then...well, I wasn't so sure. But I was interested in a whole different kind of eating followed by mind-blowing sex, preferably more than once, so the dinner plans could suck it for all I cared. I probably had a few granola bars in my bag that would tide us over.

I thought Aiden and I were on the same page. I figured

he'd throw our plans—*Addison's* plans, let's be real—out the window and drag me back to our room to hand out a few more O's.

Instead, he greeted me with a kiss and a murmured, "Hey," then clasped my hand in his and tugged me into a crowded park. Dozens—maybe hundreds—of blankets dotted with people were spread out as far as the eye could see, everyone setting up for the evening's show. It was the highlight of the entire festival—a glow-in-the-dark parade, followed by a massive fireworks showcase.

And I didn't give one single fuck about any of it.

Addison had made sure Mark from the bed-and-breakfast had reserved our place on the lawn. Our blanket lay directly in front of a large maple tree, its leaves falling like red confetti to the ground. A picnic basket sat in the middle, along with a bottle of wine, and *no*.

Absolutely not.

Aiden could not be taking me here to sit at this event for *hours* after he'd been making me hungry and needy for him all day. After he'd made me crave his cock, desperate for that fullness only he could provide. After he'd withheld it from me last night and after we'd been cockblocked this morning...

I jerked to a stop before we'd reached the blanket, our arms outstretched between us. "You can't be serious."

He glanced back at me with a raised brow. "About what?"

Breathing out an incredulous laugh, I gestured to our

picnic dinner and all the people surrounding us. "*This*," I hissed.

He stepped into me, sliding his hand around to cup my neck, his thumb just under my chin. With gentle pressure, he tipped my head back so he could meet my eyes. Then he lowered his mouth to mine, pressing a soft kiss there, before trailing his lips across my cheek to my ear. Against it, he whispered, "Let's eat, bunny."

I narrowed my gaze on him as he stepped away, not quite able to figure out his end game. But with a huff, I plopped down next to him on the blanket, accepting the glass of wine he'd poured for me. He pulled out a charcuterie plate filled with meats and cheeses, nuts and fruit, fresh bread, locally sourced honey, and homemade jam. A cornucopia of deliciousness that I reluctantly enjoyed as the glow-in-the-dark parade went on for what seemed like forever.

In an effort to distract myself, I leaned into his side and asked, "How'd today go? I mean, besides the fuckhot scene you already read me. You know I think that was excellent work."

He chuckled lowly and pressed his lips against my temple in a soft kiss. "Great. Mostly."

"Why mostly?"

He inhaled deeply before exhaling, so much angst in that single breath. "My publisher called with an opportunity. They want to send me to the Frankfurt Book Fair so I can meet with some international publishers."

"Really?" I asked, tipping my head back to look at him. "That sounds amazing!"

"They're really trying to sell it to me. They think with all the buzz currently circulating about *Heat and Desire* that we'll be able to sell a shit-ton of foreign rights for the trilogy. Which would mean a shit-ton of money. Which would mean we can complete the cottage renovations Addison wants." He tipped his head back, eyes flicking away from mine. "And I can renovate the lighthouse on the property and finally not have to live with my sister anymore."

My brows lifted at that. I knew exactly the lighthouse he was talking about, though I'd never been there, and this was the first I'd ever heard it mentioned by him or anyone else. It was on a tiny island, a few hundred yards from the resort's shore. Something that wasn't too far but you'd need a boat to get to. Which was exactly something a secretive, closed-off Aiden would love.

"That kind of seems like it would be life-changing," I said. "But how come you sound like you don't want to do it?"

He shook his head. "It's not that I don't want to—they promised any events I did wouldn't have media coverage, so I wouldn't have to worry about my identity getting out. But I literally can't do it. Addison's got my schedule blocked off the whole week they'd want me there."

"What's it blocked with?"

He grabbed his phone from his pocket and pulled up

his calendar to a date in December. Sure enough—the entire week, all day, every day, was blocked with a note that read: *Aiden required for event.*

"She always does this," he said, barely more than a grumble. "Just puts shit on my calendar without telling me what it is."

I laughed. "That's helpful."

"Welcome to my life. I think she does it now specifically because she knows it pisses me off."

"I don't doubt it. But it really doesn't matter what it is or that she has you booked for it. I'll still be here in December." I shrugged, my shoulder brushing against his chest as I did so. "I can handle whatever she's got you doing, and you can go off and be Mr. Superstar Author."

He was quiet for long moments until I finally tipped my head back to glance at him, only to find him already looking down at me. "You'd do that?"

"Handle the event at the resort so you can go off and make megabucks? Sure, why not?"

Trepidation was clear in his tone. "You wouldn't be able to tell them the real reason I'm gone... I'd probably have to make up some sort of accounting conference or some other bullshit like that."

"I know," I said, tracing my fingers over his chest through his shirt. "And I get it now. I know why you're keeping this secret, and I won't tell anyone."

At my words, Aiden's whole body seemed to relax, a

sense of relief sweeping over him as we sat, watching the rest of the way-too-long parade.

And through it all, he touched me, asking about my tattoos as he went. Brushing a thumb over the open book above my ankle, skating his fingers over the crown on my forearm, sliding his hand over the three tiny birds inked over my spine, before bringing that big palm to rest against my ass.

If it wasn't touches like that, it was wiping a crumb from my lips or sweeping the hair away from my face or cupping the back of my neck in a gesture that felt incredibly intimate and claiming all at once. Nothing overtly sexual, but it still made me crave him in a way that had me nearly crawling out of my skin.

When the parade had passed and the fireworks were about to begin—all of which happened with his dick nowhere near me—I'd had enough. "I thought you said you'd give me whatever I needed as long as I told you."

He dipped his chin in a nod. "I did say that."

"And yet here we sit, in a crowd full of people, and your dick isn't inside me."

His lips twitched at my blunt words, his amusement clear, which only made me scowl harder. "Don't be mad, bunny."

"I'm not mad," I said sharply. "I'm *turned on*. Thanks to you, by the way. Your roaming hands and your sweet words and those *kisses*. And you said—"

"Did you do what I asked you to?"

"I— What?"

He raised a brow, then repeated calmly, "Did you do what I asked you to?"

"When you texted me to take off my panties before I met you here? Yeah. For all the good it's done me."

He shifted away from me so he could lean back against the tree, his legs outstretched in front of him, and patted his lap. "Then wrap that extra blanket around yourself and come over here."

I froze for half a second before doing as he said and draping the cloth around my shoulders as I scrambled into his lap, giddy excitement bubbling up. Every single moment with Aiden felt like that, and I was a junkie addicted to my next rush.

"Someone's in a hurry," he murmured, his eyes dancing with mirth.

"Someone's horny," I corrected, grinding my pussy against the unmistakable bulge in his jeans and groaning when it bumped against my clit.

He hummed low in his throat. "Then you better take out my cock so we can do something about that."

I snapped my gaze to his before glancing at all the people surrounding us. While no one was within ten yards on any side of us, they were still much closer than I would've liked when I got up to sexual shenanigans.

"Here?" I asked. "*Now?*"

"Here," he confirmed, gripping my ass and pressing me down harder against him. "Now."

I'd never been one for exhibitionism, and I wasn't sure I wanted to start. Except that wasn't exactly true. The scene Aiden had read to me earlier today had gotten me worked up like nothing else, and it was remarkably similar to our situation. Only it'd taken place at a masquerade ball filled with dozens of people instead of at an evening picnic under a display of fireworks.

Glancing around to make sure no one could see what I was doing, I reached between us and undid the fly of his jeans, freeing his cock. Humming in appreciation, I wrapped my fingers around his impressive girth, stroking up and down his erection and watching as pleasure skated across his features. While he loved dishing it out, *I* loved watching him take it. Loved knowing that though he gave so much to me, he still needed this. Still needed the pleasure I could give him.

"Good girl," he murmured, eyes heavy lidded as I stroked him. "Now turn around so you can watch the show."

Careful to keep the blanket covering us, I did as he said, hiking my skirt up to my waist as I leaned back into his chest.

"You've been so good for me today, bunny. So good. But I made this little pussy desperate for me, didn't I?" He kissed my neck as he brushed his hands down the insides of my thighs before sliding his fingers through my wetness.

"Worked your clit over nice and sweet but left your cunt empty and aching."

"Yes," I breathed, eyes glazed as I stared up at the first firework that burst through the sky.

"Tell me what you need, pretty girl."

"You," I said without pause. "Please, Aiden. I want it so bad." I didn't even care that we were out here, surrounded by too many people to count. That fact only made me hotter...wetter.

"Then take it. Put my cock inside that sweet little cunt. Right where it belongs."

My pussy clenched at his words, desperate for him to fill me. I shifted, sliding his length through my slit and biting my lip in an effort to stifle my moan at the thought of feeling him with nothing between us. I'd never once had that, but I wanted it. More than I could articulate, I wanted it. With *him*.

Once I had his cock notched at my entrance, I sank down, my eyelids fluttering closed as he filled me in stuttered thrusts. It wasn't an easy fit. Aiden didn't have the kind of dick that could just glide right in. Even with how turned on he'd made me, I still had to work to take him. My body gave way to accommodate his size as I slid down a little more with each thrust of his hips beneath me. But that in itself was perfection. The stretch. The burn. That little bit of discomfort like a shadow lurking behind all that overwhelming pleasure.

When I was finally seated on him, panting and ready to

ride him to an orgasm that was so fucking close, he curled his fingers around my hips, stilling me.

"Aiden. What—"

"Stay just like this, bunny." He brushed his lips up the length of my neck, his mouth hovering over my ear. "Now sit and watch the show."

I blew out a disbelieving laugh, my clit throbbing with need. "You can't be serious. I'm—"

He reached down, smacking his fingers lightly against where I was spread open for him. Spread open and swollen and aching for what he could give me. "Sit and watch," he said firmly. "And don't you dare fucking move."

I had half a mind to ride him anyway. What was he going to do? Slap my clit some more? Oh *darn*. We'd already established he could make me come just like that, and at this point, I'd take even an orgasm that bordered on pain if I could just have the release. I'd nearly decided to do just that when his fingers ghosted over me, the barest brush against my clit. A soft glide in contrast to his earlier treatment.

Against my ear, he murmured, "I'll make it so good, baby. I promise it'll be worth the wait."

With a whimper, I sagged back into his chest, the fight leaving me. I stared up at the vibrant night sky, watching the tiny pops of color burst free. Fireworks exploded, one after another after another, leading to what I knew would be a breathtaking finale.

As we sat there, Aiden's cock filling me but not giving

me any relief, he stroked his hands along my body. Up to cup my breasts, his fingers toying with my nipples. His teeth scraping down the column of my neck, nipping at the tattoo behind my ear. Worse was when he'd bring his hands down the insides of my thighs but never put them where I wanted them. Where I *needed* them. Keeping me hovering but never falling, all that pleasure held just out of reach.

And all the while, my clit throbbed, my pussy clenching sporadically around him as he filled me but didn't fucking *move*.

He had me strung so tight, so ready for him to make me come, I couldn't think straight. All I knew was the sensation of him at my back, his hushed words whispered against my ear, his hands stroking my body, and his cock filling me.

All I knew was *him*.

But then he touched me. Just the barest glance of his fingertips against my clit, and my pussy throbbed at the contact. I tipped my head back against his shoulder, my whimper lost in the commotion around us.

"You think anyone's watching you?" he asked, his breath hot against my ear as his fingers toyed with me. "You think anyone knows what we're doing under this blanket? That you've been a dirty fucking girl, begging to ride my cock, desperate to come right here in front of all these people?"

"Aiden," I breathed, my entire body a live wire, aching for detonation.

"I can feel you throbbing around me. That greedy little cunt wants my come, doesn't it?"

"God, yes." I squeezed my eyes shut tight, my body hungry for him to give me what I needed. "*Please*. Please fuck me."

"I'm going to, baby. Don't worry."

"Now, Aiden. I need it *now*."

"Almost," he said, his voice tight with need as he glided his fingers up my pussy lips and down to where I was spread wide to take him. Then stroking on either side of my clit but never close enough. Never giving me the pressure I needed.

And then, finally, he moved.

He settled his hands on my waist, holding me in place as he shifted his hips beneath me. He pulled out on a soft, slow glide before thrusting back inside me, and my eyes rolled back, a loud groan leaving my lips. And I didn't even care. Didn't care who was watching, didn't care who could hear. All I cared about...all I could focus on was the single place we were joined and how amazing it felt.

"You've been so good for me. So fucking good. Are you ready, pretty girl?" he asked, his tongue circling my tattoo. "Are you ready to come all over me so I can fill up this sweet pussy?"

I couldn't answer him. Couldn't manage anything more

than sucking in lungfuls of air, my nails digging into his forearms as he stroked closer and closer to my clit.

And then, just as his fingers circled it, giving me the exact pressure I needed, his thrusts growing more pronounced, the sky lit up with dozens of fireworks, signaling the finale, and I exploded right along with them. My cries were lost in the cacophony all around us as I shuddered and shook against him, my orgasm seemingly endless as it washed through me, sucking me down into a bliss only he had been able to provide.

"Fuck," he breathed into my neck, his fingers digging into my hips. "Oh fuck, bunny. That's it. Squeeze my cock and come all over me."

Wave after wave rolled through me as Aiden continued stroking me through one release and straight into another. A never-ending sea of pleasure at this man's hands.

Finally, he settled deep even as I continued shuddering above him. With a groan, he buried his face into my neck as he exploded inside me, his cock filling me just like he'd promised.

By the time I blinked my eyes open again, the sky was dark, save for the stars scattered across it and the moon shining bright. The space around us had cleared out, and fuck me, but how long had I been lost to the pleasure he'd given me, the world disappearing around me?

"You with me again?" he asked, amusement threaded through his tone as he ran his hands up and down the outsides of my thighs.

"Barely," I managed. My body felt wrung out but somehow still tight with need.

He hummed into my neck and pressed a kiss there. "I hope you're not done for the night, bunny. Because I sure as hell haven't come close to my fill. This is our last night without my sister up our asses, and I'm going to take advantage of every single second."

CHAPTER NINETEEN

AVERY

I DIDN'T THINK there was anything hotter than watching my...fuck buddy? Temporary hookup? Short-term boyfriend? as he stood at the front desk of The Cozy Maple Inn to check us out Sunday morning. He wore a crisp navy suit that he filled out impeccably and a stern expression, a complete contrast to the kind of person who'd normally find themselves in the situation we were in.

With his mouth set in a flat line, his eyes hard, Aiden met the desk attendant's gaze without wavering. "You heard me correctly. The bed in the Cozy Garden Hideaway is broken. And that made it quite uncomfortable to sleep on, as I'm sure you can imagine."

Mark stared at Aiden for a long moment, his gaze sweeping over my 6'4" beast of a man who looked like he was the president of a bank rather than someone who went around fucking so hard they broke beds in their spare time. Then, eyes wide, Mark slid his gaze to me.

"Don't," Aiden said, his voice low but hard as he shifted to block Mark's view of me. "You don't need to look at her when I'm telling you this."

Mark cleared his throat. "Of course. I apologize, sir. But if you don't mind, could you clarify that for me? What do you mean by *broken*?"

"Exactly what I said. The bed is broken." Aiden spoke slower, as if that would help, his expression daring the other man to question him further or inquire about how it happened.

But from the look on Mark's face, he already knew. And was clearly shocked by it, no doubt wondering how the hell someone with the polished façade and stick-up-their-ass demeanor Aiden wore like a cloak could actually break a bed.

It'd been surprising for me, too. Not the fact that he'd been able to do it—I no longer questioned anything that man could do, in or out of the bedroom—but the fact that we'd fucked hard enough to break it in the first place.

After he'd gotten me back to our room following the fireworks, he'd proceeded to make me come so hard, so many times, I'd made a mess of the sheets, and my body had been one giant nerve ending, frayed and raw. I'd been shaking, my pussy throbbing and dripping wet as he'd bent me over the bed and slammed into me. Over and over and over again as I'd begged him to fuck me harder. And he had.

Christ on a cracker, he had.

Even when two of the bed's legs broke, slamming us to the floor, he'd just kept right on fucking me straight through it. He'd placed his hand over my mouth to keep my moans muffled, his hips pumping wildly against me as he whispered the filthiest words in my ear. Not stopping until I'd come three more times on his cock before he'd finally finished inside me.

Then he'd collapsed against my back, his low chuckle mixed with my fit of giggles as we'd lain on a now-slanted bed, thanks to our activities.

"I, uh..." Mark started, clearly not knowing what to do in this situation. I didn't blame him—I was pretty sure this wasn't something they generally covered in orientation. "I'm terribly sorry for that inconvenience, sir, and I'd love to comp last night's stay to make up for it."

I'd barely made it until we were in the car, the doors shut behind us, before I broke out in a fit of giggles. I pressed my head back against the seat and turned toward Aiden, a grin splitting my face. "I can't believe we didn't have to pay for the broken bed. *And* we got a free night out of it."

Aiden grinned as he started the car, shooting a glance at me out of the corner of his eye. "I can be very persuasive when I want to be."

There was no question about that, and my overworked

clit was proof enough of his *persuasion*. I hummed in agreement as he pulled out of the parking lot, guiding us back to Starlight Cove.

"There's just a little problem..." I said.

"What's that?"

"If we're not telling Addison about us"—I flicked my fingers between us and the agreement we'd come to—"what do we tell her when she asks why we got a free night?"

While attempting to fall asleep on a broken bed, we'd discussed it and decided it was in our best interest to pretend like we still weren't a thing for however long I was in town. Or however long until someone found out. If Addison wanted to shove us together repeatedly in an attempt at matchmaking, who were we to stop her?

Aiden shrugged, his hand tightening on mine over the shifter as he switched gears. "I'll tell her they were so grateful for all the events she booked that they comped it as a thank-you. That little demon loves anything that boosts her ego, so she'll be focused on that part and not the free night."

I just stared at him, shaking my head in wonder. "You're a genius."

His lips twitched, that dimple popping out as he slid me a sidelong glance before returning his attention to the road.

"Well, even though I can't tell her this, I'm grateful she meddled," I said, relaxing back in the seat, my head turned toward him. It had been a whirlwind weekend—the best I could remember having...maybe ever—filled with great conversation, great food, and great sex. Leaving me fulfilled in a way I'd thought I'd have to travel across the world to experience.

And I couldn't help but wonder, if only fleetingly, what would happen if this was my life all the time. If I stuck around, tossed my aspirations out the window, and lived *this* life instead of the one I'd been dreaming about.

Aiden glanced over at me and brought our joined hands up to his mouth, drawing my thoughts back to the present. He swept his lips across my knuckles before lowering our hands back to the gearshift. Then, with his eyes on the road, he murmured, "Me, too."

CHAPTER TWENTY

AIDEN

HALLOWEEN PASSED, October bleeding into November, and Avery and I had managed to keep our little entanglement a secret, despite the fact that we spent every night together—either in her bed or mine. I was growing addicted to her. Quickly. Even though I was well aware that we had an expiration date.

Temporary had always been my standard MO. And I didn't know why this felt so different from every other situationship I'd been in. But it was. I couldn't say how, but I knew it in my bones.

Just like I knew the placement of all eighteen of Avery's scattered tattoos, the stamps on her body that marked her life—the bunny behind her ear because her mom told her they bring luck if they cross your path, even if you can't see them, and the three star signs below her collarbone that she swore told the story of who she was, and the open book on her ankle and every other one in between. I knew she got a little needy after her seventh orgasm, and that she was just as desperate to crack a dozen as I was to get her there. I knew the list of places she wanted to travel to someday, and that she loved ice cream in the winter and hot chocolate in the summer, and that playing with her hair always put her right to sleep.

Through learning all of it and the two of us growing closer, there'd been a couple close calls of people finding out. Addison was relentless and determined to expose us. Like when she'd stormed into Avery's room at the ass-crack of dawn one morning, except my little bunny had been in my room, completely naked and dead to the world. Fortunately, I'd had the foresight to lock the bathroom door that led to Avery's room before we'd crashed for the night. Because of that, she'd been able to play it off and tell Addison she'd been sick and had set up camp on the bathroom floor.

Then there was the time we'd been taking a bath, the water hotter than Satan's balls and the bubbles sky-high, just how Avery liked it. I'd been massaging her feet as she wondered aloud where her first flight would be to when Addison had barged into Avery's room, then into the adjoining bathroom with barely a knock. I'd slipped under the water just in time and had to hold my breath for three fucking minutes until Avery had finally convinced my sister to leave.

Addison continued trying to catch us together, overstepping in ways that were too far for normal people, but not nearly far enough for her. The fucking she-devil. It was clear she was onto us and on a mission to make whatever this was between us publicly known. But catching us in the lie was proving too difficult for her.

At least until mid-November.

It was after hours, the time of night when the front desk closed, and we were only available for emergency calls. I was home alone, enjoying the quiet and working on edits, when my phone buzzed with an incoming text. I glanced over at it, assuming it'd be one of my brothers. I figured I could ignore it until I got to a good stopping point. But it was Avery's name on the screen.

AVERY:

Wish you were here. I'd love to see my stern brunch daddy drunk. You get loose and a little wild, don't you? I should ask the cute bartender. I bet he'd know.

I read her text three times, trying to make sense of it. First of all, I didn't know what the fuck a stern brunch daddy was. Second, she and Addison, along with Everly, Quinn, Luna, and Mabel were supposed to be at the police station, volunteering for some kind of sobriety test training, and not at a fucking bar getting hit on by a random guy.

AIDEN:

What fucking bartender?

I stared at my phone, willing the dots to appear that showed she was typing a reply, waiting for what seemed like forever. When the message finally came through, it didn't calm me in the slightest.

AVERY:

The one serving the drinks, obviously. He reminds me of your stupidly handsome face. Like, you could be brothers.

I hadn't even finished reading her message before I grabbed my keys, taking the steps two at a time as I headed downstairs. I'd never been a jealous guy. To be honest, I could take or leave whoever I was with, so this kind of stuff didn't bother me one way or another.

But I'd never been with Avery before.

She was different, in every possible fucking way. And there was a whisper inside me that was growing louder each day. One that didn't care that this was supposed to be temporary or that she was leaving in just a few short weeks. It still repeated a single word over and over again, until I'd started to believe it.

Mine.

AIDEN:

Where are you?

AVERY:

How about we play hide and seek and you try to find me?

AIDEN:

I'm not playing right now, Avery.

AVERY:

Uh oh. You didn't call me bunny. Am I in trouble?

AIDEN:

You're going to be if you don't tell me where you are. Now stop fucking around.

AVERY:

You know where I am.

AIDEN:

Clearly, I don't because I thought you were at the station with Brady. And the station doesn't have bartenders, cute or otherwise.

AVERY:

Of course they do. How else were we supposed to get drunk???

I was going to kill my brother for leaving out this little detail. *I* would've been their fucking bartender if I'd known they needed one because God knew that group was nothing but trouble. But Brady had passed this off as no big deal, just a couple of drinks so they had enough alcohol in them that the station could do their annual sobriety test training, and the girls would be back home in no time.

AIDEN:

I'm on my way. And tell the bartender to keep his fucking hands to himself if he wants to still have them at the end of the night.

SIX MINUTES LATER, pandemonium greeted me when I stepped inside the police station. Mabel stood on a table, swinging a baton above her head and catcalling Paul Traeger, Brady's deputy. Luna had confiscated Brady's desk and was pretzeling herself into a yoga position on top of it. Quinn and Everly were attempting—poorly—to perform some kind of stupid-ass dance. And my beautiful girl was in the middle of it all, holding up a very drunk Addison, who had her cup shoved in Brady's face.

"How many times do I have to tell you?" he snapped at our sister, his patience long gone. "I'm not the fucking bartender." Then, louder so as to address the entire room, he said, "And you're all cut off."

Mabel snorted, not pausing in whatever sort of wanna-be martial arts routine she was attempting. "If you're not the fucking bartender, you can't cut us off, you killjoy. Another one on me!" she yelled, sloshing alcohol over the side of her glass as she thrust it in the air.

"Traeger," Brady barked. "Get her down from there while I wrangle the rest of these troublemakers. And tell George to get his ass in here and gather up his wife before I throw her in the holding cell."

"He's making his way in from the parking lot," Traeger said. "Slowly."

"Of course he is," Brady muttered. "Did you contact the rest of the designated drivers? Because I want my station cleared out in the next ten minutes."

"Sure did, Sheriff," he said, his eyes still on Mabel. "Your brothers are on their way."

"One is already here," I said, striding into the fray. "Though my text came from a drunk Avery about a cute bartender, not from Traeger about driving duty."

At the sound of my voice, Avery snapped her head toward me and beamed, her smile lighting up her face, and I was so fucking gone for this girl. Her eyes were droopy, her cheeks flushed bright pink, and she wasn't just drunk. She was smashed. Along with Addison, who could barely stand. And Brady had allowed it to happen in the fucking police station.

I pinned him with a glare. "I thought you said they'd only have to drink a couple for the training."

His jaw ticked. "They did. And then Mabel suggested a drinking contest, and Addison egged everyone on. Your girl won, by the way," he said under his breath. "Drank every single one of them under the table. Even Mabel, which I didn't think was possible after that whole thing with Luna."

A smile twitched at the corner of my mouth as I watched Avery dance with a coordination-challenged Addison. And then what he said hit me, and I snapped my head toward him. "My *what*?"

He rolled his eyes, his gaze locked on Luna. "You can drop the act. Did you actually think I didn't know?"

Well. Yeah. I kind of had. Especially since Brady didn't live at the resort. Avery and I were together—but always professional—when we saw him for morning meetings, and he and I had gotten together to hang out a couple times since I'd gotten back from Vermont, but that was it. Compared to the shit Addison saw—or attempted to see—that was nothing.

"You really did, huh?" he said, shaking his head. "Well, the cat's out of the bag. And even if I hadn't known, your girl finally gave in to Addison's badgering when she was on her sixth drink."

"*Sixth*? Jesus, Brady. How fucking much did you let them have?"

"*Let* them?" He cocked a brow and gestured toward the room. "Have you *met* any of these women before? I'm just lucky a baton was the only piece of equipment they confiscated in this chaos." He glanced over to where Traeger was guiding Mabel down from the desk, the baton in question tucked safely back in his belt.

The station door opened then, and Beck and Ford

strolled in, their gazes immediately going to Everly and Quinn, respectively.

"Oh, fuck yes," Ford said with a fist pump, grinning at Quinn where she now sat, watching a video with Everly. "Someone's getting laid tonight, isn't that right, wife?"

Quinn giggled—actually *giggled*...something I'd never once heard come out of the woman—and smiled up at her husband. Ford gripped her hands and pulled her to stand, except she'd, apparently, been holding up Everly. When her bookend was removed, Everly toppled straight over, and Beck lunged to catch her before her head hit the floor.

Over his shoulder, he shot a scowl shot at Brady. "Jesus Christ. How fucking much did you let them drink?"

I raised my brows and gestured toward an angry Beck, with a very silent but very clear, *see*?

"Did you eat anything before you got wasted, sunshine?" Beck asked, lifting Everly into his arms.

She squinted and pursed her lips, pressing her fingers close together directly in front of his face. "Mmm...li'l bit."

"What's a little bit?"

"Do Starbursts count?" she asked, a hopeful note in her voice.

"No, Starbursts don't fucking count," he grumbled as he stalked toward the door, following Ford, who was busy evading a very handsy Quinn.

Ford shot Brady a wink and a thumbs-up at the same time Beck scowled his way. "We're going to have words about this tomorrow."

"Can't wait." Brady blew out a heavy sigh and propped his hands on his hips, surveying the devastation left behind by a group of six women. "I'll volunteer myself if I have to, but you can bet your ass I'm never doing this shit again."

CHAPTER TWENTY-ONE

AIDEN

AFTER WE'D DEPOSITED Addison in her room and left her mumbling about her and Avery needing to find a Taco Bell for a midnight snack so they could sleep in a sea of burrito wrappers again, Avery and I made our way to the other side of the house. It was our first night here where we didn't have to be quiet, because I knew Addison would be dead to the world until she'd jackknife in bed at 7 a.m. sharp, like she was a demon possessed. And, like someone who'd sold their soul to the devil, without a hangover. She was always ready to crack the whip the next day, regardless of how late she was up or how many drinks she'd sucked down.

Instead of letting Avery walk past my bedroom and straight to her own, I hooked a finger in her belt loop and tugged her back into my chest.

"Where do you think you're going?" I said, dipping my mouth to her ear.

"To my room."

"I don't think so. You want to explain what happened tonight?"

She tipped her head back to look up at me. "How I kicked everyone's ass and drank them under the table?"

"I was thinking more about the cute bartender you mentioned in your texts. Who was that exactly?"

She pursed her lips to the side, as if she was contemplating not answering me. When I just responded with a raised brow, she finally said, "Brady," the *duh* silent. "I thought that would've been obvious with the brother comment."

I nearly laughed at that and called complete and utter bullshit. The little instigator knew exactly what she'd been doing, taunting me with it.

"You know what I think, bunny?" I asked, gripping her hips and walking her into my room.

"What?" She glanced at me over her shoulder, her eyes dancing like she was enjoying the hell out of this. I had no doubt she was. She loved being a little brat and seeing where it got her. And I loved taking her there.

"I think you did that on purpose just to see how I'd respond."

"Why would I do that?" And I might have bought it if she wasn't shifting where she stood in an obvious attempt to get some friction on her needy clit.

"Great question." I slipped my hands under her shirt, and she raised her arms, allowing me to pull it from her body. My jaw clenched when I found no bra, her bare tits bouncing free. That pattern continued when I removed her jeans to see she was going commando. "Was it laundry day, bunny?"

"Yes," she said without hesitation, her chin tipped up in obstinance.

I reached over and grabbed the tie I'd worn today from where I'd discarded it earlier, stretching it out between my hands. "Don't lie to me."

"How are you gonna prove if I am?" She glanced at me over her shoulder, a smirk on those gorgeous full lips, as her gaze dipped to the tie and back to my face. I had no doubt she wanted to test me tonight, and she was looking forward to the outcome.

I gripped the tie in my hands. "You sure you want to go down this path?"

Instead of answering me, she bent over the bed, giving her ass a shake and allowing me a perfect view of her pussy. "What I'm sure of is I need you to C.O.H.A.L...um... To C.O.H.A.L.M... Uh..."

I raised a brow. "To what now?"

She huffed out a breath. "I forgot the letter clues, okay?"

"The letter clues? You mean the acronym?"

"Whatever! Yes. I forgot it, but I know what it means."

"And what's that?"

She rolled her lips in between her teeth, glancing up at me with the tiniest bit of apprehension written on her face.

"Well, don't get shy now, bunny. Tell me. You need me to..." I trailed off, waiting for her to continue.

"Come over here and lick my pussy like a good boy."

My lips twitched before I could wipe the amusement from my face. Goddamn, this fucking girl.

Shaking my head, I reached for her hands, pulling them behind her and wrapping the tie around her wrists at the small of her back. "Is that what you think you deserve?"

"Yes," she said without hesitation.

"We'll see," I murmured. "Keep your hands there, and don't move."

Just like I'd known she would, she listened for half a second before reaching up as far as she could, but it was enough. Enough to have her palm pressing down hard against the head of my cock, her fingers cupping my balls and giving them a gentle squeeze.

"What'd I tell you?" I asked, my voice low and rough, but I didn't step away. Not yet.

"Not to move. But where's the fun in that?"

"You're testing my patience tonight, Avery."

"Uh-oh," she said, and I could hear the grin in her voice. "I got Avery'd again. Sounds like I might be in trouble..."

I stepped out of her reach and kept my eyes locked on hers as I discarded my clothes. Watching as her eyes grew more heated with every article I removed until I was naked right along with her.

"You know you could just tell me, right?" I slid a hand over the perfect curve of her ass, digging my fingers in and giving it a squeeze.

"Tell you what?" she asked, shifting in a vain attempt to guide my hand where she wanted it.

"That you need your perfect ass or that pretty little clit —or both—spanked."

"I never said that."

"You don't need to because I already know. I'm just saying, we could get there a little faster if you would. But instead, you want to act like a brat and wait for me to handle it."

"How are you going to handle it tonight?" she asked, her tone hopeful and completely proving my point. She trusted me to give her exactly what she needed, even when she didn't want to ask for it.

"Not by licking your pussy, I'll tell you that." I squatted down behind her, sweeping my hands up the outsides of her thighs, over her hips, and then down her ass to spread her legs apart.

She whimpered at the first brush of my fingers against her pussy, rocking her hips faster, lifting them back for more pressure.

I bit back a groan as I slid my two middle fingers inside her wet cunt, circling my thumb around her clit. "No wonder you're acting like such a brat. You're fucking soaked and desperate to come, aren't you? My needy little bunny, just aching for release."

"No," she panted. "I'm not."

Obstinate little shit. And I loved every ounce of it. Loved when she was pliant for me, doing everything exactly as I told her to, but I loved this, too. Loved the defiance, loved the pushback. Loved everything she gave me, even when it was a challenge.

"Not needy or not desperate to come?" I clarified, keeping up my strokes, my thumb rubbing harder, faster against her clit. In the exact way I knew would have her flying in seconds.

"Both," she managed through panting breaths.

"So, you'd be fine if I stopped?" I did just that, pulling my fingers free from her pussy and forcing myself not to suck them clean.

"No! No, don't." She arched her back, giving her ass another little shake. "Put your fingers back inside me and fuck me with them."

I swept my hand over her pussy, the barest brush of skin on skin, not giving her what she wanted. "I didn't hear a single please in all of that."

"*Please*. Aiden, please. Please please please, I need—"

"I know exactly what you need, baby." I sank my fingers back inside, teasing that spot that made her legs shake. "And I'll always give it to you."

Without relenting, I stroked her pussy, inside and out,

driving her toward her orgasm and throwing her straight off the cliff.

She cried out, her moans echoing around the room as her release washed through her, and I fucking loved it.

"That's it, bunny. Let me hear how much you love when I make you come."

Clutching the comforter, she whimpered and moaned as she rode out her orgasm, her hips rolling against me like she was desperate for me to fill her up. And I wasn't inclined to make her wait anymore.

I stood and grabbed hold of the tie binding her wrists with one hand, notching myself at her entrance with the other. Then I split her open and sank deep with a groan.

The first thrust into Avery was always fucking heaven. The hot, wet grip of her pussy squeezing me, sucking me deep, the pulse and throb of her cunt, like it had just been waiting for me to fill it.

And then there were the nights she was so keyed up, had wound herself so tight throughout the day, it took only a couple thrusts before she was coming all over me and soaking my cock while she did it.

And thank fucking God tonight was one of those nights.

She screamed as she came again, and I didn't bother covering her mouth to stifle the sounds, my dick swelling at her obvious pleasure.

"Christ, you were a needy little thing, weren't you?" I gripped her hips, sliding my hand down to palm her ass and digging my fingers into her flesh. "Already coming all over my cock, and we haven't even gotten started yet."

"That was mostly from me," she forced out, even as her pussy still pulsed around me. "Pretty sure I don't even need you."

"No? Let's see..." I removed my hands from her body entirely and planted my feet shoulder-width apart. "Fuck yourself with my cock and see how far it gets you."

One of the things I loved most about Avery was that nothing I said fazed her. She was up for anything and everything I suggested. So without missing a beat, she did exactly as I'd told her.

She pressed her legs together, making her cunt an even tighter fit and dragging a groan from my chest. And then she started to roll those hips. Pulling me nearly all the way out before snapping back and taking me deep. Again and again, her speed picking up rhythm as near-constant moans fell from her lips. And *Jesusfuck*, she was going to make me come in three seconds flat if I didn't stop it.

With a muttered curse, I stepped back, pulling out and dropping to my knees behind her. That perfect pink pussy, dripping with how much she loved this, was presented like a gift directly in front of my face.

"Thought you weren't gonna lick—" she started, but I cupped her ass in both hands and brought one down against it in a hard smack.

Yeah, I said I wouldn't be licking her pussy tonight, but there was no way I could resist tasting her come on my tongue. And when she was fucking herself back against my cock, driving me deeper, harder, faster with every roll of her hips, her single goal to make me lose my mind, I wasn't going to last if I didn't pull out and drop to my knees.

"Shut up and let me eat your pussy in peace." I licked a path through her slit, gathering all that sweetness on my tongue and humming against her. "The only sounds I want to hear from your bratty little mouth are moans, telling me exactly how good I'm licking your cunt."

"You're not—" She cut off on a gasp when I smacked her ass again.

Then, before she could mouth off once more, I dove in, affixing my whole mouth to her and devouring her like she was my last fucking meal. But instead of giving me the sounds I wanted, she had her face pressed into the bed, the mattress muffling her cries of pleasure.

I reached up, gripping a handful of her ass and squeezing tight. Against her pussy, I murmured, "Let me hear you, bunny."

She shook her head, burying another moan into the comforter. "You told me to shut up. And I'm very good at following orders."

"What you're good at right now is acting like a brat." I brought my hand down hard on her ass again, groaning when her pussy pulsed around my fingers. "Let me fucking hear you."

It started as a whimper at first. Just the barest sound

escaping her. And then it was a moan, soft and breathy, before something louder, rougher, scraped past her throat.

"That's my girl," I murmured against her, licking her swollen clit just how she liked. "You taste like heaven, bunny. Could eat you for breakfast, lunch, and dinner, and never get tired of it."

"Aiden…" she said, the sass gone and replaced by need and desperation.

"I've got you, baby. Show me how much you love to come on my tongue so I can give you my cock." Relentlessly, I attacked her clit, her moans building in volume until I was sure the guests in the cottages could hear her. But I didn't care. I was too far gone, reveling in that affirmation of her pleasure. Wanting everyone to know I was the one who was giving it to her.

"I'm—" She choked out a sob as she shifted her hips, pressing harder against me. "God, Aiden, I'm coming again."

I groaned against her pussy, licking up every ounce of her orgasm as her moans filled the space until she was everywhere. Until all I could think, hear, see, taste, or smell was *her.*

After I'd wrung every ounce of pleasure from her body and she was boneless on the bed, I sank back inside her, groaning at how tight she was like this. How wet and swollen but still pushing back against me. Still desperate for more pleasure.

I pumped into her, my hips slapping a punishing

rhythm against her ass, but I couldn't stop. Didn't *want* to stop.

Ever.

That part was out of my hands, though. The days were flying past, the end of the year coming too quickly, and pretty soon, I wasn't going to have a choice. Pretty soon, all this would be gone.

"Tell me who knows what you need," I managed through gritted teeth, desperate to hear her say it. Desperate for her to confirm she knew.

Even if we couldn't have forever, we could have this.

We could have now.

She glanced back at me, her lips parted, eyes hazy and glazed with pleasure. "You do."

"Tell me who makes this pussy feel so fucking good."

"You." Her eyes fluttered closed on a moan when I slipped my hand around her hip and pressed my fingers to her clit.

"Tell me whose cunt this is."

"*Aiden.*"

"Whose, bunny? Whose sweet, perfect little pussy is this?"

"Yours. Oh *God*, it's yours." She cried out then, coming around my cock and pulling my orgasm straight from my soul.

With a groan, I sank as deep inside her as I could, filling her with everything I had. Losing myself in her in a way I wasn't sure I'd be able to come back from.

CHAPTER TWENTY-TWO

AVERY

I'D BEEN RIGHT, though I wasn't surprised.

When Thanksgiving rolled around, my mom was still halfway around the world with Stewart, no plans to be back anytime soon. Where once it would've bothered me, I found it just...didn't now. Not when I was here.

Plus, I was beginning to come to expect it from her. Not only expect it, but accept it. Begrudging her for what she wasn't took so much more energy than just loving her for what she was. Vivacious and fun-loving and the best kind of person to be around because her energy was infectious. But pinning her down was like trying to trap a firefly—she was too bright to be contained.

We liked to save our visits for Christmas since it was both our favorite, so I generally spent Thanksgiving with whatever friend was kind enough to invite me over to share in their family's festivities. I'd always been grateful for that inclusion, but I couldn't help but feel like a third wheel whenever I joined. Like I wasn't really part of the fray. Like I didn't quite belong.

Not here, though. Not in Starlight Cove. Not with Aiden and Addison...the entire McKenzie brood and all their significant others, actually. Through the banter and jokes, the barbs and quips, the ganging up on one another and the endless, relentless teasing, I felt like I fit.

I felt like I was home.

Which was a hell of a mindfuck because I'd always thought my home was nowhere and everywhere at once. Not a place, but a feeling. One I'd been searching for my whole life. One I wasn't supposed to find in a little town in Maine with a man who made me feel seen and heard and valued and...cherished. In a way I'd never felt before.

Beck cooked us a jaw-dropping spread, the ten of us piling into the dining room in the main inn, passing delicious food around as stories were shared. I'd hung on every one—it seemed an unspoken challenge to one-up one another and dish all Aiden's past antics in an attempt to embarrass him.

But through it all—through tales of him turning a hallway in high school into a makeshift slip and slide and losing his trunks as he slid down it, or walking around with orange hair because Ford put bleach in the shampoo bottle—he just sat, his hand on my knee a comforting weight, that damn dimple winking at me when his siblings recalled something particularly funny. And a tiny part of me whispered that she wanted to stay here forever.

AFTER EVERYONE HAD GOTTEN their fill and we'd cleaned up, we gathered in the parlor. Addison suggested playing charades since it was about the only thing we could do with all ten of us at the same time. Everyone in agreement, they started naturally splitting off into pairs while I stood just outside the circle.

I hated this part. It was something I'd always dreaded in school. I could jump from group to group and prided myself on being the life of the party, but this was different. I might not have always been picked last, but I'd *never* been picked first.

Just as I was starting to shift on my feet, an uncomfortable knot forming in my stomach, Addison jumped up, shooting her hand in the air. "I call Avery!"

At the exact same moment, Aiden said, "Avery's with me."

They snapped their gazes to each other, Addison's narrowing on her brother, while Aiden just met her glare with an unflinching one of his own.

My bestie crossed her arms over her chest. "She's with *me*."

Aiden mirrored her position and shook his head. "Not tonight, little D."

She huffed in disbelief, throwing her hand out. "Now you're calling me that stupid-ass nickname too? First of all, I'm not a dictator! Second, it's dumb, I hate it, and it's not even true! Don't try to pretend like I don't have the biggest D out of everyone in this room."

Levi snorted at that while Ford let out a loud guffaw, the rest of her brothers basking as Luna, Everly, and Quinn all piped up with their dissent.

"And if she's with Aiden, that means I'm stuck with the guy who can't even guess a fucking teapot!" Addison pointed an angry finger at Levi.

"Jesus, Addison." Keeping his eyes on the book he was reading, Levi breathed out a heavy sigh as if dealing with his sister was the most exhausting thing he'd done all day. "This again? That was months ago."

"Yes, this again! Everyone else might come to family game nights to have a good time and blah blah blah, whatever, but I come to *win*. And I know for a fact Avery and I would wipe the floors with every single one of you."

"Doesn't matter," Aiden said with a shrug. "She's with me. You're the one who kept trying to throw us together—"

"And it worked, didn't it?" Addison cut in, tossing her arms out to the sides, having not a single clue Aiden and I had been together long before the Vermont trip. "I'm a fucking matchmaking *genius*."

Aiden continued as if she hadn't spoken. "So you're going to have to deal with the consequences. And the consequences today are that you're paired with Levi because *Avery*," he said firmly, taking a seat on the couch and tugging me to sit in his lap, "is with *me*."

Addison's mouth dropped open. Her gaze bounced between me and Aiden when I didn't make a move to leave his lap or remove his arm from where he had it banded around my waist. "Seriously? What happened to chicks before dicks?"

I cringed and shot her an apologetic smile. "I love you. You know I do. But...well, he's got a really great dick."

"*Avery*!" Addison yelled, slapping her hands over her eyes as if that would help. "I can't believe you just said that! I get that you're with Aiden now and I love it, but we need to set some boundaries, because that shit is *not* okay." She spun around, eyes still covered, and swung a pointed finger at the rest of the room. "And that goes for anyone else banging one of my brothers, because I've heard too much!"

Luna grinned unrepentantly from her perch on Brady's lap, Everly blushed and leaned into Beck's side, and Quinn pursed her lips from where she sat between Ford's legs, clearly hiding a smile. The McKenzie boys' reactions were varied but all basically boiled down to them puffing out their chests at the thought of their dicks being gossip material. Well, everyone but Levi, who ignored us completely and continued reading his book.

"Fine. I'm with Levi," Addison said, then stabbed a finger in his direction. "But I swear to God, you better get your head out of your ass, man. That means you stop reading *this*." She grabbed the book from his hands before glancing down at it. "What is this, anyway? Is it the book Mabel kept going on about?"

Before I could even glance to check out the cover, I felt Aiden stiffen beneath me, and I knew exactly what book it was.

His.

"Oh my God," Everly said, leaning forward, eyes wide. "It's so good. I don't normally love fantasy, but I'd *live* in this world if I could."

"And the sex scenes, am I right?" Luna raised a brow and fanned her face.

To my shock—and, I was sure, Aiden's absolute horror—murmurs of agreement went up from everyone in the room, Ford offering his approval for the number of times *Heat and Desire* had gotten him laid, with Beck and Brady both agreeing. And then everyone fell into a discussion on the masterful character- and world-building and how the sexual journey between the hero and the heroine was about so much more than just fucking—it was about exploring their deepest desires, the parts of themselves they kept hidden from everyone else but shared with only each other.

And they were right. Aiden had a gift. He wrote the kinds of books I could get lost in. Could spend hours... days...inside the world and still not have it be enough.

So badly, I wanted to tell everyone that it was their brother's books they loved. Their brother who they were raving about. Their brother who'd created the world they wanted to live in, the characters they wanted to befriend, the book they'd escaped into.

I hadn't ever thought about this part of his secret. About him not being able to receive any of the accolades he so rightly deserved. Not being able to accept any praise.

Because I was the only one in this room who knew who he really was. Knew the secret part of himself he never shared for fear it would hurt the very people raving about it.

I slipped my hand over his, linking our fingers together, and gave it a tight squeeze. Letting him know he wasn't alone. That he wasn't by himself on what I knew had to have been an incredibly lonely journey.

I was with him.

At least for another twenty-nine days.

CHAPTER TWENTY-THREE

AVERY

ON A SLOW AFTERNOON IN EARLY-DECEMBER, I was working on the average occupation projections for next year. Not my favorite part of the job, but something that needed to be done. I was sitting in the parlor, curled up on the couch and poring over the numbers when I came across something that had managed to slip my notice in the couple months I'd been working at the resort.

Cottage Thirteen.

As I looked at the lack of data for that particular cottage, I realized I'd never once helped a guest who had stayed in it. Never scheduled a fishing excursion or an adventure tour. Never replaced a light or took a maintenance request or set up an anniversary stay inside it.

I scrolled back through the records, finding it was never available for booking. Not once, in as far back as this program went, which was six years. And yet it also never showed that it was occupied or that the resort received any revenue from it. It was like it didn't even exist.

The mystery had sunk its claws into me, and I had to solve it. I started poking around the main inn for Aiden or Addison. Or anyone, really, who might know something about the elusive Cottage Thirteen.

Unfortunately, Addison was in the Bayside Room, filming one of the required interviews for the documentary, and Aiden had responded to my text asking where he was with a message that he was on the phone with his publisher and he'd be a bit. Which meant I couldn't ask the two people who'd know what was going on to help solve this mystery. But now that I'd uncovered this, I wanted to get to the bottom of it, and I didn't want to wait.

So, I did what anyone with a hyperfixation problem would do—I grabbed my coat and headed out to investigate myself.

I would've liked to say that my skin had hardened to the Maine weather in the time I'd been back home, but that would be a bald-faced lie. Four years in Mississippi had ruined me. I froze anytime I stepped foot outside, especially these past few weeks as the temps had dropped. Today wasn't any different, despite the fact that it was—according to the local weirdos anyway—a pretty nice day. "Pretty nice" being mid-thirties, which wasn't nice at all if you asked me. I zipped my coat and pulled up my hood, uncaring if I looked like a waddling penguin as I made my way toward where Cottage Thirteen should be.

It didn't take long to walk there, and sure enough, the small cabin sat right between Twelve and Fourteen, just as I'd assumed it would. It had the same exterior as all the rest—white siding, navy shutters, tiny evergreen trees bracketing the porch, and a welcome mat in front of the door.

It didn't look abandoned or like something that shouldn't be on the reservation site. It looked like someone had stayed there recently...was currently staying there, actually. But without any record or revenue coming in, were they supposed to be?

I climbed the porch steps, made my way to the front door, and knocked twice. My brows drew down as the door crept open, obviously not having been latched properly.

"Hello?" I called, my voice tentative but loud enough to carry to whoever was inside. "This is Avery from the front desk. Is anyone—"

My words cut off as the door inched open farther, and I got a better glimpse at the inside of the cottage...and the man sprawled out on the floor in front of the couch. Without a thought about how stupid this probably was—what kind of idiot barged into someplace with a strange man?—I rushed inside and straight for him.

He was maybe in his sixties...possibly seventies, if I went by his worn face alone. But his hair was still dark, only a couple slivers of gray throughout the unkempt strands, and he had a scraggly beard that hadn't seen a razor in what I would guess was years. He looked worn-out and run-down, like he didn't take care of himself. Worse, like he was digging himself an early grave on purpose.

Once I was by his side, I dropped to my knees next to him, and that was when the odor nearly knocked me on my ass. I wrinkled my nose, the overwhelming stench of alcohol undeniable as it hit me like a wrecking ball.

Biting back a cough, I pressed my fingers against his neck to check for a pulse. But I was nearly positive this man—who we had absolutely no record of staying in this cottage and was more than likely a squatter in an unoccupied cabin—was just passed out and not dead.

"Sir, are you okay?"

The sound of my voice must've roused him because he groaned, his eyes blinking open with the kind of slow, uncoordinated movements that spoke of being wasted to the world. And then before I could get any more words out, before I could tell him who I was and why I was there, he lashed out with a shout of surprise.

Flailing hard, he shoved me, sending me sprawling straight into a table. My head hit the corner, knocking off it hard enough that a burst of pain shot through my skull.

"Fuck," I groaned, my head throbbing as stars danced in my vision.

"Who the hell are you?" the man yelled, his words slurring together even as he tried—and failed—to roll to his hands and knees in an effort to stand. "Get out! You don't belong in here!"

That was the understatement of the century, and something I wished had come to me before I'd stepped foot in here. Before I'd even walked this direction. Before I'd left the main inn without telling anyone where I was going. Because *Jesus Christ*. Who the hell did I think I was, the first idiot killed off in a horror movie?

I needed to leave. Immediately. Needed to get out and find Aiden or Addison, but my head was throbbing, water was running into my eyes, and I couldn't quite make sense of it all. I reached up to swipe it away, the liquid coating my fingers.

Only, when I pulled them away, holding them in front of my face, the wetness covering my hand wasn't water.

It was blood.

Aiden

JUGGLING a secret publishing career was getting harder and harder every fucking day. Especially with all the events my publisher wanted me to consider doing as *Heat and Desire* continued to outsell the rest of the list, as well as with book two's release coming up. The Frankfurt Book Fair was all I'd agreed to so far because they'd promised me no media coverage at the events I'd be doing and in the meetings I'd have. And even then, the only way I was able to do it was because Avery was here to help shoulder my workload at the resort.

Part of me wondered if it was even necessary to keep a lid on this anymore, or if I should just come clean. After the impromptu—and incredibly uncomfortable—book club discussion on Thanksgiving wherein everyone bragged about how much sex they were having thanks to my book, it had become blatantly obvious exactly how accepting my family would be about the secret life I'd been leading for years.

But they weren't the ones I was worried about, and they hadn't been for a while. It was everyone else in the world who had my guard up, my instincts telling me to keep this whole thing under wraps. I didn't want the resort to go the way of Mabel and George's newspaper—namely, a solid dip in revenue thanks to their being the current and continued focus of an amateur smear campaign run by a small handful of catty, puritanical residents of Starlight Cove.

Those kinds of people weren't just in Starlight Cove, though, and I knew all too well the power of a viral video. All it would take was one. The last thing the resort needed was someone picking up this story and making a not-so-amateur smear campaign about this small-town resort and the "pervert" who ran it.

As much as it sucked, the sad reality was that most people were too fucking judgmental. And that went double for anything pertaining to sex. Never mind that everyone was a product of it. Never mind that they enjoyed the hell out of it. It was only okay to do so if it was locked up and shoved under the bed, never to be spoken of in the light of day.

I truly didn't know how much longer I'd be able to keep this from everyone, though. After I'd agreed to attend the book fair, my publisher had been pushing for a book tour to launch *Storm and Shadow*, book two. But if I did that, there'd be no more hiding behind a pen name and an innocuous author photo that didn't give any clues to my identity.

The entire world would know exactly who A.M. Kinsey was. And exactly what he had to lose.

But I'd cross that bridge when I came to it. Fortunately, my publisher had been appeased by my upcoming attendance at Frankfurt, but even that was playing with fire. I'd had to make up a convention in California to justify my absence, and Addison only relented when Avery said she would handle things at the resort. If she hadn't been here to help, I didn't know what I would've done. And she wouldn't be here forever.

Hell, she wouldn't even be here next *month*.

The thought sent a sharp stab of pain through my chest, a boulder falling into my stomach at the thought of her gone. Out of my life, when it felt like she'd just come into it. But it was one of those weird contradictions where it also felt like she'd always been here. I couldn't remember what life had been like before she'd come spinning into it, all sunshine and sass, and made me fall head over fucking heels for her.

Because, of course, she had. Of course, she'd be the one. Of course, I'd finally fall for someone I couldn't keep.

But I'd known that going into it, so I shoved it aside, pushing the thought down deep. Just like I'd been doing for weeks. Months. We had this time together, and I refused to let the shadow of a future without her sour it.

Once I'd finished my call and looked around, not finding Avery in the inn, I pulled out my phone and thumbed to my last message with her when I'd told her the call might take a while.

AVERY:

OK lmk how it went when you're done.

AIDEN:

Just finished. Where are you?

I'd just hit send on the message when the front door opened, bringing in a gust of cold air. I glanced up, the flash of Avery's red hair in the entryway making a deep ache bloom in my chest, and I reached up in a vain attempt to rub it away.

Slipping my phone back into my pocket, I strode toward her. "Hey. I just sent you a text. Where were you?"

She didn't answer. Didn't even lift her eyes to look at me when I stepped into the entry. Instead, she stumbled, tripping over absolutely nothing, and braced a hand against the wall.

"Whoa, bunny. Are you—" My words cut off when she turned toward me, tipping her head up enough for me to see the blood running in a steady stream down the right side of her face. It was everywhere—smeared across her cheek, all the way to her chin, back into her hairline, dripping onto her coat.

My face blanched, my entire body going cold as I cupped her jaw, tipping her head back so I could see better. "Avery, what the *fuck*? What happened?"

She reached up, gripping my forearm as she shook her head. "It was my fault. He wasn't expecting me, and I didn't know anyone would be there."

I stilled, my entire body running cold even as anger boiled hot and bright inside my chest. "What do you mean *he*? Someone did this to you?" I'd never felt this kind of rage in my life, but I was grateful for it. Because whoever did this? I was going to kill them. "Who the fuck was it?"

"I don't know. I haven't seen him before, but he was in Cottage..." She swallowed, her face paling as she slowly blinked up at me. "Aiden. I don't feel so—"

At her words, she went limp, and I jerked to catch her just before she could fall, scooping her into my arms as her eyes fluttered closed.

"Addison!" I yelled, not caring who heard. Needing someone to. Needing *everyone* to. "Addi—"

"Jesus, Aiden, what?" she snapped, strolling in from

the back of the house. "What's so—" Her words cut off on a gasp as she rushed to my side, eyes frantic on Avery. "Oh my God! What happened?"

"I don't know. Where's Quinn? Is she at home?" I asked, my voice little more than a bark. Praying she was around because she'd be able to get here a hell of a lot faster than if we called for an ambulance.

"I think so." Addison's hands hovered above Avery, a rare moment of uncertainty from someone who was usually sure about everything.

"Call her." I'd never been more grateful that our sister-in-law, the doctor of Starlight Cove, lived just a two-minute walk away. "Tell her to get her ass over here *now*."

CHAPTER TWENTY-FOUR

AIDEN

AN HOUR LATER, I was pacing in my bedroom, hands on my hips as I grilled Quinn—again—on whether she was *sure* Avery didn't have a concussion or needed to be admitted for observation.

"Aiden," Avery sighed from where she lay in my bed, exasperation in her tone. But she had a giant fucking bandage on her head, so I got to be a little overprotective.

"What? I want her to be sure."

My sister, for the first time in recent—or even distant—memory, nodded in agreement from where she sat on the edge of the bed next to Avery.

"For the fifth time, Aiden. Yes, I'm sure." Quinn's voice was hard, her patience with me clearly gone. "I know you're worried, but I take my job very seriously. I wouldn't risk the safety of a patient just so I didn't have to go into the clinic on my day off."

I blew out a heavy breath. "That's not what I meant. I just—"

"I know what you *just*," Quinn cut in, her tone firm but not unkind. "But trust me. I've checked her over thoroughly, and she's fine. I promise. No concussion, and she doesn't even need stitches. Head wounds just always bleed like a bitch and look scarier than they are."

"Okay, fine." I crossed my arms over my chest. "What about the fainting, then? Shouldn't we be worried about that?"

Quinn shook her head as she packed up her medical bag, clearly ready to end this conversation. "It's not unusual. The pain from the injury combined with the shock of it all is likely the culprit. She just needs to take it easy for the next twenty-four hours and manage any lingering pain as best she can. It would also be good for someone to keep an eye on her. Make sure she's still feeling okay, that she's eating and drinking—no alcohol, of course. She'll be as good as new in no time."

I pressed my thumb and forefinger against my eyes. "As good as new with a gigantic fucking gash on her head."

"I'll call in an order to Beck to get you something to eat," Addison said, glancing back to look at Avery. "What sounds good?"

"Cinnamon-sugar toast?" Avery asked, her tone hopeful.

"On it." Addison left the room, her phone already at her ear.

Quinn stopped by the bed and smiled down at Avery. "I'll give you a call later tonight to check in on you. But if you start to feel off, just give me a call. I can be here in two minutes."

"Okay. Thanks, Quinn. I feel all right except for a killer headache, so I'm sure I'll be fine."

"I have no doubt." Quinn walked over to me then, laying a gentle hand at my elbow. "Trust me, Aiden. I would not leave this room unless I was one hundred percent sure she'd be fine. But you have *got* to relax or you're only going to make her more tense, and that's not good for anyone."

With that, she patted my arm before strolling out of the room. Addison's voice carried from down the hall, so I shut the door, closing out everyone but Avery and me. I pressed my hands against the frame and hung my head, my body still trying to process the rush of endorphins that had exploded inside me the second I'd seen Avery's face covered in blood. The sight was going to haunt me for the rest of my life.

"Aiden? C'mere."

I couldn't do that. Not yet. Not until I knew. "Tell me what happened, bunny. Do you remember? You said a man did this." I turned around to face her, unable to hide the anger rolling through me. "I need to know who."

She stared at me for a moment before nodding and scooting over to pat the spot next to her. When I didn't make a move toward her, she huffed and rolled her eyes.

"Aiden Christopher. Come over here and cuddle me, please. And I promise I'll tell you all about my stupid attempt at sleuthing."

Just like everything with Avery, I couldn't deny her. So despite feeling like I wanted to crawl out of my skin, I strode toward her and dropped onto my bed. She didn't even wait for me to drape my arm around her before she was curling up against my side, a contented hum leaving her.

"Much better."

"Good," I murmured, pressing my lips to the crown of her head, careful to avoid the bandage Quinn had placed there. "Now tell me, bunny. I'm going out of my mind here."

She let out a sigh and tipped her head back to meet my eyes. "You know how I was working on the projections for next year? Well, I couldn't find any data for Cottage Thirteen."

At the mention of that particular cabin, I stiffened beneath her, a dozen different scenarios floating through my mind, my anger bubbling hotter with every one.

"Which I thought was really weird, you know? It's never available to be booked, so I assumed it was always occupied. Except the resort never got paid for it, so I went investigating—"

"What do you mean, you went to investigate?"

She cringed. "I sort of went over there? I knocked, but

then the door opened like it wasn't latched, and I found him—"

"*He* did this to you?" I asked, my voice cold and low, threaded with an undercurrent of rage.

Her mouth dropped open as she sat up and stared at me. "You *know* him?"

Knew him.

Hated him.

And was absolutely going to fucking kill him.

I HAD THOUGHT about this a lot. Had probably spent what equated to days of my life thinking about it. About what it would be like the first time I spoke to my father again after ten years of nothing but silence from him. After ten years of unanswered calls and dodged welfare checks. Ten years of disinterest and abandonment from him while we struggled through the hardest part of our lives.

And during it all, we gave him a place to stay. We paid his bills, delivered food to his door, took care of his laundry. Addison switched out the exterior decor and flowers to Mom's favorites in an attempt to make the cottage feel like a real home for him. A man who hadn't even bothered to attend her high school—or college—graduation.

The caretaking we all did for him was a dirty little

secret. One we—myself included—held close to our chests. It was something every one of us, save for Levi, took part in but pretended like we didn't.

Patrick McKenzie was our version of Fight Club—the only rule we had was that we didn't talk about it.

Which was why I hadn't told anyone where I was going. Hadn't warned anyone I was about to break our decade-long silence. Hadn't wanted anyone there as witness to what I was about to bring to my dad's doorstep.

When I made it to Cottage Thirteen, I didn't bother with a knock. Besides the fact that my father didn't pay for that kind of privacy, he didn't deserve it after what he'd done.

The door banged open with a sharp thump against the wall, and my dad's gaze found mine immediately. Not looking the least bit surprised. Didn't look surprised when I stormed in and grabbed him by the front of his flannel shirt, either. I ignored the stench of alcohol that seeped from his pores as I jerked him to stand in front of me.

Then I cocked my fist back, weighed down by years of pent-up aggression toward him. The fear over seeing Avery covered in blood, having her pass out in my arms. Then everything prior to it. The years when he'd escaped into himself after his wife died, not caring that we'd lost our mother...the only parent who'd given a shit about us. Then there were the years before that. When we were kids and he'd be passed out on the couch by lunch, when he'd miss school conferences and baseball games and family sailing outings because his gin had been more than enough for him.

He didn't even dodge the first punch I landed. His lip split, producing a not nearly satisfying enough amount of blood. Not when I'd seen exactly what Avery had looked like coming from this place. Not when I could see evidence of her blood still on the fucking floor.

Worse, the punch wasn't as cathartic as I'd hoped it'd be. It didn't offer any relief, didn't allow this balloon that had stretched inside me to pop and release all this bottled-up anger. Especially when he just stood there, not fighting back. Just taking it. Like he deserved it. Like he *wanted* it.

I gripped his shirt tighter and held him against the wall, my other arm cocked back, fist clenched and ready to drive into him again. Over and over until this anger inside me was finally gone. "Give me one fucking reason why I shouldn't beat your ass right now and give you back double what you gave her."

He stared at me for long moments, his eyes full of wonder, as if he didn't recognize me completely. Which wasn't a shock. I'd been barely twenty-four the last time he'd seen me, mourning the loss of my mom. And while the ten years that had passed since had played a part in my changing appearance, I knew it was really more to do with *life*. The life we'd struggled through, even in our mom's absence, and even without him. The life we'd had to figure out on our own, because we hadn't had another choice.

"I'm your father," he said, his voice tired and scratchy, his breath reeking of booze.

"Bullshit!" I yelled, shoving him hard against the wall. "You haven't been a father to me a day in your life. You weren't around before Mom died, and you haven't been around since. And you sure as fuck aren't going to start now. So I'm going to ask you again—give me one fucking reason why I shouldn't lay you out right here."

"Because you're better than this," Brady said at my back, and it spoke to how pissed off I was that I hadn't heard him come in. The floors creaked under his boots as he stepped up behind me. "And he's not worth the repercussions."

I blew out a humorless laugh. "Guess that means you're here as the sheriff for a welfare check."

"No. I'm here as your brother. And you don't need to go down this path. Not for him."

I stared at our dad for long moments, my fist still cocked back, his shirt clenched in my hand. Unsure what to listen to—the part inside me that wanted this man to pay. For everything he'd done to my family, for what he'd done to the woman I loved. Or to the voice of reason standing at my back, my older brother...my best friend. And the one person who'd never steered me wrong.

Brady reached up and rested his hand on my shoulder, giving it a firm squeeze. Telling me without words that while our dad may not have ever been there, he had been. He would be.

And just like that, the fight drained out of me, replaced by the overwhelming need to flee. I needed to get out of there. Needed to be back with Avery. Needed to wrap her in my arms and remind myself she was okay.

"I want you out," I said, voice hard as I released him with a shove. "You don't get to stay here like a fucking leech on this family when all you've done is cause us grief and pain. For ten fucking years. We're done."

I turned around and stalked toward the door, Brady following behind. Just before we stepped over the threshold, I glanced back, my gaze doing a quick scan of the cottage he'd been in for a decade with little to no outside contact.

It was messy, with bottles of alcohol and cans of beer littered about. A collection of white, silver, and red chips were spread out on a side table—probably a dozen or more of each—next to a mostly drunk bottle of gin. I'd done enough research years ago—back when I'd still carried a flicker of hope that he could be more than what he'd been for us...hope that he could get help—so I knew exactly what they were. Sobriety coins from AA, none of them designating anything longer than thirty days of sobriety, which was all too clear based on the surroundings.

"I don't care where you go," I said, acceptance finally washing over me. Acceptance that I'd never have the kind of dad I'd hoped for. The kind who'd show up at baseball games or teach me how to change a tire or boast about my accomplishments. That was a dream I'd kept alive, just a smolder of embers in a fire that had burned out long ago, and today extinguished it entirely. "I want you gone by the end of the day."

CHAPTER TWENTY-FIVE

AVERY

IT HAD BEEN a long time since I'd felt this...protected. This cared for. This looked after. And I didn't hate it.

While my mom had always been my most favorite person in the world, she hadn't exactly been a caretaker. And it had taken me almost the entirety of my twenty-six years to realize that while she was amazing at a lot of things, that wasn't one of them.

And now, it was undeniable. Especially when faced with Aiden's reaction to what had happened to me. He didn't brush it off. He didn't sweep it aside. Did he overreact? Maybe. Probably. But since I couldn't remember ever before having anyone overreact on my behalf, I wasn't even going to pretend my chest didn't warm from it. At least a little.

When he'd stormed out of his room following my half

explanation, I knew he'd hit the point of no return. It took a lot for Aiden to get mad—I'd never seen it in my time here, and that spoke volumes. Frustrated? Yes. Overworked, stressed, impatient? Also yes. Irritated? Almost daily. But this had been different.

That man in the cottage—whoever he was—was obviously already down on his luck, an alcoholic if I had to guess, and didn't deserve Aiden's wrath for what had essentially been an accident. And Aiden shouldn't have to deal with the repercussions of whatever he'd planned on doing to take care of it.

Because of that, I'd called Brady. I'd known if anyone could talk sense into Aiden, it would be his older brother.

So as soon as Aiden had stormed down the stairs, I'd grabbed my phone and called the sheriff, letting him know the situation, and he said he'd handle it.

And since my temporary boyfriend was currently behind me, soaking in a steaming hot bath and not in jail on assault charges, the eldest McKenzie had come through.

Though the tub in our shared bathroom wasn't as big or as luxurious as the one that had been in the Cozy Garden Hideaway, it was good enough. I rested back against Aiden's chest, his legs on either side of mine, bent so they could fit. While the tub was a perfect fit for my five-foot-six stature, it was comical watching Aiden attempt to fold his much taller frame into it. But he did it. For me.

Without question. Without hesitation. Just like everything.

When he'd come back, twenty minutes after storming out, he'd cupped my face in his hands and pressed a soft, lingering kiss against my bandage, then my lips. Then he'd closed his eyes and rested his forehead against mine, breathing deeply before murmuring, "How about a bath, bunny?"

He'd slid in behind me with barely more than a wince at the near-scalding water, his hands not leaving my skin for even a second. He brushed them up and down my arms, swept them over my stomach, massaged my shoulders...his touch a gentle but firm presence reminding me he was with me.

With me, but silent, not having strung together more than ten words since he'd gotten back.

"So..." I said, dragging out the word. I'd waited patiently for him to tell me what was going on. But, as he often did, he'd retreated into his head, had gotten lost in his thoughts, and I was all too willing to pull him out of them. "How long is this elephant going to be in the room with us?"

His hands stilled for the briefest moment before returning to their path over my thighs. "I don't even know where to start," he admitted.

"How about we start with the biggie." As much as I wanted to, I didn't meet his gaze. Somehow sensing this would be easier for him if I weren't looking. If he could whisper it into the darkened room without the pressure of my eyes on him. "Who was that man, and what was he doing in Cottage Thirteen?"

Aiden's touch grew firmer now, his hands a comforting weight against me, and I sensed it was more for him than it was for me. "That man," he started, then took a deep breath and exhaled slowly. "Is my father. And he's been in Cottage Thirteen, without any contact with me or any of my siblings, for ten years. Since our mom took one of our boats out during a storm and died at sea."

I gasped and turned over, no longer able to sit with my back to him. I'd known about their mom—it had recently happened when I'd met Addison—but I hadn't known this. I rested my hands against his chest, over the heart that was beating steadily beneath my palm. The one I had come to love, despite trying with everything in me not to. And I offered him the only thing I could. "Oh, Aiden. I'm so sorry."

He reached up, sweeping the hair back from my face, and shook his head. "There's nothing for you to be sorry about. He's an alcoholic—he's always been an alcoholic—and he will always choose alcohol above everything else. Including us. I'm the one who should be apologizing for getting you wrapped up in this in the first place."

"Well, I was the idiot who went stomping over there like fucking Veronica Mars."

His lips twitched at that. "Yeah, please don't ever do that again."

"Promise."

"We still should have told you about it when you started working here." He blew out a heavy sigh. "Not that it's an excuse, but the thought didn't even occur to me. We've spent the past decade never talking about it or him, so it's easy to forget."

"Never?"

"Never," he confirmed. "We each played our roles in his life while pretending none of us was doing it. But not anymore. He's gone—or he will be by morning."

This was a part of their life they had shoved into a box, sealed it shut with chains and a padlock, and thrown away the key. It had to be, because Addison shared everything with me, but she hadn't shared this.

"So," he said, "it looks like between the two of us, your dad is definitely winning Father of the Year."

A huff of a laugh burst out of me, and I shook my head. Aiden had absolutely no idea. No idea what kind of person my dad was or why I also hadn't spoken to him in a decade. No idea just how similar our paths were. We both had these huge father-shaped holes in our lives, had both dealt with absences from the people who were supposed to care for us. We had a shared history that had fundamentally affected the people we were now.

He'd just given me a huge part of himself. Had shared something with me he never spoke about. Something I had no doubt he'd kept between himself and his siblings... no one else.

Except me. He'd shared that with *me*.

I could do the same.

Lowering my gaze to the smattering of dark hair on his chest, I ran my fingers through it and tried to work up the nerve to say what I needed to. "Actually, I think they probably both tied for worst."

I swallowed down my apprehension, my stomach tying itself in knots, because the last person I'd told this story to had been Addison. And that had happened eight years ago, following our first college party when we'd been blitzed out of our minds.

But I wasn't drunk now, and unfortunately, my head wound wasn't bad enough that I'd be able to forget about this come morning.

As if sensing I had more to say, Aiden kept quiet. He ran a hand down my back, settling his palm just above the curve of my ass in a way that made me ache for him. Not just for sex—though that was always something I craved with him—but for the comfort he provided me, without fail.

"You don't have to tell me," he murmured. "This doesn't have to be a tit-for-tat situation. Just because I shared why my family is fucked up doesn't mean you need—"

"When I was sixteen, my mom and I found out the reason my dad never stuck around for longer than a day, never visited more than a couple times a year, and never moved to our town to live closer to us, was because he had another family. In Connecticut." Avoiding Aiden's shocked eyes, I swallowed back the anger that still bubbled up when I thought about that day. "A boy and girl, one older than me, one younger. He kept that secret from us—from everyone—for years. But then his wife found out about me and my mom, and she gave him an ultimatum. No surprise that he chose them. Cut off all contact with us without so much as a goodbye."

"And that's why you hate secrets so much..."

I pressed my lips together and nodded.

"Jesus, Avery. I'm so—"

"You don't have to say you're sorry. I'm not. Anymore, at least. I'm so much happier without him in my life. My mom is, too. He'd never really been there anyway. I'd only see him a few times a year, and only for a couple hours at that. It took me a long time to realize that *I* wasn't a problem. That I wasn't unlovable." As much as I tried to stop it, my voice still cracked on the last word.

Aiden made a rough sound in the back of his throat. "Fuck, bunny. Don't say that. It's the furthest thing from the truth. How else could you explain a grumpy ass like me falling?"

It took a moment for his words to seep in, a handful of seconds for my brain to register what he'd said. But when it did, when I realized exactly what he was saying without actually saying it, my stomach flipped, a flurry of butterflies somersaulting within it. And I knew there was no more denying it.

I loved him, too.

While I thought I'd been in love before, it was now blatantly obvious I never had been. Couldn't possibly have been because they never generated a fraction of what I felt burning inside me for Aiden.

As much as I wanted to tell him that...as much as I wanted to let him know he wasn't just a grumpy asshole—that he was the perfect man, at least for me—I didn't.

I couldn't.

I was leaving, and no amount of declarations would change that. I had a dream that was finally in my grasp, and I'd learned the hard way not to give that up for anyone.

So instead, I just pressed my lips against his, pouring everything I held for him into it and hoping he felt my love even though I couldn't say the words.

AFTER AIDEN DRAINED the bath and dried us both off, neither of us bothering to redress, he gathered me in his arms and carried me to his bed, despite my protests.

I rolled my eyes, even as I looped my arms around his neck and played with the curling ends of his hair. "This feels excessive. Pretty sure Quinn didn't say my legs were useless tonight."

"Humor me." He set me down on the mattress, then braced his hands on either side of me, his gaze darting all over my face, pausing on the bandage covering my wound. "How're you feeling? You want some more painkillers?"

"I'm okay."

He grunted in a way that told me he didn't believe me. "Tell me what you need."

Instead of answering him with words, I hooked my legs around him and tugged him between them, shooting him a sly smile. "This is good."

He scowled down at me, the firmness of the gesture weakened by the fact that I could feel his cock hardening against me. "You're supposed to be resting."

"I'm lying down... Doesn't that count?"

"Not when you've locked your ankles around my back and are trying to grind your pussy up against me."

"Well, I wouldn't have to work so hard if you'd help me out."

"Bunny..." he said, his tone a warning.

One I didn't heed.

"Please, Aiden." I wrapped my arms around his neck and tugged him down for a kiss, allowing a tenor of vulnerability into my voice that I usually kept buried. "I just want to be with you tonight."

For long moments, he stayed still as a statue above me. Just when I thought he'd tell me no, he made a gruff sound in the back of his throat and dropped his face into my neck. "Fine, but we're taking it nice and easy. I'll make you feel so fucking good, but you're just going to let it happen. Can you do that for me, bunny?"

"Yes," I breathed, eyes fluttering closed as he brushed soft kisses across my skin. Over my collarbone, between my breasts, to my belly, and then lower still. His beard scratched against my inner thigh as he pressed his lips there, then against the other, then in between, right where I was aching for him.

He spread me open obscenely but licked me soft and sweet, guiding me on a slow, steady climb to my orgasm instead of the forceful shove over the cliff it usually was. I came with a low whimper, my hips rolling against him and my fingers in his hair as he lapped up everything I gave him, his groan of satisfaction making my stomach flip.

When he moved above me, settling himself between my legs and sinking deep as he kissed me, I wondered if it would ever be like this with anyone else. If I'd ever feel this connected...this safe...this loved...with anyone else. Or if Aiden was the single man who owned my heart completely, in this life and the next.

No matter how far I traveled. No matter where I went.

I knew there would never be another love like this.

THE BUZZING of my phone woke me from where I had my face buried in Aiden's chest. He reached over and plucked it from the nightstand, glancing at the screen to see who was calling.

"It's your mom," he said, his voice low and raspy with sleep.

With a groan, I flopped onto my back. "I swear, she gets halfway around the world, and she forgets what an early morning wake-up call is."

"She loves you and wants to talk." He pressed a kiss to my forehead and handed me the phone.

"Wish she would love me a little later," I grumbled, grabbing the phone from him before swiping to answer. "Mom, you know it's ass o'clock in the States, right? I get that you're roaming all over the world, but come on."

"Oh shit!" she said, and I could picture her smacking a hand to her forehead. "I forgot. I'm sorry, honey. Were you asleep?"

"*Yes*, I was asleep. It's really fucking early."

"I won't do it again. But since I've already got you on the phone... Do you want the good news or bad news first?"

"This again?" I rolled my eyes at Aiden, who lay next to me, his arm bent beneath his head as he kept his eyes trained on me. "Bad first."

"I'm no longer seeing Stewart."

"Oh. Well...that's a bummer?" My statement came out more question than anything, and Aiden raised a brow, clearly wondering what she was saying since he couldn't hear her end of the conversation. Figuring it'd save me the time of having to recount it, I pressed the speaker button, and her voice filled the room.

"Not for me, it's not. He got way too controlling, and his true colors came out. For one thing, he's a liar. As in, he never got you into that flight training program thing."

My mouth dropped open as I split my gaze between Aiden and the phone, a mix of emotions erupting inside me faster than I could catalog them. "Are you serious? Mom, I changed everything for this! I quit my job and moved halfway across the country. And now you're—"

"Time for the good news, I think."

"If you're going to tell me you're shacking up with some other guy and *that's* the good news, I'm going to lose it."

"Well, I *am* with another man—Claude, who I met in Paris after I kicked Stewart to the curb—but that's not the good news."

I blew out an exasperated sigh, my patience gone. "What is it, Mom?"

"Claude wants to hire you immediately!"

"For what?"

"To be a flight attendant!"

"Claude owns an airline?"

"Honey, Claude owns a *jet*. His flight attendant just broke her leg, though, and he needs a replacement right away. Isn't that *great*? He said the requirements are different for private jets, so you don't even have to worry about the regular training. As long as you can take the safety courses, you can start immediately."

"What do you mean by immediately?" I asked, a pit forming in my stomach.

"He wants you to start tomorrow..."

I blanched, my gaze snapping to Aiden's to find him staring at me, all expression wiped from his face.

I'd known my time in Starlight Cove was winding down, even though I'd done my best to ignore it. But I was supposed to have more than two weeks left. Seventeen days, during which I'd gorge myself on Aiden so I could satisfy my need for the next year or twenty.

And now, suddenly, that was gone.

But what other choice did I have? My contract with the resort didn't extend past Christmas, and I couldn't just throw my life up to chance like my mom did. As much as I'd love to live my life the same way, with complete and utter abandon, I was always aware of things like bills and responsibilities.

The longer it took for me to respond, the stiffer Aiden grew, his shoulders squaring off, his mouth firming, eyes shuttering. And I knew what this was. He was shutting down. Blocking me out. Protecting himself.

Part of me wished he'd tell me to stay. Promise that we could keep on doing exactly what we'd been doing and everything would be fine. But the other part of me—the part that'd had this dream since I was twelve years old—wanted to grab hold with both hands and see where it took her.

Turned out it didn't matter, though, because Aiden didn't say a word. He might've been lying right next to me, his body heat seeping into mine, but he was a world away.

In the castle he'd built for himself, never allowing anyone else to enter, and I was staring in from the outside.

So I did the only thing I could.

I swallowed down my fear and uncertainty, my hesitation and doubt. "Just tell me where, and I'll be there."

CHAPTER TWENTY-SIX

AIDEN

I'D FORGOTTEN what it was like to not get a full night's sleep.

In the time Avery had spent in my bed, her presence lulling me into dreamland, I'd forgotten what my schedule had been like before she'd come into my life. Forgotten how it was to fall into bed exhausted, only to lie there for hours, staring at the numbers on my clock change while the amount of time I had before my alarm went off rapidly diminished. Or to sleep for an hour, only to wake up at three in the morning and not be able to get back to sleep.

I'd taken for granted how it felt to lie there with her in my arms. To fall asleep with the weight of her body on mine, her soft breaths against my chest, and the scent of her hair filling my nose.

I was exhausted, both from the lack of sleep as well as everything that had fallen back into my lap since she'd been gone. Things she'd taken care of in the time she'd been here that I now had to shoulder once again.

But I had to learn to deal. She'd made her choice. Seemingly without a second thought. She didn't want to be here, and she'd made that abundantly clear when she fled without a backward glance, breaking the contract she'd signed with the resort more than two weeks early and not even once mentioning the event she'd promised me she'd take care of in my place.

She'd left so quickly I couldn't help but wonder if I'd embellished how good we'd been together. How we'd clicked, both inside and out of the bedroom. How it had felt like she was the other half of my soul I didn't even know I'd been missing. Wondered if maybe what we'd had hadn't been anything special to her, and that was why she'd so easily chosen that other life.

Even with how much I hated it...even with how much it hurt—especially after everything I'd shared with her, after cracking open my chest and laying its contents at her feet—I couldn't begrudge her that choice. I wasn't about to stand in the way of what she'd been dreaming about since she was a little girl. I wanted the best for her. I always would.

I just had to accept the best for her wasn't me.

I also had to accept that I was completely and utterly fucked in her absence. I'd spent the past five days trying to figure out how I could be in two places at once. How I could handle what was needed for the resort while still meeting my commitments to my publisher. And the short answer was, I couldn't.

There was no way I could do this on my own.

Which left me with only one choice...

I found Addison sitting on the couch in the parlor, all her shit spread out on the coffee table in front of her.

Strolling into the room, I cleared my throat. "We need to talk."

She barely spared me a glance before returning her attention to her tablet. "What's up?"

I shifted on my feet, running a hand through my hair. It didn't matter how long I'd had to come to terms with this. Didn't matter that I was no longer given any other choice. Forcing myself to speak the words that I had kept hidden for years was exactly as difficult as I'd thought it would be.

"We need to grab one of the other guys to fill in for me next week because I won't be here."

"Because of that conference in California?" She rolled her eyes, swiping a hand through the air. "There are dozens of accounting conferences all over the country, Aiden. At any given time of the year. Hell, there's probably one next month. You can go to that one instead."

"I'm not going to California."

Her brows rose, even as she kept her attention on her tablet. "That was easier than I thought it'd be."

None of this was what I would call anything remotely resembling easy.

"No, what I mean is I'm not going to be in California

next week because I'll be—" I took a deep breath and blew it out slowly, knowing there was no coming back now "—in Germany."

She froze, her finger hovering above the tablet screen, and slowly turned her head to stare at me. "You're what now?"

"Going to Germany."

"I heard that. And yet it still doesn't make sense. Why the fuck would you be going to Germany?"

"So I can attend the Frankfurt Book Fair."

With a sigh, she braced her elbows on her knees and dropped her head into her hands, massaging her temples. "I don't know what kind of joke this is, but it's not funny. I have a lot of shit to handle before next week, and I don't have time for—"

"You remember the book everyone was talking about on Thanksgiving?"

With a huff, she dropped her arms and turned an exasperated look at me. "What about it?"

I'd spent so much time worrying that Avery would spill my secret and blow my cover. That she'd destroy years of careful plans and throw everything I'd kept hidden out into the world. But in the end, she hadn't needed to tell anyone. I did that all on my own. And the relief when I finally said the words—when I finally spilled the secret I'd kept for years—was palpable.

"I'm the author."

She snorted and shook her head. "No, you're not.

That's written by A.M. Kins—" She gasped, her eyes going wide, no doubt realizing just how close it was to Aiden McKenzie. Mouth agape, she stared at me with a look of utter shock written across her face. "Holy shit. Holy *shit*."

Basically what I had been repeating to myself nonstop for the past two days.

"My publisher is sending me there to meet with foreign publishers about expanding into different languages. They've already booked my flight and my accommodations...have set up all the appointments I'll be attending. So we need to figure this out because I have to be there."

"Well, of course you do!" she snapped, like any other possibility was absolutely not an option. She grabbed her phone, her thumbs flying across the screen. "What I want to know is why the hell I'm just now hearing about this. Why the hell would you keep it a secret?"

Because we were brought up thinking the kinds of books I wrote were trash. Because I was worried about what other people would think. Because, after years, it had seemed easier to keep up the lie than it would be to just tell the truth.

Because I'd been scared. I was *still* scared. Especially now...when we had everything to lose.

Instead of saying all that, I narrowed it down to my current worry. "The resort."

She snapped her gaze to me and huffed out a

disbelieving laugh. "The *resort*? What does that even mean?"

I gestured behind me to where we'd had that conversation with Mabel back in October. "You heard what Mabel said when she was here. You know just how many subscribers the newspaper has lost because a handful of people were offended that she'd *suggested* my book. How do you think those same people would react if they knew the author was one of the owners of the resort?"

"I think bookings would go through the fucking roof."

"Yeah, exactly. They'd— Wait, what?" I shook my head. "No, people would—"

"Lose their shit because the author who spiced up their comatose love life runs a resort where they can escape to and have even more hot sex while possibly catching a glimpse of the elusive author himself?" She raised a brow and then gave a definitive nod. "I agree. This is *gold*. I've already thought of a dozen angles we can go in for our social media."

"And what about the people who won't see it that way?"

She lifted a single shoulder in a shrug. "I've also got counterpoints for any assholes who want to try me. I'll happily eat them for breakfast."

Addison was a shark and a honey badger all rolled into one. Tough as nails, obstinate as hell, and not giving a single fuck what anyone else thought. A giant pain in my ass most days. But she was also a fierce mama bear to our family, despite her being the youngest, and despite the fact that *we* were supposed to protect *her*. Family was the most important thing to her, and she'd sharpen her claws on her enemy's teeth and dig them into anyone who threatened that, without hesitation.

So, yeah, she was a force to be reckoned with, but she was *our* force, and I didn't know how this resort—how this family—would run without her.

"It's all making so much more sense. *This* is why you've been such an incompetent idiot lately. I thought you were just getting old."

"I'm thirty-four, Addison," I said dryly.

She lifted a brow as if to say, *exactly*. Baby sisters were the worst.

With her gaze still on her phone, she said, "This trip had to have been booked for a while, but you're just now telling me about it. What was your plan?"

My plan? My plan was a girl with sunshine in her eyes and fire in her soul. My plan was the woman who'd danced into my life like a whirlwind and altered it forever.

Memories of Avery flitted through my mind—her slapping her hand over her T-shirt the first time we'd met, like that would stop me from seeing what I'd already seen, her laughter when my siblings had been ragging on me at Thanksgiving, and the light in her eyes when we'd shared dinner on the rooftop. How she looked under me, taking everything I had to give her. How she whispered my name in the dark. How perfect she tasted, how sweet she smelled.

I cleared my throat, shoving back the thoughts I didn't need to be thinking. "Avery was my plan," I said, talking about so much more than just this.

Silence filled the room, and I glanced at Addison, only to find her narrow-eyed stare fixed on me instead of her screen.

I shifted under her scrutiny. "What?"

She pressed her lips into a flat line and shook her head. "It was more than a fling, wasn't it?"

I recalled moments with Avery—tiny details that had made me fall in love with her. How she'd had this amazing way of making you feel like you were the most important person in the room.

And then I thought of the phone call that had changed everything.

How her face had given nothing away. How, with barely a pause, she'd told her mom she'd be there. How she'd packed up her life here in two hours and left without more than a soft brush of her lips against mine, a murmured thanks, and a smile that spoke of mischief and adventure. Of excitement and anticipation.

Just not here. Just not with me.

I shook the thoughts from my head and strode out of the room. "Not for her."

Group text between Brady, Aiden, Beck, Ford, Levi, and Addison

2:17 p.m.

ADDISON:

Time to stop fucking around, boys

BECK:

You're the youngest one out of all of us. You don't get to call us boys.

ADDISON:

And yet I just did

SOS SOS SOS

We've got a code red situation over here

BRADY:

Is this actually a code red situation, or is it like the time you ran out of peanut butter cup ice cream when you had your period and demanded one of us pick some up for you?

ADDISON:

That was literally a code red situation

And you can't pretend otherwise

LEVI:

that was an unnecessary visual I could've lived my whole life without

ADDISON:

Thanks again to Ford for being the only decent one of you assholes

FORD:

Happy to be of service.

BECK:

Suck up.

FORD:

She's in charge of handing out my resort tasks. Fuck yeah, I'm sucking up.

ADDISON:

FOCUS

We need all hands on deck this week

The documentary is wrapping up

And it's going to be an absolute shitshow around here

I can't handle that and the resort on my own

BRADY:

Good thing Aiden is there, then

ADDISON:

Aiden won't be here

Hence my SOS

I need everyone's help

That means Levi can't hide on his boat

LEVI:

that's my job

BECK:

"Job"

ADDISON:

Ford can't hide at the fire station

FORD:

Okay but that actually is my job...

ADDISON:

Brady can't hide in his police car

BRADY:

Also my job.

ADDISON:

And Beck...

Okay, Beck can hide at the diner

But only because we're going to need him there

BRADY:

And Aiden...?

ADDISON:

I'm going to tell you something

But you should probably sit down

Are you sitting down?

Yes?

Last chance...

...

Aiden

Will

Be

In

GERMANY!!!!!

FORD:

At the Frankfurt Book Fair?

ADDISON:

At the WHAT?

How the hell do you know about that??

And how are none of you acting surprised at what I just said???

ADDISON:

Hello?

ADDISON:

HELLO???

LEVI:

this should go well

ADDISON:

One of you better tell me what's going on RIGHT NOW

BRADY:

We already knew.

ADDISON:

You WHAT

FORD:

Relax, little D.

ADDISON:

I swear to God, Ford, I will kill you

BECK:

We sort of figured it out the weekend after Thanksgiving.

ADDISON:

THAT WAS ALMOST A MONTH AGO

LEVI:

it sure was

ADDISON:

AND YET YOU DIDN'T TELL ME

BECK:

Gee, I'm not sure why…

BRADY:

We figured Aiden had his reasons not to share. Were we right?

ADDISON:

It doesn't matter!

FFS you should've told me

And his reasons are stupid anyway

If assholes want to push their puritanical bullshit onto us, I'll be there to push back

BECK:

I kind of hope they do. Maybe then you can take some of your aggression out on them instead of us.

ADDISON:

I'm going to find you all and aggressively murder you if I don't get some answers to my distress call

BRADY:

I'll be there.

FORD:

With bells on.

LEVI:

yeah fine

BECK:

Can't, but I'll make sure none of you starves.

ADDISON:

I don't say this enough

But you're not assholes all the time

FORD:

Aww, we love you, too, little D.

ADDISON:

You just had to ruin it, didn't you?

CHAPTER TWENTY-SEVEN

AVERY

I WAS DOING IT. Living the life I'd wanted since I was a little girl. Experiencing all the things I'd spent years dreaming about. Traveling to places around the world I never thought I'd see.

So it should've felt better than this, right?

If it was something I wanted so bad—badly enough that I'd given up everything for it—why had I spent the entire time I'd been gone thinking about what I'd left behind rather than what was in front of me?

Not even the wow factor of walking onto Claude's impressive jet, with its luxurious leather seats and an entertainment system to rival any mansion's, had taken my mind off Aiden.

Nothing had, including my daunting first days on the job. Since private flight attendants didn't have to go through the same protocols those in the public sector did, and because of how quickly Claude wanted me on board, my training had been significantly condensed. I'd had an accelerated course focusing on just the essentials—safety protocols, emergency procedures, and all the basic shit I'd need to be able to do my job. Once I'd finished that, Margo had joined us—broken leg and all—on my first few flights to ensure I ran things how Claude wanted them and didn't fuck up.

And through it all, through takeoffs and landings, through overnight stays in London, Monaco, and Budapest, I'd felt restless. Unsettled. And absolutely, one hundred percent untethered.

In my fantasy world, I'd be exploring the sights of all these amazing places I traveled to. Soaking in the cultures, relishing in the delicious food, and learning the experiences of others.

In reality, I saw the inside of a very nice private jet and the four walls of my hotel room, and that was it. I mean, it was a nice hotel room. A really fucking nice hotel room—the exact kind you would expect a billionaire to reserve. But it was still just a room. Just a generic place to call home before I jetted off to somewhere else I wouldn't be able to explore.

It wasn't the soft flannel sheets beneath me or the furnace of a man at my back or his softly murmured words in my ear that I'd become used to. That I'd come to crave.

It just...wasn't enough.

After a whirlwind ten days, I was on my first break,

back in my childhood home in Maine, and restless in a way I wasn't sure how to fix. I'd just finished making my sad little dinner of boxed mac and cheese when my phone rang with an incoming FaceTime call from Willow.

Her smiling face filled the screen as soon as I answered. "Oh, thank God. I was worried you were too fancy to answer my calls, Miss Jet-Setter. Now tell me everything! Is it amazing? What's it like? Do you ever get to enjoy the flights? Like, sit on those seats that look nicer than my furniture? Or are you always—" She cut off, her brows snapping down as her eyes darted around my face. "What's wrong?" With how it came out, it was less of a question and more of a demand.

I shifted in my seat, spooning a bite of mac and cheese and avoiding her eyes. "What? Nothing."

Willow just sat there, staring me down. "Did you forget who you were talking to? I'm not just anybody, you know."

She wasn't. She was one of the best people in my life, someone who had the uncanny ability to listen to problems without judgment and help figure them out. But how could I voice what the problem was? How could I tell her that after not even two weeks, I was ready to give up on this dream I'd had for more than a decade?

"Avery?" she said, her voice softer now. "Seriously... What's going on?"

I stared down at my bowl of mac and cheese and shook my head. "I think I really fucked up."

"With the job? I'm sure it's not nearly as bad—"

"Not with the job. The job is...fine."

Willow's brows flew up, her wide eyes fixed on me. "*Fine*? We are talking about you flying all over the world in a billionaire's private jet, right?"

I laughed then, a sound that bordered on hysterical, and shook my head. "It's ridiculous, isn't it? This should be exactly what I wanted. It's *supposed* to be exactly what I wanted. But I can't help but feel like I'm missing something."

Willow was quiet for long moments. Then, quietly, she said, "Something? Or someone?"

I huffed out a breath, not at all surprised to feel the sharp sting of tears in my eyes, the lump in my throat. "How do you do that?"

She shrugged and shot me a soft smile. "It's a gift. Now how about you tell me what's going on."

So, I did. I filled her in on everything I'd left out during our chats while I'd been in Starlight Cove. Even though I'd shared some things regarding Aiden, I hadn't shared everything. It had felt like so much was just ours, and I'd wanted to keep it that way. Keep it safe in our little bubble, where just the two of us could go.

But now, I opened up to her about our time together. How he'd made me feel...cherished. For the first time in my life. How he was nothing like I expected, and everything I never knew I needed.

When I was finished, when I'd poured out everything I was feeling until I felt like a husk, I stared at her with hopeful eyes. Wishing she'd tell me where to go from here.

"You love him." She said it with such finality, my answer was irrelevant, but I gave her one anyway.

"So much it hurts."

"You know it doesn't have to hurt, right?"

"It does when we're not together."

"And why aren't you together again?" she asked, brow raised.

"I just started a new job. I'm finally doing the thing I want to do. And—"

"And it's boring and hollow and not what you want anymore."

"No, it's—"

The look on her face was enough to cut me off. Just that purse of her lips and the quirk of her brow, her arms crossed over her chest as she stared me down, challenging me to contradict her.

"Don't even try to pretend I'm not right," she said. "It's not what you want anymore. Listening to you talk about that trip y'all took to Vermont? Where you went to that festival to gather ideas and bring back to the resort? You got to meet all those people and explore and use that beautiful brain of yours to come up with new ideas. You were excited and passionate and *alive*. That's the Avery I know. Not whoever this is right here."

She was right. Of course she was right.

But I'd left.

I'd bailed without truly giving my life in Starlight Cove a chance because I was scared. Scared of what I'd give up if I didn't leave. And scared of what I might lose if I stayed.

But I'd lost him anyway, hadn't I? Not only that, but I'd made that choice for both of us.

"What if he's already written me off?" I asked, my voice barely a whisper. "What if he doesn't forgive me for leaving?"

"There's only one way to find out..."

ONCE I'D MADE up my mind to go back to Starlight Cove and to Aiden, I couldn't get there fast enough. It'd already been nearly two weeks, and I was crawling out of my skin to see him again. And *I'd* been the one who'd left. I couldn't imagine how he was feeling, having been the one left behind.

I needed to get to him. Immediately. Needed to see him and tell him I screwed up and that I was sorry. So fucking sorry.

But first, I had to get through Addison.

The resort was chaotic, too many people around and none of whom were the ones I was looking for. I'd asked around for Aiden, but no one had seen him, which meant I was going to have to beg my bestie to tell me where he was.

I found her in the back office, shuffling papers in a way

that said she was looking for something and needed the answer yesterday.

"Levi, did you get Cottage Thirteen all cleaned—" She lifted her gaze toward the door, her mouth pinching into a tight line when she saw it was me standing there and not her brother. "Oh. It's you."

Not the warmest welcome, but I could work with it. At least she wasn't throwing a stapler at my head.

"Hey..."

She froze for long moments before slamming the papers down and bracing her hands on the desk as she fixed me with a glare. Apparently, I had spoken too soon.

"Hey? *Hey*? That's what you have to say after you left like that? After you bailed on us? On *him*—" She held up a hand and shook her head. "You know what? I'm not going to do this. I can't talk to you right now, or I'm going to explode into full-on Cuntasaurus Mode, and I swore I wouldn't do that to you again after that time junior year when you broke the heel on my favorite pair of shoes because you thought it'd be a good idea to wear them on a hiking date with that dumbass from psych."

Fuck, she'd been mad then. She hadn't talked to me for three days. And then she'd only given in because I'd come home with a bag full of her favorite snacks and promised her I'd never borrow anything again without asking.

"In my defense, he didn't *tell* me we were going hiking. He told me we were—" At her glare, I rolled my lips in and nodded. "Right. Not the time."

She turned her attention away from me, dismissing me entirely. "Look, we're slammed right now. They're wrapping up the documentary and—"

I gasped, slapping a hand over my mouth as I stared at her with wide eyes, all the pieces clicking into place. This was the week Addison had blocked out on Aiden's calendar. The one I'd promised him I'd cover for so he could go do his famous author thing and have his siblings be none the wiser. The one I'd completely bailed on.

"Oh shit! The— Uh…the thing. That he needed to do. The one I was going to cover for…"

"The very one."

"Why didn't anybody call me?"

"Because you quit," she said, no warmth in her tone. "And because I'm pretty sure my brother would rather eat glass than drag you back from what he thinks is your dream, no matter how you left."

"Fuck," I said under my breath, pressing my fingers to my temples. This was so much worse than I'd thought. Not only had I left him behind, but I'd flaked out on something he was counting on me for. Something he'd entrusted me with. But he'd handled it…let me do what he thought was my dream. What *I* thought was my dream.

He'd put me first, even when I hadn't deserved it. Even when it made things more difficult for him. It was exactly what I'd been looking for, and I had it. With Aiden, I had it. And I'd walked away from it like an idiot.

"Yeah, fuck."

"I know it's not an excuse, but everything happened so fast," I said. "My mom called and suddenly I didn't have a job in January like she'd promised, and then she hit me with this opportunity. The thing I've wanted to do my whole life. I didn't even think—I just left."

"Yeah. You did," she said flatly. "And for what? What was so important that you had to leave this behind? That you had to leave me behind? That you had to leave *him* behind?"

When she put it like that, it didn't make sense. But that was the thing about hindsight. When you were staring it down, though, facing it head on, things didn't look so black-and-white.

I bit back my fears, forced down my apprehensions, and told her the truth. "Because I thought it was what I was supposed to do. It was what Aiden and I had agreed on. Three months, nothing more."

"Well, it was more than that to him."

"It was more than that to me, too."

"And yet you still left."

I swallowed down the lump in my throat and nodded, because I couldn't deny it. I *had* left. But if I hadn't...if I hadn't explored the possibility, I would've always wondered what would've happened if I had. And that would've hung over our heads like a bomb waiting to go off, me always wondering what if...

"I did. But I think I needed to to see what I was giving up. To understand that it doesn't matter if I throw away this opportunity because I'll have my chance at a thousand more. But I only get *one* opportunity with your brother. One chance with him, and I almost blew it. I need to—" I stopped myself and shook my head, rubbing my fingers over my eyes. "You know what? I get that you're pissed at me, and I'm sorry. I'll spend the next year trying to make it up to you, I *promise*. But Aiden is the person I should be telling this to, not you."

Addison stared at me for long moments, her arms crossed over her chest, gaze scrutinizing. Then she nodded, almost to herself, and grabbed her phone. "You're right. It's too bad you didn't come to this realization yesterday. Before he left for another continent."

I gasped, bringing my hands up to cover my mouth. "Fuck. He's already..."

"In Germany."

My brows flew up, because his cover to her and all his siblings was that he'd be at a conference in California. "And you..."

"Know about the books?" she asked, though she didn't lift her gaze from her phone. "Yep."

"And you're..."

"Totally cool with it? Also yes."

I breathed out a sigh, so relieved for Aiden that he finally had that weight off his shoulders. Relieved...and guilty as fuck because he'd had to tell them. Because I hadn't given him a choice.

"Well, this isn't going to be great," she said, her tone all business. "The earliest flight you could make doesn't leave until tomorrow night, which means you wouldn't get to Germany until Monday morning, and that's if you don't have anything hold you up. And since his return flight is on Monday, you'd probably pass each other on the way to and from the airport." She pursed her lips. "You could also just wait here for him to get back and save yourself a fuck-ton of money. Or..."

"Or?" I asked, not bothering to hide the hopeful note in my voice, because waiting here wasn't an option. I needed to see him now...yesterday...as soon as fucking possible.

She shrugged. "Seems like a waste of a perfectly good billionaire contact and your mom's sugar daddy if you can't hijack his jet for something like this..."

I stared at her for a moment, eyes wide, then breathed out a laugh. I squeezed her tight, peppering kisses all over her face, before stepping back and pulling out my phone, dialing the person I needed.

She answered on the second ring, and before she could say anything, I cut in, "Mom? I need the biggest favor of my life."

CHAPTER TWENTY-EIGHT

AIDEN

THE PAST THREE days had been a whirlwind, and I was fucking exhausted. Between the flight over, being jet-lagged as fuck, then a packed schedule filled with panels and pinging between publisher booths, and more cocktail parties than I ever wanted to attend again, I was wrung out.

But I was here—the first public appearance of A.M. Kinsey—and I was doing the thing. At my siblings' urging, I was enjoying it—or trying to—no longer paranoid about cameras or worried the media or influencers would find me out. Addison had already shouted it to the world, wanting to get in front of the narrative and make sure the announcement came out on our terms.

When I'd told my publisher that, they'd been thrilled. Thrilled enough to stuff my schedule full of public appearances. They got me slotted in at the last minute for a signing where I'd sat, meeting fans and taking photos, until I'd run out of books. Then there were the dinners and the networking and all the fucking socializing.

It was a humbling and awe-inspiring experience. Something I was immensely proud of but somehow still felt empty without Avery by my side.

She would've made this whole thing easier. Better. With her laughter and her whispered comments designed to make me smile and her *light*. She'd bring her sparkle into a place that felt drab...that felt exhausting...and brighten up the entire space—me right along with it.

But Avery wasn't here.

Which meant I was traversing this exhausting day on my own, and I was only halfway through my afternoon of publisher meetings when all I really wanted to do was be back home.

Actually, if I was wishing for things, it wasn't Starlight Cove I wanted, but Avery. I'd hoped the days passing would've tempered this pain a little...would've made her leaving easier to swallow, but all it'd done was push me further and further away from the last time I'd held her in my arms and felt her lips on mine.

And thinking of things like that wasn't conducive to anything because she'd made her choice.

In the end, she'd picked what she wanted, and it wasn't me. I needed to get that through my thick skull, or I'd still be pining for her in fifty years.

With what I felt for her, I wasn't sure I wouldn't be anyway.

My last appointment had just cleared out, which meant I had about thirty seconds to myself before the next one would slip in. Opulent Enterprises. Didn't sound like a foreign publishing company to me, but what did I know? I was so fucking tired, all the appointments I'd had were starting to bleed together. I was just glad my agent would be brokering any deals and all I had to do was the meet and greet...smile and discuss plans for the rest of the series.

The door opened, and I stood from the chair, making my way around the way-too-fucking-large conference table to greet my next appointment. I was halfway there, hand outstretched, when my steps stuttered, my brain taking longer than it should have to compute what it was seeing.

Because there, in the door I'd watched half a dozen men and women clad in their finest suits walk through, stood Avery. In jeans and a hoodie, her face free of makeup, hair in a high ponytail, and eyes tired and hesitant but hopeful.

I couldn't drink her in fast enough, my gaze roving over every inch of her to catalog anything that had changed. I wanted to ask her what she was doing here. Why she was in Germany. Wanted to know how she liked her new job... if it was everything she'd dreamed about. If she had a matching pain in her chest that just wouldn't go away.

But what came out was, "You're not with Opulent Enterprises."

Her lips quirked up into a tentative smile. "I'm not..."

"How'd you get in here?" Still not the question I wanted to ask, but this was far easier than anything I truly wanted to know.

She gave a short shrug. "Turns out, my mom's sugar daddies are good for something. And Claude is kind of a romantic. He hooked me up with the pass to come here and the appointment to see you. I think he said I was a reporter? Or...I don't even know. Or care. I just needed to get in here."

"Yeah?" I crossed my arms over my chest and regarded her with as much detachment as I could, my armor back in place—something I hadn't realized until now had been gone around her. "Why's that?"

She swallowed, her nerves apparent in the tightening of her eyes, the pinch of her mouth. "I needed to see you. I needed to tell you... God, Aiden." She shook her head, her lips rolling in as her eyes filled with tears, and I had to force myself not to go to her. Not to wrap her in my arms and offer her the comfort I knew she needed. "I'm so sorry." Her voice broke on the last word, and she cleared her throat to try again. "I'm sorry I left. I'm sorry I didn't talk to you first. I'm sorry I bailed on you and left you to figure this out on your own." She gestured around us and took a step closer to me. Close enough that she had to tip her head back to stare up at me. "I'm sorry I ran after I promised you I wouldn't."

That was what stung. She'd told me—she'd promised me—she wouldn't. And she'd done it anyway.

"Why'd you do it?"

She brushed the back of her hand across her face, swiping away an escaped tear. "I was scared."

"Of me?" I asked, voice rough.

"No, Aiden. Of *us*. Of what we were together—of what you were...*are*...to me."

"And what am I, Avery?"

Tentatively, she reached out to me, hovering a hand over my chest. When I didn't step back, she placed it directly over my heart, and I had no doubt she could feel just how hard it was beating. Slamming a million miles an hour against my chest cavity, just trying to get closer to her.

"Everything," she said, her voice cracking on the word. "You're everything to me."

I made a rough sound in the back of my throat, wanting so badly to hold her. To kiss away her tears. To wrap my arms around her, bury my face in her neck, and never let her go.

But I didn't want to do this again.

When she got scared, or her emotions got too big, I didn't want to have to worry about her running. Not from me and not from us and not from whatever life we'd built together.

"You're the whole fucking world to me, bunny," I managed through a tight throat. "But you left."

"I know I did. It took me all of twenty minutes after leaving to realize it was probably the worst mistake of my life, then another day to realize there was no probably about it. And I'd estimate I've spent a grand total of three years thinking about all the mistakes I've made, so that's saying a lot." She stared up at me, those gorgeous whiskey eyes so full of remorse and regret and pain. But there was hope, too, and love. "I'm not going to do it again."

Unable to stop myself any longer, I cupped her face, swiping away her tears with my thumbs. "How do you know?"

She wrapped her fingers around my wrists and turned her head, kissing first one palm, then the other, before meeting my gaze again. "Because I know what it's like to live without you. And I don't ever want to feel that again."

A breath escaped me in a whoosh as relief swept over me, tenderness and anticipation bubbling up as she mirrored exactly what I was feeling myself.

"Good," I said, voice gruff.

"Good?" She darted her eyes between mine, a hopeful lilt to her voice.

"Yeah, good." I stared down at her, at this beautiful woman who'd stolen my heart the first night we'd met and who'd have it until my last dying breath. "Because I don't want to spend another night out of your bed. I don't want another morning where I wake up without your face being the first thing I see or another night where your lips aren't the last thing I taste. And I don't want to think for another fucking second what this life would be like without you. So let's not do that, okay?"

She nodded quickly then, a surprised huff of laughter bursting out as tears streamed down her face faster than I could catch them. "I love you, Aiden. More than anything."

"I love you, too, bunny." I pressed my lips to her forehead, her nose, each of her cheeks, before hovering them over her mouth. "So fucking much."

I kissed her then, her face cupped in my hands, her lips pliant under mine. She opened to me immediately, slipping her tongue into my mouth, and I groaned at finally tasting her again.

After long moments, when we were both panting and I was hard as a fucking rock with absolutely no option to handle it right now, I pulled back and gazed down at her. "I just have one question."

"Anything."

"Why would you have to ask your mom's sugar daddy to borrow the jet—aka your office—instead of your boss? Isn't he the same guy?"

She breathed out a laugh and shook her head. "He *was* my boss, and it *was* my office. But I quit."

I froze, my entire body going still as I studied her. I'd been ready to do whatever I needed to in order to make this work. Travel around the world so she could live her dream... I was pretty sure I could be a stowaway on

Claude's jet. If he was as much of a romantic as she said, he probably wouldn't mind. But we were in new territory now...

"Have another promising career on the line?" I asked.

"Yeah, actually. I do." She grinned up at me, eyes bright. "One where I handle guest relations for a gorgeous beachfront resort and get to travel with the man I love and gather ideas to bring back while he writes the hottest sex scenes I've ever read and then calls me in the middle of the day to read them to me before acting them out with me."

My lips twitched, my cock twitching right along with it at the memory of that day... "That seems oddly specific. Did you have to submit a résumé?"

Her laughter was the best fucking sound I'd heard all day—all *week*—and I wanted to soak it in. Wanted to bask in it. Wanted to do whatever it took just to hear it on repeat.

Before I could, someone knocked on the door, and I swore under my breath as I glanced at my watch. "Fuck. That's my next appointment. I still have another two hours of this."

"Oh, of course!" Avery said with a nod. "I should go so you can do your thing. I think this badge will let me walk around, so I can—"

Before she could step back, I wrapped an arm around her waist and held her to me. "No fucking way."

"I—" She blinked up at me, eyes wide. "What?"

I guided us over to my seat and deposited her in the

chair directly next to mine. Then I settled in next to her, her hand encased in mine. "If you think I'm not keeping you right by my side after two weeks without you, you haven't been paying attention or I haven't been direct enough." I called out for my next appointment to enter before turning back to her and dropping my voice into a low murmur. "I love you, and I'm not letting you out of my sight until we're back in Starlight Cove."

CHAPTER TWENTY-NINE

AVERY

WHEN WE MADE it back to Aiden's hotel room, it was a mirror of our first night together, all frantic hands and claiming kisses as we divested each other of our clothing as fast as humanly possible. As if we'd never have enough time to fit in everything we wanted to. As if we'd already known then that one night would never, ever be enough.

Fortunately, it didn't have to be. Because now? We had forever.

Almost as if he'd heard my thoughts, Aiden slowed his lips, gentled the glide of his tongue, eased the brush of his hands as he swept them over my body. He walked me backward until my knees hit the mattress and I fell back on the bed, his hungry gaze sweeping over me in a soft caress I felt everywhere.

"We're gonna go nice and slow tonight, bunny." He braced his hands on either side of me, lowering himself until his words ghosted across my lips. "I want to savor this. Want to spend an hour just playing with your tits. Another hour licking up that sweet little pussy. Another mapping the tattoos all over your body to see if the bunny is the only one that makes you wet. I want to make you come so many times your throat is raw from screaming my name. And then I want to do it again. And again. And again."

"I'm willing to accept those terms," I said, breathless, because he'd already started, his hands cupping my breasts as he licked languidly at the tips before sucking them into his mouth.

"Good," he rumbled against me. "Because tomorrow or next week or next year, I want to be able to recall your sweet moans and pleas for more. Want to remember exactly what it felt like sliding inside this perfect cunt."

I was panting now, my body arching toward his as he did exactly what he promised, laving attention all over my breasts until the string connecting them to my clit grew tighter. Sharper. Until the ache that had started as a low simmer built and built, my pussy clenching around nothing and desperate for a release.

"Missed these perfect tits," he murmured against me. His short beard rasped over the delicate skin, juxtaposed with the soft brush of his lips, the gentle glide of his tongue, then amplified by the sharp scrape of his teeth against my nipples.

"Aiden..." I was strung tight, my body desperate for the

relief it knew he could give but also loving this attention. Relishing the unhurried build. *Reveling* in it.

"Do you think I can make you come like this?" he asked, his voice low and rough.

It was another callback to our first night, when I'd questioned his ability to make me come with his fingers. But if I had known then what I knew now, there would've been only one possible answer...

"I'm counting on it."

He smiled against me then, his eyes bright as he flicked his tongue across a nipple. "That's my girl."

He cupped my other breast in his palm, his thumb brushing back and forth over the hardened tip. And then he switched sides. Over and over again. He moved back and forth, never allowing a moment to pass when he didn't have his hands or mouth on me. He split his attention between them both until I was strung out, just a ball of need, my breaths growing faster as I stared down at him in wonder. In shock that this...was actually going to happen.

"Oh my God, Aiden." I dropped my head back to the bed and closed my eyes, arching my back so he could suck more of my breast into his mouth. Focusing on the feel of him when he did exactly that.

"You're close, aren't you, bunny?"

But I couldn't answer him, all my attention on the feelings he was coaxing out of me. And disbelief that he was making it happen... I was going to come without even a brush of him against my clit...was going to come with nothing inside me, nothing winding me up but this attention he was giving me.

The orgasm built softly, a slow, unhurried climb up a hill rather than the race up a mountain. And when it came, when I rolled right over the top rather than shooting straight off a cliff, it was gentle waves lapping at my skin, soft pulses sweeping through my body.

Aiden groaned against me as I moaned his name, his tongue swirling light circles around my nipple. "There's my perfect girl." He switched sides, licking softly across my other breast. "Good job, baby. Knew you could give me one just like that."

Breathless, I reached down, cupping his face in my hands and tugging his mouth to mine. I kissed him, hungry and raw and aching for him like I hadn't ever before. Longing for him in a way that had me needy, desperate to feel him everywhere.

"I need more," I admitted. Because he'd spoiled me. From that very first night, he'd made me crave everything with him. And he'd given it. Time and again.

"That was just the warm-up, bunny. I've got you." He slid down my body then, pressing kisses against every inch he passed, murmuring how much he missed every one, until he settled those big, broad shoulders between my thighs. He hummed low in his throat as he swiped a thumb over my slit. "Fuck. I missed this pretty little pussy, too. Has she missed me?"

"Yes." I threaded my fingers through his hair and

tugged him where I wanted him, desperate to feel his mouth on me. But he didn't budge.

Instead, he licked a slow, teasing line up one side of my pussy, then down the other. The barest brush against my skin, and I groaned because it wasn't nearly enough.

He chuckled against me, his eyes dancing as he stared up at me from between my spread thighs. "Do you need something, bunny?"

"I need you to make me come." I tightened my fingers in his hair, attempting to move him where I needed his attention, but once again, he stayed right where he was.

"Pretty sure I already did that."

"That's not what I mean."

"No? Then I think you're going to have to be more specific. Tell me what you want, and I'll give it to you, remember?"

"I want your tongue."

He licked against the seam where my leg met my body. "Like that?"

"*Aiden.*"

"What, baby?" His words were playful, cajoling. And then all teasing left his tone when he said, "Tell me what you need."

"You."

"You have me. Always." He swiped his thumb over me again, the barest caress against my clit before he dipped it inside me, the teasing strokes not nearly enough. "Tell me what you need right now."

"Lick my pussy. *Please*," I said shamelessly. Desperately. "Make me come all over your mouth."

Those handful of words were like a gunshot in the room signaling the start, and he groaned against my inner thigh before scraping his teeth over my skin. "Good girl. That's my good fucking girl." He turned his attention to where I wanted it, licking up my seam, just a tease of what was in store. "That's what you're going to do, isn't it? Gonna come all over my tongue and give me exactly what I've been craving. Gonna do it over and over so I can taste you for hours."

Then he made me do exactly that. He spread me wide with his thumbs and attacked my clit with the kind of focus that had me falling in minutes. And then he did it all over again, his lips and tongue and fingers everywhere, working me up and pushing me over the edge, one after another after another.

When I was a panting mess, somehow both boneless and still strung tight with need, I gripped his hair again, tugging him away from my pussy. Needing to finally be filled by him. "I want you inside me."

He came without hesitation this time, climbing up on the bed and settling between my spread thighs. A low hum of satisfaction left his lips as he stared down at me, sweeping the head of his cock through my slit. "Look at this gorgeous cunt. I made a mess of it, didn't I, bunny? Made you soak the fucking sheets."

That might've been something that embarrassed me

before, to end a session of fucking with an honest-to-God puddle beneath me on the sheets. But with how Aiden said it, in that awed tone filled with reverence, I could only preen under his praise.

He pressed his cock against my entrance and pushed the barest inch inside, stretching me wide. The move stole my breath and reminded me exactly what he was packing and exactly how long it'd been since he was inside me.

"*God*," I breathed, eyes wide as I stared up at him, once again wondering how the hell he was going to fit.

"Been too long, hasn't it, baby?" He divided his gaze between my eyes and where he was splitting me open, my pussy lips spread tight around his cock.

"Yes." My breaths were panting out of me now, my hand wrapped around his wrist where he was gripping my hip. To push him away or pull him closer, I wasn't sure. I ached for him, for the stretch only he could give me, and he did...sliding deeper with each thrust even as I cried out.

He groaned as he watched himself disappear inside me. "You can take it."

I nodded, a short, jerky movement, too lost in the sensations skating through my body.

Reaching down, he thumbed my clit as he worked his cock deeper, cranking me up and making me needy for him all over again. Until, finally, I was lifting my hips to meet his, seeking more. Seeking it all. "There you go, pretty girl. Show me how much you want every fucking inch."

I wrapped my legs around him, hooking my ankles at the small of his back and urging him deeper...deeper... until his hips were flush with mine.

"Fuck," he swore under his breath, a hint of wonder threaded through his tone as he stared down to where we were joined. "You feel so fucking good, bunny."

My pussy pulsed around him as he continued stroking my clit, my next orgasm already breathing down my neck.

"Say it." His words were low, rough. "Say it while I'm inside you."

I didn't need him to elaborate what he meant, didn't even question it. Because it was bubbling out of me, overflowing as he filled me. "I love you."

"Again."

I whimpered, my eyes fluttering closed as my body wound tighter. "I love you, Aiden."

"I love you, too," he said, his voice scraped raw. "So fucking much. Now, are you ready to give me another one?" He stared down at me, his eyes filled with a love I'd spend the rest of my life thanking every deity in the world for.

I wrapped myself around him. Legs around his hips, arms hooked under his, hands caressing up and down the length of his back. Not wanting an inch of space between us. Needing to feel him everywhere.

He moved inside me then, in slow, deep strokes, grinding against my clit with every thrust and taking me exactly where I needed to go.

And through it all, I kissed him, caressed him. Poured every ounce of my love for him into it all. Into the brush of my lips against his, the glide of my tongue into his mouth, the clutch of my hands on his skin, holding him as close as I dared, so there was nothing between us, not even air. Answering his question in the only way possible...

Everything.

I was ready to give him everything.

EPILOGUE

AVERY

TO CELEBRATE the release of *The Realm of Storm and Shadow*, Aiden and I, along with his siblings and their significant others, were all at One Night Stan's. Back where it all started, except this time, it felt like we had come full circle.

Where some things were the same—like the fact that I was *ridiculously* attracted to Aiden, thought he had the most gorgeous eyes I'd ever seen, and I wanted to climb him like a tree—so much was different from the last time we were here. The biggest of which was that his writing career was no longer secret.

By the time Aiden and I had returned from Germany, Addison had already managed to spread the news far and wide. Every resident in Starlight Cove—as well as hundreds of thousands outside our little pocket of Maine

—knew exactly who Aiden was and exactly the resort he was partial owner of.

And, as she'd predicted, bookings skyrocketed. As for any prudish assholes who wanted to rain on his parade, she had no problem putting them in their place. In fact, I was pretty sure she lived for it. She certainly was tonight.

She was acting like Aiden's personal bodyguard, verifying everyone's intentions before they could get within ten feet of him. Which meant the mayor's wife and her cronies weren't even allowed into One Night Stan's tonight. And when they complained about it, Addison told them—loudly—to suck her dick and then get lost.

Basically, my bestie was living her best life.

The other difference between tonight and the night we'd met was that I wasn't sitting next to Aiden, dumbfounded at how fucking hot he was and planning to spend my evening with my battery-operated boyfriend while reading ridiculously smutty fictional situations.

Instead, I sat in his lap, his hand cupped possessively on the inside of my thigh, much higher than was probably appropriate for a public setting. And while there may be battery-operated toys in my future tonight, it wouldn't be the only way I'd be getting off. I'd also have his tongue, his fingers, and that gorgeous, glorious cock doing wicked things to me before the night was through.

"So, Aiden," Everly said, leaning toward him from her perch in Beck's lap. "I know book three doesn't release until later this year, but..."

When she didn't continue, he raised a brow in her direction. "But?"

"Well, I mean... Do you think—" She cleared her throat, darting a glance away before returning her gaze to him. "Would you maybe consider..."

"She wants the book, man," Beck said when she didn't continue. "And I want it too, if you know what I mean."

"Hey, if they get it"—Ford pointed to Beck and Everly before gesturing to himself and Quinn—"we do too."

"I would definitely take it," Quinn agreed with a nod.

Luna shrugged. "I mean, if you're giving it out..."

"I'm not giving it out." Aiden shook his head. "I can't just give you the book."

"But can't you?" Everly asked, a bright smile on her face.

Brady shrugged. "If you did, I'd be willing to look the other way on your next speeding ticket."

"I could build you something?" Ford said hopefully. "Anything you want. I'll help with the lighthouse reno on my days off."

Beck nodded. "And you can eat for free whenever."

"I already eat for free." Aiden rolled his eyes.

Levi's brows shot up. "Shit, man. You've got all three of them begging for early smut? I'd maybe cash in on that."

"Did someone say we could get book three early?" Mabel leaned toward us from where she was sitting with her girl gang in a nearby booth.

I laughed under my breath, knowing my boyfriend

was absolutely, one hundred percent hating this attention. But so damn proud of him for what he'd accomplished. I placed my hand over top of his on my thigh, linking our fingers together and giving them a squeeze.

"Unfuckingbelievable," Aiden grumbled under his breath, low enough that only I heard.

I glanced at him over my shoulder and smiled. "Apparently, men—and Mabel—will do anything if it improves their chances of getting laid."

"She's right," Beck said, with Ford, Brady, and Mabel all murmuring their agreement.

Aiden shook his head. "I can't give the book out early. It goes against my contract. So you guys will just have to get it up for each other the old-fashioned way."

"Okay, but do you think you could put us out of our misery and let us know if Aurelia is alive or not?" Mabel asked, her tone hopeful. "How you left us on that cliffhanger was just cruel."

"It's a romance, Mabel," Aiden said.

"So?"

"So, there's always a happy ending, even if it takes a trilogy to get there."

Mabel narrowed her eyes at him. "I'd rather hear you actually say the words. She's alive, right?"

"I think I liked it better when no one knew who I was," he said.

"Yeah, but then you'd be sitting here while we

discussed the book right in front of your face, and it'd be like Thanksgiving all over again," Addison said.

"But at least I wouldn't know how much sex everyone's having thanks to my words. It's fucking weird."

"It'd be weirder if we did it in secret," Beck said.

Ford nodded. "Yeah, like some kind of underground smut ring."

"Is that a no to spilling the beans?" Mabel asked. "Maybe you can toss us a bone this weekend at book club. We'll be in the parlor...you can just pop on over."

"When can we leave?" he asked me.

I breathed out a laugh and shook my head. "It's *your* party."

"Exactly. So the rule should be that I get to leave whenever I want."

"In a hurry?" I asked.

Using the hand that wasn't gripping my thigh, he reached up and cupped it lightly around my throat, tugging me back against his chest. He pressed his lips against my bunny tattoo. "Yeah, actually. I'd like to go home so I can fuck my girlfriend."

Eyes wide, I reached around and slapped a hand over his mouth, too late, before glancing around.

"Yeah, we all heard that." Ford nodded.

Aiden shrugged, unrepentant. "Payback for all the shit I'd rather not know about what you're doing thanks to the fictional sex I write about."

Mabel's group shuffled out with waves and murmurs of

excitement for Saturday's book club. The woman herself stopped at our table, hands braced on the back of Aiden's chair. "So proud of you, Aiden. And I can't believe our little town produced *two* famous people! A *New York Times* best-selling author and a pro hockey player. Speaking of, did everyone see the news?" She dug around in her purse and pulled out a copy of the *Starlight Cove Gazette*, dropping it on the table between Addison and me.

The headline read: HOCKEY PRO TO RETURN TO STARLIGHT COVE AFTER TEAM CONFIRMS HE'S OUT FOR SEASON

Addison stiffened next to me, her body going ramrod straight as her mouth pressed into a flat line. Just like she always did whenever Chase came up in conversation. And I had to stop myself from reaching out and offering her comfort, because she'd hate every second of that. But I could give it to her silently.

Chase might've been Levi's best friend and some big shot sportsball player, but he was also the man who'd had my bestie crying every night the first month of freshman year, and I hated him on principle. So, no. He wasn't going to get a warm welcome back in Starlight Cove from me, accomplished pro hockey player or not.

"Whoa," Aiden murmured in my ear. "What's got you all stiff, bunny?"

I jerked my chin toward the newspaper and turned my head so I could speak in his ear. "That motherfucker."

Aiden's brows flew up before he chuckled under his

breath. "There's definitely a story there, but you can tell me some other time why you hate my brother's best friend. Right now, we need to get home so I can help you burn off some of this anger."

I hummed under my breath and shot him a grin. "Always thinking of me, huh?"

His eyes grew serious then, even as conversations continued around us. He squeezed my thigh and kissed me slow and sweet. Reminding me of exactly who he was to me—the anchor to my wings, the calm to my chaos, the shelter to my storm. My complete opposite, my perfect balance. And forever giving me a safe place to land.

"Always."

Thank you for reading Reckless Heart! Do you want more of Aiden and Avery? Scan the QR code below to get their bonus epilogue spanning four years delivered straight to your inbox!

OTHER TITLES BY BRIGHTON WALSH

Starlight Cove Series

Defiant Heart

Protective Heart

Fearless Heart

Reckless Heart

Holidays in Havenbrook Series

Main Street Dealmaker

Havenbrook Series

Second Chance Charmer

Hometown Troublemaker

Pact with a Heartbreaker

Captain Heartbreaker

Small Town Pretender

Reluctant Hearts Series

Caged in Winter

Tessa Ever After

Paige in Progress

Our Love Unhinged

STAND-ALONE TITLES

Dirty Little Secret

Season of Second Chances

Plus One

ABOUT THE AUTHOR

Award-winning *USA Today* and *Wall Street Journal* bestselling author Brighton Walsh spent a decade as a professional photographer before taking her storytelling in a different direction and reconnecting with her first love—writing. She likes her books how she likes her tea—steamy and satisfying—and adores strong-willed heroines and the protective heroes who fall head over heels for them. Brighton lives in the Midwest with her real life hero of a husband, her two kids—both taller than her—and her dog who thinks she's a queen. Her boy-filled house is the setting for dirty socks galore, frequent dance parties (okay, so it's mostly her, by herself, while her children look on in horror), and more laughter than she thought possible.

www.brightonwalsh.com

tiktok.com/@brightonwalshbooks
instagram.com/brighton_walsh
facebook.com/brightonwalshwrites

Made in the USA
Las Vegas, NV
23 September 2023

78009596R00217